So far on her tour of Europe, Althea had been ~~~~~~~ brigands and shadowed by an unknown assailant with homicidal intent—not to mention being pursued by an odious fortune hunter who would not take no for an answer to his avarice—as she traveled on strange roads in foreign lands.

Never, however, had she felt so desperately in need of a guide as now. Never had she been so close to a man before, other than in dancing and a few hasty kisses snatched by importuning young men at various parties. But this was no importuning young man she faced now. This was the Earl of Montmorcy, who did not importune but simply took what he wanted. And this was like no kiss she had ever known. Never had a kiss felt so wonderful and right.

Finally he let her go and Althea managed to say in what she hoped was a calm voice, "This ought not to have happened."

But how could she expect this mocking man to believe her, when she did not come close to believing it herself?

ALTHEA'S GRAND TOUR

ALTHEA'S GRAND TOUR

Emily Hendrickson

A SIGNET BOOK

SIGNET
Published by the Penguin Group
Penguin Books USA Inc., 375 Hudson Street,
New York, New York 10014, U.S.A.
Penguin Books Ltd, 27 Wrights Lane,
London W8 5TZ, England
Penguin Books Australia Ltd, Ringwood,
Victoria, Australia
Penguin Books Canada Ltd, 10 Alcorn Avenue,
Toronto, Ontario, Canada M4V 3B2
Penguin Books (N.Z.) Ltd, 182–190 Wairau Road,
Auckland 10, New Zealand

Penguin Books Ltd, Registered Offices:
Harmondsworth, Middlesex, England

First published by Signet, an imprint of Dutton Signet,
a division of Penguin Books USA Inc.

First Printing, October, 1994
10 9 8 7 6 5 4 3 2 1

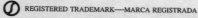

Note: In all the reference material I could find regarding nineteenth-century Switzerland, everyone from Maria Edgeworth to Hilaire Belloc to Goethe spelled *Chamonix* as *Chamouny*. In particular, a gentleman named Galignani compiled a *Traveler's Guide to Switzerland* in which the town's name is also spelled with the *y* rather than *ix*. So, I have used that earlier spelling of the town in the novel, as it seemed more faithful to the period.

Chapter One

The select of the *ton* shimmered and glittered beneath the soft glow cast by hundreds of wax tapers high above their heads in the Granvilles' ballroom. Gowns of every hue were set off by the black garb of well-bred and somewhat bored-looking gentlemen as couples moved through the patterns of a quadrille.

On the far side of the long, high-ceilinged room a group of fashionably dressed men stood clustered before an extremely tall, beautifully painted screen, deep in conversation.

"Face it, Haversleigh, she's as dull as ditchwater. Not even her respectable dowry will make it palatable for you there," the socially eminent Lord Spencer-Jones avowed.

Foggy Thornback, who had just joined the select group of gentlemen standing so casually while all the time casting side glances at passing ladies, stared at one face, then another. "I take it you are discussing the local Juno, the Antidote of the First Water?"

"Right you are, old chap," Haversleigh replied, wincing only a trifle at Foggy's booming voice. "Although she is a lovely creature—if you don't mind acquiring a stiff neck from looking up at her." He chuckled at his witticism, sharing knowing looks with the others in the little circle of friends. Since the Honorable George Haversleigh was not above five feet and six inches, he seldom towered over any young lady, having to be satisfied with those of modest height.

"Needs a fellow like Montmorcy, if y'ask me," Thornback

boomed in his amiable way once he had ceased his loud laughter.

"Think she'd manage to talk to him? Seems to me she could not say boo to a goose," the elegant Lord Spencer-Jones offered in a bored voice. "However, I daresay she would remain quietly at home and not give a fellow a speck of bother. Cannot imagine she would ever do anything daring—too spiritless, don'cha know."

"Sounds devilish dull to me," Foggy replied with a frown crossing his plump face. "I'd not fancy that. Don't care much for dreary females."

"I say," Lord Finlay inserted, "does anyone chance to know where Montmorcy is? He has been away for simply ages."

"Took off to the Continent now that Nappy is out of the way," Haversleigh said, referring to the incarceration of the once-dreaded Napoleon. "Lucky chap, Montmorcy—with pots of money, tons of good luck, and handsome looks to boot. Wish I knew how he does it."

"Well, at least he does not have to face Miss Ingram, for he neither needs her money nor her name," Lord Spencer-Jones concluded. Since his father had been obliged to adopt the name of the heiress he married, Spencer-Jones knew whereof he spoke. Only the exceedingly high *ton* of his father's family had saved the name from social disgrace. And besides, lack of money and the quest for the same was an all too familiar matter to many of the peerage for that to be quibbled about.

The gentlemen then turned the conversation to the matter of traveling abroad and the topic of the unseemly tall Althea Ingram was dropped.

Behind the exquisite screen painted in a classic Italian style, Althea Ingram, the young woman who had silently suffered the snide little digs and slurs on her appearance and personality, shut her eyes and clenched her fists in silent rage.

"Pay them no heed," her companion Cecily de Lisle begged, placing a gentle hand on Althea's arm. She had rapidly discovered that being chaperon to her tall cousin was no easy task. Poor Althea tried on one hand to appease her jealous new stepmother by remaining discreetly in the background, while on the other she attempted to please her father by finding an acceptable husband. It seemed a near-hopeless task.

"I had not thought, when I came to study this lovely screen, that I would be subjected to such crass stupidity," Althea declared in her soft, low voice. She turned a bitter look on her dearest cousin and continued, "I believe I would like to leave now."

"You cannot," Cecily countered, shaking her head even as Althea took a step away from their place of concealment. "If one of those nasty men sees you exit from behind this screen, then leave the ball, it will be tittered about from one end of London to the other. If you think you have a problem now, that would be far worse," she concluded with a sage nod.

"What am I to do?" Althea said quietly, her voice reflecting the anger and hurt within her. "Were I a delicate, fairylike creature such as you there would be no dilemma. Instead, I am belittled for something I cannot help—my height. As though I would choose to be this tall." But Althea stood ramrod straight, refusing to stoop one bit in an effort to diminish her five feet and ten inches. She might not be pleased with her height, but she refused to give anyone the satisfaction of knowing it.

"You might try for a bit more conversation and sparkle, for I know you are capable of that," Cecily chided.

"Of course, and I would bring down my dear stepmama's wrath should I be so foolish." Althea exchanged a look with Cecily that the other found uncomfortable. "I fear dear Beatrice does not wish me to shine. Although, you would think she'd be glad to be rid of me, see me married off to someone—anyone. She does not like me about, that is for certain. Nor does it please me to reside with her."

"Well, if your papa did not spoil her so, it might be easier for you." Cecily frowned at memories of Althea's dear papa indulging Beatrice with all manner of expensive gifts and flowers enough to fill a conservatory.

"She produced an heir, and as her odious cousin, *dear* Jemima, so often says, that is something my own mother failed to do. It never does to have two women beneath one roof and now there are four! Heavens, 'tis a wonder my father ever comes home, what with all the dissension that goes on within the house."

"It is not your fault if Beatrice cannot bear to share the attention of your papa." Cecily peeked around the screen now that the booming voice that belonged to the genial Mr. Thornback had faded from hearing. "They have gone away from here. I do believe it is safe for us to casually drift across in the general direction of the ladies' retiring room if you wish."

"I *wish* to crash a pot of ferns over the head of the not-so-Honorable George Haversleigh, if truth be known," Althea muttered in her quiet way. "And I shouldn't mind doing the same to that odiously stuffy Lord Spencer-Jones as well. What an obnoxious little man."

They slipped from behind the elegant screen with the poise of young ladies carefully bred not to reveal their emotions, even when severely irritated.

Althea, head held high and delicate color tinting her ivory cheeks, glided smoothly across the polished floor. Her dark brown hair, drawn into a sleek and somewhat unfashionable chignon, gleamed with a discreet sprinkle of diamonds across the back. Her gown flowed smoothly about her, with the diaphanous scarf she carried floating in the faint stir of air created when she moved. She looked remote and regal, like a high priestess of a pagan religion, thought Cecily as she hurried along behind her.

"Oh, please," Cecily finally pleaded in a breathless wisp of a voice. "Do remember that I have not your ability to cross the room in that effortless walk you have. Tall you may be, but you are wondrously graceful."

"I am sorry, Cecily. I forget too easily, I fear." Althea immediately adjusted her pace to a gentle stroll.

"Particularly when you are angry."

"Which seems to be all too often as of late," Althea admitted. She turned to her widowed cousin who had so providentially stepped in when Althea had been desperate for companionship. "Something must be done. But what?"

"We shall put on our thinking caps. Surely something will come to mind," Cecily said gaily with a genial smile for a passing dowager.

"I believe the easiest thing would be to merely put on my caps, period, then settle in that charming little manor house left me by my grandmother. Would you join me there, Cecily?" Althea asked only partly in jest.

"I refuse to give up just yet," Cecily swiftly replied, nudging Althea into the retiring room after a glance down the hall. "That dreadful Foggy Thornback is coming, and I fancy you would not wish to confront him at the moment, my love," she explained at her unseemly haste.

"He is the least of them, I imagine. Well? Is my flounce torn? Do I have a smut on my nose?" Althea demanded with a wry smile, referring to the usual reasons given for a young miss to seek refuge in the retiring room. She glanced down at her elegantly simple gown of creamy ivory trimmed in coquelicot riband and sighed.

"Neither, and I think you have recovered quite admirably. I suspect most young women who heard such a nasty assessment of their appearance would have had strong hysterics. Men," Cecily concluded derisively.

"That would only have made matters worse." Althea gave herself a searching look in a tall cheval glass before turning to face her cousin again. While Cecily might be small, she was most resourceful.

"Can you think of anything I might do? To be thought boring and dull is beyond anything horrid. I vow I should like to do something outrageous if it did not distress dear Papa too much. While I have an ample allowance from the money Grandmama settled on me, Papa pays most of my bills. One does not upset the bill payer without incurring a penalty."

"It is only proper that he foot your expenses, my love," Cecily said in her most soothing voice.

Althea paused in her ambulating about the room to stare off into space. "I believe I should like to go far away from London."

"Into the country at the height of the Season?" Cecily declared with surprise.

"No, no. I mean really far away. Like the Continent."

"You want to go to Paris?" Cecily asked with a slight frown, then brightened as she considered the possibilities.

New gowns of the very latest style, bonnets of ravishing beauty and design, and dainty slippers to dazzle the male eye when cunningly revealed. She nodded with increasing enthusiasm.

"No," Althea said with growing determination. "I wish to do the Grand Tour, just as my dear Papa did when he was about my age." She ignored Cecily's gasp of dismay to continue expounding her idea. "You shall be my equivalent of a tutor, and we could have a smashing time." She watched her chaperon with a calculating gaze, wondering just what she would have to do to convince Cecily that this was the solution to Althea's dilemma.

Cecily gave her cousin a dubious look. "Oh, I do not think so. Imagine all the arrangements, the trouble, all that is needful for such a monumental trip."

"We could plan together, and I do believe it cannot be too difficult, for there are so many people who travel," Althea declared, as though that would make it so. "Papa would know. And he could provide me with letters of credit from our bank, perhaps find me a courier. I believe I should like to cross France and see the Alps. Lord Byron has written marvelous things about them." Her enthusiasm bloomed as she continued, "And think of those Alpine lakes in Switzerland we might paint—for you know I do very well at painting. I should like to see Geneva, I believe."

"And then we could come home?" Cecily asked with hope, for she knew that one so determined as Althea would accomplish her goals.

"By no means," Althea said indignantly. "Papa went to Italy. Think of romantic Venice, with the canals and all," Althea said vaguely with a wave of her hand.

"They probably stink," Cecily inserted with the hope of halting Althea before she became too carried away. At the rate she was going on, they might end up in Greece, or—heaven forbid—Turkey! That promised far more danger than Cecily dared to contemplate. Even Egypt seemed to be dangerous, albeit exotic, to her thinking.

"Well, then, we could go to Rome. Imagine, Cecily, the Forum and Coliseum, the romance of the ages." Althea paused, lost in her rising excitement. "I heard of someone who went to visit the sculptor, Canova. I should like to view his workplace, I believe. I might even commission a statue done— of me." She laughed a trifle self-consciously.

"Oh, my," Cecily said in a faint voice, for it was quite clear that Althea was developing a decided partiality to the idea of foreign travel. It would be best to spirit Althea away from here and hope that by tomorrow this entire scheme would be forgotten. It must be the result of that wretched conversation they had overheard. "I shall check the hall again, and with any luck at all we can sneak out of here. The Granvilles' ball has suddenly become not the place to be."

"At least, for us," Althea said in a grim voice. The pain was tolerable, however the knowledge that she'd not likely find a husband within the accepted circle hurt deeply. She wished to marry and have a family as much as the next girl. To think her height would stand in the way of achieving such happiness was more than a girl should have to bear. It was not as though she was an ugly or deformed antidote; rather it was her height that interfered with her hopes. Well, she had best come to terms with her future. It did little good to rage over what could not be altered.

They might joke about Lord Montmorcy, but Althea had vivid recollections about the time she first met him. He had taken one glance at her and muttered, "Good God, an Amazon!" Subsequent encounters had been no better, with John Maitland, now the Earl of Montmorcy, treating Althea with an almost unsettled regard, as though she disturbed him in some manner. She could only wish she might, for he was indeed a handsome man, and the one time she had chanced to dance with him had been pleasant. He was exceedingly tall— Althea's head came nicely to his shoulder. And he possessed unusual green eyes that had the power to reduce Althea to helpless silence with no effort at all. Most likely he thought her a silly nodcock with not a thought in her head.

Cecily whispered, "The hallway is clear for the moment. Come, let us slip along the hall and down to the entry. Even if we must wait for our carriage, it would seem best to wait there."

"Who knows, some desperate fortune hunter who has lost all hope of an eligible connection might seek me out. Poor Cecily, you are ignored, although you are the prettiest woman in the room." Althea gazed at Cecily with fond regard.

"Well, I have neither money nor fascinating looks, it seems," Cecily replied with her usual good nature. "Come now, do not dawdle or we shall be discovered."

"I should like to bid Lady Granville good evening, but I believe it would stick in my throat to tell her that it was a divine party." Althea chuckled, then drifted down the stairs with her customary grace.

Cecily checked behind them, then watched her elegant cousin as she swirled to a halt before the butler, sweetly requesting their carriage be summoned. Following at a more comfortable pace, she wondered just how she would convince Althea to forget this nonsense about a Grand Tour of the Continent. It was not done for women to go haring about the world, never mind that Lady Hester Stanhope had done such. Look what had happened to her!

"Miss Ingram, leaving the ball so early? I vow it will seem empty without your charming presence," the Honorable George Haversleigh stated with more than a trace of pomposity as he neared the foot of the stairs directly behind them. "I am desolate," he declared with a bow that seemed mocking to Althea. How the dratted man had managed to sneak down upon them like that neither woman could fathom.

"Do try to bear up, Mr. Haversleigh," Althea said bracingly. "It would be a tragedy if the world were to be deprived of your company." She gave him a sugar-sweet smile, then accepted her cape from the butler. With a queenly nod and regal grace she swirled around the open door and down the front steps as though marching off to view the troops.

"Good evening, Mr. Haversleigh," Cecily said absently while wondering just what she ought to pack in her trunk. "I trust we shall meet again some year." There was no doubt in her mind after that fatuous remark by George Haversleigh that Althea would not be reasonable about the trip nonsense.

The not-so-Honorable George, as Althea had called him earlier, stood with his mouth open, wishing the other chaps had been there to witness the amazing sight of Althea Ingram tossing off a bon mot like a royal before exiting the house in dramatic form. She had been cutting and almost bitter in her manner, but she appeared oddly magnificent, like some female warrior off to do battle. And what did Mrs. de Lisle mean about seeing him some *year*? She must be confused. Then he remembered what had brought him downstairs and hustled off in the direction of the billiard room.

The heiresses were a bit thin on the ground tonight, so he'd decided he might as well enjoy himself before heading in the direction of White's. A good game or two of billiards was just the thing to do before sitting down to an evening of cards.

Once settled in the carriage, Althea cast a sidelong glance at her cousin. "You see how it is? I shall never find a husband in London. If not here—where? I might as well resign myself to single blessedness."

"Like Jemima?" Cecily thrust at Althea. Plump and plain Jemima Greenwood was a cross both young women had been forced to bear since she had come to visit, and then remain, with her truly adored cousin, the lovely Beatrice. It was doubtful that Jemima would ever wed, remaining a comforting companion to her precious cousin.

"Please," Althea said in a pained voice, "leave the poor obsessed Jemima out of this. I find her devotion to my stepmother almost unnerving, were it not that she is so busy running errands for dear Beatrice that it allows us some manner of peace."

"Well, then," Cecily prodded.

"Well, then I shall travel. Not as daringly as Lady Hester Stanhope, you may be assured. I have no desire to investigate the interior of a Turkish harem or the private life of an Arab sheik as I have heard she has done. But in my own modest way, I intend to enjoy the world, see what is out there." Althea tilted her chin with a resolve that was most familiar to Cecily.

"Oh, dear," Cecily said, but with a game smile that told Althea that she would not be deserted.

"Do you ever consider what restricted lives women live in this country? We may be presented, attend balls and shop, direct our households once married, and go calling, or on visits to country homes. Diversions are not many, you must admit." She gave Cecily a challenging look that good woman was able to avoid answering when the carriage drew to a halt before the Ingram home.

If Cecily had the slightest hope that Althea might forget her scheme, that hope was dashed the following morning when they came down to breakfast. It was the one time of day when Althea might have the ear of her beloved father without incurring the wrath of her stepmother.

"Papa," she said in a most bland manner, "did you find your Grand Tour edifying? And did you enjoy it a great deal? Was it worth your while to take it?" She buttered her toast, then sipped her tea with the calmest face in the world, not at all as though she planned something momentous.

"Indeed," Lord Ingram said with a happy sigh. "Why, it was the highlight of my life." He ignored both marriages and the birth of his two children in that sweeping statement, something Althea might have argued at one time.

She listened avidly while he told her again of the excitement, the stimulating meetings he had while in France, the pleasure of the views to be seen, the charms of Italy.

When he had done talking, she dropped her words into the ensuing silence with the effect of a bomb.

"I should like to do the same."

"What? My daughter travel abroad without suitable escort? Wait until you marry, girl. That is when you may travel. Not hare off alone." He sought to take refuge behind his morning paper, but Althea would not give up.

"Papa, I might not ever marry. You know I have had no offers these past two years. I would more than anything like to see a bit of the world. Oh, please, Papa. I have treasured your tales of adventure and the beauty to be seen for so long, wishing I might also partake of such a trip."

"I would be with her," Cecily chimed in with resignation to an uncomfortable and possibly dangerous journey.

"And I know whoever *you* hired to be my courier would do an admirable job of it, I am certain. And there would be outriders and a coachman. I would be no more at risk than going on our roads at home," Althea said persuasively.

From the doorway Jemima stared at the scene before her. She entered at her usual brisk trot to join the trio at the table. Ignoring the quickly concealed look of dismay that had crossed Mrs. de Lisle's face, she looked directly at her cousin-in-law. "Cousin Thomas, I would think that an admirable plan. In fact, it sounds so wonderful, I should like to go with Althea. With Mrs. de Lisle and myself along as chaperons, Althea ought not be censored. Indeed, I believe it would be a most educational time for us all."

Althea stared at her stepmother's cousin with barely concealed horror at what she proposed. Surely her father would not condemn his dear daughter to months spent in Jemima's company. But a look at his face brought her hope crashing to grief. She knew he must chaff at times from the presence of the hostile females who intruded on his marital happiness. He must long to be alone with his adored Beatrice. Baby William held forth in the nursery, and unlike most fathers of the day, Thomas was an unfashionably doting parent. She knew that if she wished to flee England, not only Cecily but Jemima would be in the carriage.

"Cecily cannot face backward, and I also tend to become ill if I must. Our maid should be along. How do you propose to join our group," Althea daringly inquired.

Jemima gave a dismissing wave of her hand. "The maid could travel with the baggage and other paraphernalia that must be carried with you . . . us," she concluded with triumph. "I will be happy to face the rear as I am never ill when traveling."

Her final hope shot down, Althea looked again at her father. He had the grace to look uncomfortable, yet Althea could see that indecision, that torn expression in his eyes.

"I fancy I could make the arrangements for you—letters of credit you will need, a courier to arrange housing for you as you travel. My secretary can handle the countless details, for I believe he once acted tutor on a similar trip.

"Then I may go?" Althea said, hoping against hope that he would allow her to go with Cecily and not Jemima.

"The three of you ought to have a splendid time," he said firmly. "You do realize it will take many months? Perhaps upward to a year?"

"Yes," Althea said with a narrow look at Jemima, "I am aware of that fact." Then she said to the usually doleful woman, "Surely you'd not wish to be away from Beatrice all that time? Think of missing baby William's first steps."

Now it was Jemima who looked torn and indecisive. Then some notion must have hit her for she suddenly firmed her mouth before saying, "I believe it to be my duty to go along with you. It is unseemly for two young women to go alone."

Althea might have questioned Jemima's wisdom but for another glance at her father's face. He looked so wistful she had not the heart to deprive him of time alone with his Beatrice.

Jemima it would be.

"Well, then, we had all better do some planning. Before I take off for the shops, I must make lists of what we will need." Althea finished her toast and tea, then rose from the table while awaiting her father's final words on the subject. "Could Mr. Pursey be available to us soon, Papa?"

"Pursey will no doubt be very pleased to assist you. You will have more lists in hand than you bargained for, I daresay." He finally succeeded in retreating behind his newspaper when Althea and Cecily swept from the room.

Jemima gave her relatives a narrow look, then determinedly applied herself to an ample breakfast. One never knew what would be available in foreign parts.

"Of all the horrid things to happen," Althea whispered to Cecily when they were in the relatively safe confines of Althea's room. Neither trusted the servants, who had all been hired by the new mistress and knew where to place their loyalty.

"Drat Jemima, anyway," Cecily muttered as she crossed the room to stare out of the window across the rooftops of London. "Will the cities of Europe appear much different, I wonder," she mused to Althea.

"We shall find out. Oh, Cecily, do you realize what is ahead of us? Even if we are plagued with Jemima, we shall have a splendid time of it. I shan't allow her to dampen our journey with her sour-grape view of life."

"Perhaps we may meet up with other English citizens while traveling—tall gentlemen." Cecily gave Althea a teasing grin, her eyes sparkling with delight.

Althea stiffened as though struck by a dead fish. "I sincerely hope not. No complications, please." She glanced at the door, wondering if someone was out there eavesdropping. "I was once called an Amazon by a so-called gentleman. It was not the most happy of occasions."

Cecily giggled at the affronted expression on Althea's face, then sobered. "I know it must have been dreadful for you, but think—were not the Amazon women reckoned to be most forbidding to men? While 'tis true they were deemed tall, they were a force to be dealt with. Warriors, I believe. Perhaps that is how he viewed you?"

"I doubt it," Althea replied, but recalled that odd expression that had lingered on his face as though he felt uneasy and somewhat perplexed at his reactions upon meeting her. She turned her attention to the tasks facing them, but ventured to say, "Should I take a bow and arrows along, do you think?" she said to Cecily, forgetting she had not followed along in Althea's thoughts.

"Heavens, I should hope not," Cecily cried, not caring if anyone heard her.

"Well, perhaps looks can kill as well," Althea muttered as she pulled out another paper to begin her own list. "Let me see, now, we shall need some sturdy, yet attractive clothing in which to travel. It will not do to look provincial, yet we would not wish to appear too prosperous. And in addition to those letters of credit we must have some letters of introduction to influential people along the way. And I intend to cut my hair—for it will be easier to care for when short."

"Have you considered our route, then?" Cecily asked with caution, knowing better than to argue with Althea on the matter of cutting hair.

"South through France to the Alps and across to Italy."

"Italy," Cecily echoed. "It seems a dangerous trip to take."

"Oh, pooh. This is eighteen-sixteen. What could possibly happen?" The likelihood of meeting the man she detested crossed her mind, then was dismissed. Europe was an enormous area.

Chapter Two

Althea watched her cousin whisk out of the door, then turned her attention to the scene from her window—a view that was nothing more than the brick facades of the houses across the street. However, it offered a familiar, soothing sight to her eyes and allowed her mind to drift where it would.

What was she to do about Jemima? The plump, dour woman was hardly the sort one wished for a traveling companion. She would doubtless complain the entire trip. Why she had taken it into her head to demand she be allowed to travel with them was beyond Althea. Well, she had tried to make it plain to Jemima that she was joining them on sufferance. It was not very kind, Althea supposed, but one did not associate kindness with Jemima. Although it was true that she doted on Beatrice and would do anything in the world to assist her pretty cousin. Odd, that quirk in the sullen Jemima.

Then Althea dropped the puzzle of Jemima's peculiar request and turned her attention to something her father had said before he had turned her over to Mr. Pursey.

"Shouldn't mind it were you to run across Montmorcy. Mind you he's tall enough to be a grenadier, but he has a good mind and comes from an excellent family. His height certainly ought to commend him to you, at any rate." He had frowned, giving Althea a most singular look. "I trust you will not regret this journey. It will not be easy for you, but I cannot say I am sorry you wish to repeat my Tour, for it was wondrously educational."

"Are you implying that you would like Lord Montmorcy to possibly join our party, look after me—and the others?" Althea asked in a deceptively mild tone her father knew well.

"Not look after you—like a nursemaid. But you cannot hire the sort of trustworthiness that occurs naturally in a man of his station. I knew his father well and have met the son once or twice. He is an honorable man, although I know you were displeased with him when you first met him." Lord Ingram gave Althea a cautious look while somewhat nervously rubbing his hands together.

"You know I met him and was less than delighted?" Althea said, amazed at what her father managed to glean when he wished.

"Yes, well, remember, he approached you on a dare. Absurd young cawker allowed his friends to egg him into inviting you to dance. Stands to reason you might hold it against him. All I ask is that, should you meet him, you not hold that foolishness against the lad."

Althea had refrained from gasping her outrage with only the firmest grip on herself. "I shall endeavor to behave as proper, Papa," she managed to reply. Only the dry, papery voice of Mr. Pursey inserting his offer to assist her with her list of needful items saved her temper from exploding as it longed to do.

Poor Papa had not the slightest idea that she had not known of the infamous wager. Had she, she might have done something drastic, so perhaps it was as well. It did offer an additional reason for disliking the man nearly everyone else in the world seemed to think so wonderful.

The cool green of his gaze had haunted her for many a night until she realized that he had not the slightest interest in her. He had never once called on her. He simply disappeared—off to the Continent she learned later.

Now, that sense of outrage returned. So *that* was why Lord Montmorcy was so startled when he confronted her, to find that she was far taller than the average miss. And that infamous remark, "Good God, an Amazon!" must have popped out from a quite astounded mind. And *he* was an example of fine English manhood to shine before others? Bah!

But it hurt. The man she had admired, been struck all of a heap over, had not only asked her to dance on a dare but had been confounded by her. Which must have been why he had that odd expression in his eyes. Well, if she did chance to confront the man she would . . . push him off an Alp!

She whirled about to pace around her room, picking things up, then setting them down again. She had known the comfort of retreating to this little abode for years. She would miss it, for here she was always free from Jemima.

Back to Jemima again. As Cecily declared, Jemima would simply have to get along with their plans and if she didn't, they could nicely inform the pouting pigeon that she was the one who had insisted she be allowed to join them. That argument ought to settle most anything that came up.

A tap on the door was followed by Cecily, peeking around it with arms full of fabric. "What think you? Shall I take my cardinal or this woolen superfine cape along? And what of boots? My jean half boots are well enough for ordinary travel, but do you not think we should see a shoemaker for something more substantial if we are to cross the Alps, as you said we might?" Cecily had entered the room, carrying two cloaks, one a bright red, the other a dull blue. As she concluded, she eyed Althea with the expression one saw on a hopeful but wary puppy.

"Indeed, you may need both cloaks. And stout boots are of the first order. I intend to bring at least two pair along. Although Mr. Pursey cautioned me that it would be best not to be overburdened with clothing. I believe he urged us to 'keep it simple.' However, I have a notion to order a divided skirt," Althea announced with an equally wary look at her cousin.

"You would never!" Cecily gasped in horror at the very notion of something so daring.

"I think it might prove practical if we must take to horseback at one point or another. We cannot expect to find sidesaddles in remote areas I should think, and even if Pursey put them on his list, I cannot see bringing them along. They take too much space. You might consider such a skirt as well," Althea concluded with a speculative note in her voice.

"Jemima would never wear such a garment, nor will she take kindly to the prospect of riding on a horse," Cecily mused with a nod that implied she would consider the divided skirt but promised nothing.

"I know," Althea said solemnly with a wink at Cecily. "I fear I am a very wicked girl and should be whipped for my unkind thoughts about my stepmama's cousin.

"I doubt that anyone—other than Beatrice—would find your thoughts the least reprehensible." Then seeing the long sheet full of precise notations in Mr. Pursey's hand, she peered over for a glance. "Have you made any headway assembling what we shall need?"

"Papa provided the sheets made of sheepskin to place atop a cot if need be, and I have three sets of sheets and pillowcases, three pillows, blankets, bedside carpets, gauze netting to protect against insects, two of those traveling chamber-locks—for Papa said the inns are not always as safe as might be and it is well to be protected—towels, tablecloths, napkins, and all that is necessary to eat with, down to a teapot and salt spoons.

"Do you intend to take a pistol with you?" Cecily asked, twisting her dainty hands together in a nervous gesture.

Althea nodded. "Papa gave me two very good little pistols and all to go with them in a neat box. 'Tis about the same size as the box that holds our gold. I do hope I do not mix them up!"

"It is necessary to carry gold along? What about letters of credit?" Cecily looked askance at the thought of carrying something so very tempting to thieves.

"We shall need both, my dear worrier. The men we hire are to protect us from harm, or so says Papa."

Cecily cast a worried look into the first of the trunks that stood at the foot of Althea's bed. It was nearly full of not only the basic items on the list, but also contained a medicine chest that they hoped not to need. She lifted the lid. "I trust we shan't require that tooth-file. Mercy, how dreadful to have the toothache while traveling."

"Mr. Pursey said we must take along whatever could be useful in the event of an emergency, for such may not be obtainable if we are off in the wilds of nowhere."

"Oh, Althea, must we? Do you really wish to do this trip? Just look at that medicine chest." Cecily poked about the inside. "A rhubarb grater, James's powder, vitriolic acid, and liquid laudanum to list just a few. Why we shall be traveling apothecaries!" She plumped herself down on Althea's bed, her face crumpled with worry.

"You would not cross the Channel without your oils of lavender or chamomile flowers, would you?" Althea had been equally dismayed when she had first viewed the list handed her by Pursey. She could but hope all the labels remained securely glued on each bottle and that no one would take ill from the time they left until the time they returned.

"No, no, but the others—paregoric elixir and ipecacuanha, emetic tartar, calomel, all the rest—give me the shivers, I tell you." The cloaks slithered to the bed when Cecily fluttered one fragile hand to her throat.

"Do you know what to administer when?" Althea casually inquired, hoping her older and wiser cousin might have that sort of knowledge.

"To some degree. You had best take along some sort of book to assist us. What may I do to help, since you seem bound to quit this city as soon as possible." Cecily retrieved her cloaks, then rose from her perch.

"Gather what we might need for mending and writing letters to home or keeping a journal—for I am reliably informed we must do that. And you might see if Cook has assembled the tins of spices we could use. Oatmeal as well, I should think. And do not forget sugar and tea. Plenty of tea."

"They do not have tea?" Cecily exclaimed in a scandalized voice that revealed her horror of such uncivilized people.

"Not the sort we buy from Fortnum and Mason, love."

Any additional requests were brought to a halt when a tap was followed by Jemima's entrance into the room without a wait for Althea's permission to enter.

"I would like to inform you that I shall bring along my own necessities. Mama always said a few drops of oil of lavender would drive away bugs. I intensely dislike bugs," Jemima said with a grimace. "Do you have a bottle?" She peered into the trunk already packed with most of the supplies but for what Cecily would organize.

"Indeed, but one can never have too much oil of lavender, I

perceive. What other gems of wisdom did you reap from your mama?" Althea said in an effort to be agreeable.

"Should you think a carafe of water is bad, four drops of vitriolic acid will make it wholesome, she said."

"I believe I shall adhere to tea," Cecily murmured. "My mama always declared it best when in doubt."

"*My* mama said you can never be too careful while traveling. It is best to trust no one—other than an Englishman, that is." Jemima clasped her plump hands across her middle and stared at Althea and then Cecily.

"You will be pleased to know Papa gave me two of those traveling chamber-locks, the sort you can slip onto any door and you will be safe from unwanted entry."

"Oh, that is good," Jemima said with transparent relief. "Naturally you will have the trunks brought to our room each evening and that will help to keep your gold and papers safe, for we would of course dine in our rooms."

"Jemima, I fear I have done you a disservice. I believe you will be a most welcome addition to our little party," Althea said in a most handsome apology.

Jemima flushed a bright pink and looked away from them. "I shall try to be agreeable, Cousin Althea."

She left the room shortly after that, promising to locate her mama's book on treating ailments. As well, she offered to obtain the finest candles possible for their carriage and their rooms, plus the latest thing in tinderboxes.

"Well, did you ever?" Cecily wondered aloud.

"No. And I shall make an effort to bury my suspicions regarding that girl. What a pity she is so plain and plump."

"Perhaps were she to wear her hair in a more attractive style?" Cecily suggested hesitantly.

"I fear it would take more than that to snabble her a husband. I have heard the most platter-faced miss can wed quite well if she has sufficient dowry."

The two women exchanged significant looks, for poor Jemima was but modestly dowered.

"Her manners must please, at any rate. That was very nicely done of her, to offer her mama's precious book."

" 'Tis to her advantage as well to have a book of remedies

about. I shall seek out our herbal and tuck it in, for one never knows, does one?" Althea said thoughtfully.

"By which I take it to mean that you do not quite trust the new Jemima?" Cecily strolled to the door, opening it to see if a servant lingered nearby. When she saw the hallway was clear, she nodded to Althea, then concluded, "Nor do I. Time will tell just how much of a leaf she has turned over."

"Come shopping with me," Althea begged. "I desire a stout parasol and we wish tinted spectacles, for Pursey said they are much needed in the Alps. And," she added, "I still intend to order that divided skirt. Will you as well?"

"By all means I shall go with you," Cecily replied, accepting the challenge. "But not to order that skirt!"

"Well, hurry, then. I am impatient to be gone." Althea, feeling driven for some reason, made little shooing motions to Cecily.

"What about Jemima?"

"You said she'd not take to a divided skirt, and I shall be quite noble and buy her a stout parasol and a pair of tinted spectacles," Althea replied with her more customary good nature.

"At this rate, we shall be off within the week."

"Not any too soon, to my thinking."

"I hope you will not be sorry," Cecily said in a firm voice.

"If I am, you shan't hear a word about it," Althea promised gaily. She ignored that curious little ache that she had carried tucked away ever since she had met the dratted Lord Montmorcy. She felt assured they would not meet again. Then she placed her faithful old bedside clock into the trunk near the very top. When traveling it was wise to know what time it was.

"I shall buy one of those pretty little watches one pins to one's bosom when we arrive in Switzerland. I have been told they work very well," she commented to Cecily.

With that sound observation, she gathered up what she needed and went down to the entry to await Cecily who had paused in her room to collect her reticule and spencer, and their shopping expedition. If at all possible, she intended to depart within the week, come what may.

Actually, arrangements went quite well, considering that Jemima had made a cake of herself when they went to the office of the French Ambassador at No. 2 George Street on Portman Square. The Marquis d'Osmond himself came to assist them and sign their passports. Jemima insisted on trying her deplorable French on the man, and he barely contained his pain at her execrable accent.

With personal effects to a minimum, only one maid along so as to reduce the size of the retinue, and the admonitions of Lord Ingram ringing in their ears, the three young women, with their courier—supplied by the estimable firm of Messrs. Delavand and Emery—left London.

"I still say that if you truly wish to hurry to the Alps, we had been better off taking the tour that Delavand and Emery offer," Jemima said with a sniff. "Think on it. In sixteen days, with provisions and lodging included, we could be safely in Geneva."

Althea gave her traveling companion a narrow look. "I have no desire to spend sixteen days cooped up in a carriage with two strangers—for they require six people for the trip, rising at five every morning, even if they assure us that we shall always sleep at some town come night!"

"Mercy, Jemima," Cecily said, "the others might have been men!"

Jemima gave them a peculiar look, and Althea was left to wonder if perhaps the young woman found the notion of traveling with men appealing.

At Dover they spent the night before taking a packet to Calais. The courier, Mr. Winton, had arranged their accommodation and the next morning set about obtaining their passage on the boat and overseeing the loading of their carriage and trunks.

Fortunately for Cecily the sail across the Channel was relatively smooth, with pleasant winds, if a cloudy sky. The three women remained on deck straining to see the last of England, although none would admit to a tear or two.

In Calais Mr. Winton herded them through the business of the customs house, waving their passports in the air with great authority.

"I had no idea it was so slow and trying an ordeal," Althea admitted to Cecily.

"Mama said that foreigners always try to best the English, for they sense we are superior and resent it," Jemima announced in her high-pitched voice that tended to carry farther than she realized.

Althea glanced about the area where they awaited their carriage and winced at the expressions she noted on a few faces. "You do know that a good many of these people speak English?"

"Well, I speak French, so what has that to say?" Jemima snapped back at her.

"It is well that Mr. Winton is to handle all our arrangements for us. He will travel ahead, thus assuring that when we arrive we will find all in readiness," Cecily inserted. "Otherwise, it might do well to permit Althea to be our spokeswoman, as it is her trip, her money, and her excellent French that accomplishes so much."

Althea had not thought herself accomplished in that language, but knew she was far more proficient than Jemima, so she modestly kept her mouth shut and bowed in Cecily's direction.

"Are we to take the route through Dijon?" Jemima demanded. "Mama said it is the shorter one."

Althea gave Jemima a look of dislike, wondering how Jemima's mama had become so expert in so many areas, and then smiled—rather grimly, it must be admitted. "No, I fancy to travel by way of Lyons, through Fontainebleau. And after reading the little guide book I found at Hatchard's, I believe I should like us to stop at Chambery. Would you not wish to view a glacier? I find the notion most appealing. I understand that from Chambery we can take a pretty little trip into the mountains to view the glacier, perhaps even climb up on one if we wish."

Jemima sat in thought for a few minutes of total peace, then surprisingly nodded agreement. "I believe that would do quite well."

Althea exchanged a look with Cecily full of questions she could not ask.

"Well, it sounds dangerous to me," Cecily commented after a few moments.

When they reached Paris, the three women watched from the carriage windows with curious eyes as they drove through the cobbled streets, fearing to cause comments if they displayed too much curiosity and seem vulgar. Yet even Jemima was excited.

"Now remember," Althea admonished, "since I organized the trip, it is best for me to present our passports to the Prefecture of Police. It was not well-done of you, Jemima, to speak so boldly to the English Ambassador when we called upon him. Goodness knows what he thought of us."

Since there was no way she might leave Jemima behind at their hotel, all three women—plus Susan, their maid—proceeded to the quai des Orfèvres for a countersignature on their passports. Jemima maintained a blessed silence, permitting the policeman in charge to remain ignorant of the horror of her slaughter of the French language.

It was a different matter when they reached the office of the Minister of Foreign Affairs at the rue du Bac for the final signature. Jemima objected to paying the sum of ten francs just to have a man sign the piece of paper.

Althea listened in appalled silence when Jemima broke into her simply awful French to give voice to her complaint.

Before the gentleman could respond, Althea politely thrust forty francs into his hand and gave a very Gaelic shrug, as though to say she could not help matters in the least.

Since the man had kept his gaze on the petite and lovely Cecily, who had managed to flutter about in a feminine manner quite appealing to a gallant Frenchman, it was doubtful that he had paid much attention to Jemima anyway, or so Althea consoled herself as they left the building with the required signatures.

"Jemima, I think it admirable that you desire to practice your command of French," Cecily said in her conciliatory way. "However, it seems you have an accent the local Frenchmen find hard to comprehend. Perhaps when we go farther south it will be better for you."

"Bravo," Althea murmured as they entered the carriage—

Althea, then Cecily, followed by Jemima and Susan, for Mr. Winton had a nice regard for precedence and knew that Althea must come first. He joined the coachman after closing the door, but not before urging them to enjoy Paris a bit.

"I, for one, desire to see a fine mantuamaker and a milliner as well," Cecily announced when they reached the security of their room again. She glanced with unconcealed curiosity at the crisp note Althea had been given upon their return to the hotel.

"An invitation to attend a small affair at the home of the ambassador was waiting for us. Shall we go?"

"When?" Cecily demanded.

"Tomorrow evening." At their dismayed gasps, she continued, "Come, all three of us deserve a Paris gown, and perhaps if I wave enough money under her nose, that fine French mantuamaker will discover she has three pretty dresses for us. I cannot bear to be thought provincial."

Althea made a gay whirl about their room, reveling in the fact they had left England and were truly on their way to adventure.

As she had discovered some years back, money was able to accomplish a great deal. By the following evening each of them wore a charming new gown that bespoke a Parisian flare. When she entered the home of the British ambassador, Althea felt able to face the throng of people, for as suspected the party was anything but modest in size.

Once past the ambassador and his charming wife, Althea circulated about the lovely rooms, trailed by Cecily and Jemima like colorful shadows. The mantuamaker had actually managed to make Jemima appear less plump, but had been able to do nothing regarding her sullen expression.

"I hope we are not served things like frog legs and such," Jemima complained. "I cannot think why the French must eat such nasty things. Why can they not eat good food as we do at home? And the sauces," she continued, oblivious to a few glances coming her way, "why must every bit of meat and vegetables be hidden from view and unrecognizable to taste?"

Althea silently blessed an older Englishwoman who took Jemima aside to point out some gorgeous flowers in an arrangement and chat with her, claiming she knew Jemima's parents. Once alone, Cecily was besieged by handsome gentlemen while Althea was given puzzled looks by gentlemen who obviously were too polite to comment on her height and didn't know what to make of her.

"I understand you charming ladies are to travel the Grand Tour," said a suave Italian gentleman who had been introduced as the Comte de Bosio. The words were general, but there was little doubt he spoke to Cecily.

"True," Cecily replied, fluttering her fan at the intent regard from so handsome and polished a gentleman.

Althea did not mind being ignored. She took a step back to study the throng of people dressed in such fashionable garments and possessing a high degree of elegance.

"I say," boomed a hideously familiar voice. "Fancy seeing you here, Miss Ingram."

"Mr. Thornback," Althea managed to say without sounding horrified. "I had thought you to be in London."

"Heard you were to travel and fancied to do a bit of a trip myself. Are you taking the Dijon route south?" he asked with the air of one who has taken innumerable journeys. Althea doubted he had crossed the Channel before in his life.

"Well, I have not firmed my plans. Are you?" Althea countered smoothly. Which was true. Their intentions had not been carved in stone.

"Dijon, for certain," he declared with a nod of his head. "There has been a spot of trouble with banditti on the Lyons route once you near Chambery. Understand the road is carved though some pretty narrow rock walls. Not safe, y'know," he concluded sagely.

Althea decided that encountering the odious Foggy Thornback was far worse than facing a group of banditti; however she kept this to herself.

"Your father come along?" he asked, looking about the room for Lord Ingram.

"No," Althea replied sweetly, giving Foggy a level gaze. "We travel just the three of us—with our maid, and the courier, Mr. Winton, of course. Papa felt it important to be at home just now. And I so wished to leave dreary London for new experiences and a taste of adventure."

Foggy had turned an alarming shade of red while listening to her words. "Alone? Four defenseless women? Alone? I say, miss, you do need protection. Of course, on the Dijon route it will be little worse than at home. But, ain't the thing to do, to go alone."

"I expect we shall manage quite nicely, thank you," Althea had the satisfaction of saying. "This is eighteen-sixteen, you know, and the war is past." She said not a word about which route she intended to take.

"If you were to take the Lyons route, you might be wise to look up Montmorcy," Foggy mused as though reading her mind. "Understand he is doing a walking tour of the Alps. Been there close to a year now and not finished as yet." Foggy looked as though he could not quite fathom why anyone would wish to walk anywhere, let alone spend a year wandering through alpine country.

"Indeed," Althea said in a voice that could have frozen water. "I shall take great care not to disturb Lord Montmorcy. I am convinced we shall not need his assistance in the least—although what good he might be is more than I can see," she added in an undertone.

"Why, Mr. Thornback," Cecily said, popping up at Althea's side with welcoming speed. "What a surprise. We did not think to see anyone we knew while in Paris."

The comte, who had remained close to Cecily, now inquired, "And do I dare hope that will you grace this city for long, fair lady?"

"Alas," she said with a pretty little laugh, "Althea wishes to head southward to Geneva on the morrow."

"No, no. You must remain here." When he caught sight of Althea's expression, he sighed and said, "You travel through Dijon?"

"Oh, no," Cecily replied, oblivious to Althea's nudge. "Althea has planned for us to go through Lyons. I should like to see that town, possibly buy some silk."

"Ain't safe," Foggy admonished with a dismal shake of his head.

"I beg leave to differ with you, Mr. Thornback. I predict we shall arrive in Geneva no worse for wear than you," Althea declared somewhat rashly, goaded by Mr. Thornback's odious manner.

"Well, hope you see Montmorcy, then," Mr. Thornback said morosely.

Not if I see him first, Althea vowed.

Chapter Three

"I protest, dear ladies. You cannot leave Paris so soon. You have just arrived," the Comte de Bosio declared in his pleasant tenor voice. "There are all manner of things to do—riding in the park, strolling along the boulevards, attending the charming parties the elegant Parisians host, so many things. Surely you wish to visit the fascinating shops and mantuamakers that help make this city famous?"

Ignoring Cecily's nudge, Althea shook her head. "I cannot wait to be away from the city. It reminds me too much of London," she added with a pointed glance at Mr. Thornback.

"Pity, that," the comte said with a rueful and very Italian shrug of his elegantly tailored shoulders. "But then, I, myself, must leave this lovely place for my home."

"You are returning to Italy, Comte?" Cecily inquired in a breathless and very pretty voice. Wisps of her lovely blond hair haloed the charming little evening cap she wore, enhancing her likeness to an angel.

"Ah, my little bird of paradise, I cannot linger in this social heaven forever. My family and home await me."

If she had not felt such sympathy for Cecily, Althea might have chuckled at the disappointed expression that flitted across her cousin's face.

"Your wife must miss you," Cecily said quite properly.

"Oh, I am not married," the comte assured her. "My family is a large one, and I am the head of it since my papa died. I have many brothers and sisters, and my sainted mama still lives. We have a very large house, you see," he added when he observed Cecily's confused face.

"Oh," Cecily said politely, not quite understanding much other than noting the handsome Italian was not married.

They continued to chat, with Althea most thankful when Mr. Thornback left for more interesting locales than the ambassador's rather staid party.

The comte insisted upon escorting the ladies to their hotel, pointing out that Paris at night was not a friendly place, no more so than was London.

Cecily beamed a radiant smile at the kind and fashionable gentleman and placed her hand on his arm with a look of utter trust. Althea bestowed a worried look at her cousin, feeling more the chaperon than the one looked after.

The ride was unexceptional, except that Althea and Jemima sat in silence while Cecily and the comte chatted twelve to the dozen about anything and everything.

Once back in their rooms, Cecily turned to Althea and frowned. "I do not see why we must hurry away from here."

"The weather, you know," Althea said, grasping at something she had overheard. "I wish to see the glacier before the snow becomes too mushy. Besides, once the comte is gone, you will find the city lacking in appeal, I vow."

Cecily drew herself to an imposing height, if one was not five feet and ten inches looking down on five feet and one. "He is a very nice man, and I truly enjoyed his company this evening. I hope," she declared defiantly, "that I see him again." With that she whirled about and disappeared into the dressing room that Jemima had just exited.

"What was that about?" Jemima wondered aloud.

"I really do not know," Althea replied absently, while considering the matter of her dearest cousin. Of course she must mind being unwed. A woman as pretty and lively as Cecily would attract any man, such as the comte, who of course was not eligible as a husband, being Italian and quite foreign, even if he was handsome and charming. But there must be other, better possibilities to be found.

Althea decided she had best keep her eyes open for a likely

gentleman. After all, Cecily deserved a bit of happiness, and Althea could jolly well find herself another companion.

In the end it took another two days for Mr. Winton to locate the proper horses, the outriders, and what other provisions she had requested be provided. This permitted an excursion to the boulevards, a chance to inspect a few more shops and purchase an enormous oiled-silk parasol that the comte declared a necessity when one went into the mountains, plus a delightful— at least to Cecily and Althea, who understood French very well—visit to the theater. Jemima went along, reluctant to be left alone for any time. But she managed to cast a damper on the occasion, however slight.

Cecily protested when roused at four on the morning of their departure. "Surely we are not thieves who must creep from the city before daybreak!"

"I thought you wished to view Fontainebleau. If that is the case, we must leave early." Althea whisked herself into a practical traveling gown of fine merino in a pretty shade of dark blue. An attractive spencer of blue and gray print went over it, and by the time Cecily had managed to change into her shift and petticoat, Althea had donned a smart traveling hat trimmed with a knot of deep blue ribbon.

She picked up her gloves and walked to the door. "I shall go down to settle any bills remaining that Mr. Winton has not seen to, while you consume your rolls and chocolate." She gestured to a table where it could be noted that part of the food had already disappeared.

"So early in the morning?" Cecily gasped, unable to imagine anyone up and about to do business so early in the day.

"Of course," Althea calmly replied as she opened the door. "I informed them last evening that we would be departing early. Someone will be around; you can depend on it."

Thus it was that when Cecily and Jemima presented their barely awake beings in the doorway of the hotel, Althea stood by the traveling carriage with an expectant face, waiting for them. Susan sleepily trailed behind them, toting numerous small portmanteaus that had been the last to be packed.

"Let us be off, my dears. You may sleep in the carriage, for

I am reliably informed that the road south of here is in excellent repair."

A surprising number of carriages were heading out of the city at this hour. Daylight was just creeping over the trees and tops of the buildings, giving the streets and buildings a tender glow absent in the harsher light of day. Here and there one could still see evidences of the past war—ruined buildings not rebuilt with tumbled brick and plaster in untidy heaps, and maimed men sleeping in sheltered corners of the street, ex-soldiers, most likely. Althea remained alert, watching everything she might see while the others nodded off in a light slumber.

It was seven and a half posts to Fontainebleau. Here, not even Jemima could remain sullen when faced with such faded splendor.

"What a pity they tried to destroy such beauty," Cecily cried when she circled the rooms that were rapidly falling into decay. "Such hatred of the aristocracy ought to be a warning to our royalty."

"I believe they do worry, but it seems our Prince looks the other way. He must, or else he'd not spend so foolishly," Althea said by way of agreement.

" 'Tis a sobering sight," Jemima confessed as she stared at the crystal and gold chandelier that was all that remained in one of the salons, most likely because no one had been able to cart it away.

"Come, let us have a little picnic far from the sad splendor of this once glorious palace," Althea coaxed.

Leaving the vast expanse of dingy windows and moldering paneling, the women returned to their carriage and went some distance toward the main road. From here they could view the splendid palace through the morning mists and imagine it as it once was not so very long ago.

Jemima had just begun to complain about the modest repast consisting of excellent cheese, fresh bread, fruit from a market stall, and pale, delicate wine when the sound of a carriage was heard.

Springing up from her cushion, Althea hastened to the carriage from which she extracted one of her pistols. When Cecily and Jemima saw she had armed herself, they huddled

together in fright. The coachman and outriders as well prepared themselves to protect their employer and her friends.
The several guns were carefully aimed at the approaching carriage, a light foreign make with a trim young fellow at the rib-
bons who looked askance at the armed men greeting him.

The well-built carriage slowed to a halt; the door opened,
and they were hailed by a friendly face and tenor voice. Guns
were stowed and all relaxed.

"The comte," Cecily breathed in pure delight. She rose and
crossed the grass to greet the gentleman. Althea followed
slowly behind, prepared to return her pistol to its box.

Jemima remained on the rug that had been placed over the
rough grass and summer wildflowers. She found another bit of
cheese and bread, took a little more fruit, then contemplated
the arrival of the comte with a passive face.

"I thought I might encounter you three here," he declared,
ignoring the men who staffed the traveling entourage and the
shy maid who peeped from behind a bit of shrubbery.

"You remembered that Cecily wished to view the palace,"
Althea said with absolutely no surprise.

"I was late in departing," the comte said by way of an apology after agreeing that he had indeed recalled Cecily's desire.
"The ambassador came over with a request that I deliver some
important letters to one of your countrymen. I had mentioned
that I intended to travel through Geneva," he admitted with an
almost sheepish glance at Althea, "and he hoped that the gentleman might be located from there. Perhaps you know him?
Lord Montmorcy?"

"It wanted only that," Althea muttered.

"We do know who he is," Cecily said with care and an admonishing glance at Althea.

"I have met the gentleman, but not seen him for some
time," Althea admitted. "I understand he finds tramping the
alpine peaks far more interesting than tending his estates or
entering into society," she said with more sharpness than she
realized.

"Perhaps you will help me to locate the gentleman?" the
comte said with a smile, quite ignoring Althea's ill grace when
presented with her countryman's identity.

"Of course we will help you," Cecily replied with a gay smile and a look of reproach when Althea gave a sniff of disdain. "We shall be in Geneva as well and will certainly have access to the English community while there."

"Would you care to join us for our little picnic?" Althea offered with her more customary charm, after realizing that the comte could hardly be responsible for Lord Montmorcy's lack of character.

"But of course. The so-charming Signorina Greenwood is already partaking, I see.

They turned to see Jemima stuffing the last of her bread and cheese into her mouth, her other hand clasping a full glass of wine. There was not a hint of expression on her placid and quite plump face.

"I purchased plenty for all," Althea said. Knowing what an appetite Jemima possessed, she had instructed Mr. Winton to buy extra of everything.

In short order the comte was regaling them with tales of life in his Italian home that had even the dour Jemima chuckling while he sipped his wine and sampled the fine cheese and bread.

When Althea noticed the passage of time, she rose reluctantly. "I fear we must be on our way if we are to reach our destination before dark."

"And you plan to stay at . . . ?" the comte smoothly inquired.

"Montargis," Cecily promptly replied, ignoring the annoyed glare from Althea.

"I shall make my confession here and now," the comte said, facing Althea with every courtesy. "I truly worry about you ladies, and I have decided to follow you in my carriage. We shall make a merry entourage as we progress through France to Geneva, no?"

"We do not plan to go directly there, but stop in Chambery, so to view the glaciers," Althea blurted out before she realized that this information gave him the opportunity to adjust his plans accordingly.

As she suspected, the comte merely smiled and bowed to

Cecily. "I would deem it a pleasure to escort Signora de Lisle in her view of the glaciers."

His use of the aristocratic form of address was not missed by Althea, nor, she suspected, Cecily. That lady smiled beatifically and fluttered her lashes like a young maiden.

Double drat, Althea fumed inwardly. Cecily was apparently far more susceptible to the elegant and too-charming Italian then she'd realized. What if the dratted man merely intended to befriend them only to make off with their gold when they reached a remote spot on the road?

Men, she observed to herself, certainly had a way of complicating life for a woman. And the comte's accent was becoming more *Italian* the farther south they went and simply oozing Italian charm.

The two carriages rattled into Montargis as the sun was setting, the glow giving the little town a romantic hue. Althea bustled into the inn, only to be stopped just inside the door by the comte.

"Signorina, permit me," he said softly in English. "I know you would prefer to eat privately in your room, but in France they force you to pay dearly for this privilege. If you will dine *table d'hote* you will find that not only is it cheaper—about four francs including an excellent bottle of the *vin du pays*— but the food will be better and twice as well-served."

"I see." Althea appreciated his concern for her purse, for she had suspected she paid far more than necessary for the service and food while in Paris. His statement also served to reinforce her belief that the comte was perhaps slightly pressed for funds. Since he amused Cecily and, she admitted, the rest of them as well, she nodded her agreement. "Very well. You will join us, of course?"

"With pleasure, Signorina Ingram." He bowed and bustled off to see the host of the inn where Mr. Winton had arranged for them to spend the night.

The following morning Althea had to admit that allowing the comte to more or less join their party had proven to be a wise decision. The food served was utterly delicious, in spite of Jemima's muttered complaints about sauces concealing what you ate and deploring the garlic that seemed to be put into everything but the morning hot chocolate and rolls.

The next few days passed in pleasant travel with pauses to view monuments, pretty villages, charming sights, and to halt at little booths along the road where one might purchase the finest of wine for mere pennies.

When they entered the city of Lyons, Cecily commented over the narrow streets. The road led them to the Place de Bellecour where the comte explained the guillotine had been erected during the revolution. When Cecily learned that over three thousand had been executed on this spot, her eyes brimmed with tears, and she looked more angelic than ever as she sniffed into a dainty handkerchief.

Althea found the place, now bustling with traffic and street vendors, a touching sight as well. She fancied she could almost hear the carts rumbling into the heart of the city, bearing the aristocrats to meet their deaths.

Jemima spoke first. "I am most hungry. Do you suppose we might get on our way? I trust that Althea will wish to be on the road at first light again."

Cecily protested. "You promised we might buy some silks, Althea."

So, rather than leaving at first light, the ladies indulged in a bit of shopping, finally leaving the city two days later with an assortment of fine velvets and satins that would make Beatrice's eyes stare with envy. Of course Jemima bought lengths of fabrics for her cousin as well, thus making Althea feel the veriest wretch.

The trip to Pont-Beauvoisin turned out to be most picturesque. The road twisted upward from Lyons through ever steeper mountains, with dark woods of firs on either side and rocks jutting skyward in stark splendor. Waterfalls cascaded over precipices and down along crevasses, causing Jemima to moan with worry.

"I know we shall be set upon by thieves," she cried.

Unable to convince her otherwise, and indeed becoming a trifle anxious herself, Althea again had cause to bless the comte for insisting he travel with them. What a pity he was not quite eligible, for if he was, he would be most agreeable as a spouse for her dearest Cecily.

The following day, feeling assured that nothing untoward had happened the day before, they set out for Chambery with high expectations. The scenery grew wilder, and even Althea fell silent as she peered from the window of the carriage at the spectacular sights from the carriage windows. However, she had taken the precaution of stowing her box with the pistols at her feet, just in case.

They reached an area where the road passed through a narrow stretch cut between rocks and so winding that you could see no more than a short distance ahead when it happened.

Althea had been peering out of the window, admiring the rugged scenery. From around the bend came a wild-looking man on horseback. When she looked behind them, she discovered an equally nasty individual dashing at them from that direction. A movement from atop a nearby rock caught her eye, and when she raised her gaze, she was horrified to see a grisly-looking man training his gun on her carriage. Ahead of her carriage the comte had halted, his driver fearing to proceed.

As was wise, she reflected while loading her pistol and preparing to defend herself and the other women as best she could. She could not entirely trust the outriders, who after all were French and might not be happy to fire on a fellow Frenchman in defense of Englishwomen. While they had been respectful, Althea had sensed a certain animosity in their behavior to her.

The command came in French and translated to Jemima was much the same as the old "stand and deliver" used by English highwaymen for years.

"Oh, mercy, we shall all be murdered for our gold," she moaned.

"Be quiet, you silly girl," Althea sharply admonished. "Say nothing, for you do not know if they might understand English, at least a word or two. And the word *gold* is universally comprehended," she added softly.

The comte left his carriage and hurriedly walked to open the door to Althea's. "What do you have that you can give them for appeasement? Those outriders of yours have taken to their heels. I doubt your coachman will help from behind that boulder."

"I suppose it is pointless to say I should like to shoot it out?" she said in an attempt to be amusing. Yet a part of her wanted to defend what was hers. Why must she beggar herself and the others just to mollify a few ruffians.

"You would fight them?" the comte said with wide-eyed admiration for this Amazon of a woman.

Althea tossed off her hat and now left her carriage, ignoring the gasps and alarums of the other women. She stared at the bandittos with loathing, her gun concealed in the skirts of her merino traveling dress. How fortunate she had practiced shooting—albeit at a target.

They shifted uneasily in their saddles, motioning with their guns and in general trying to convey something to Althea in an atrocious accent she had great difficulty in comprehending.

Rather than admit she understood French, which she began to doubt they spoke, she said loudly in English, "I do not understand you. Speak slowly, please," she concluded as though addressing a child.

"Mama mia," the comte said softly at her side. "Are you mad, woman? These are fierce men; they will kill as soon as breathe."

"Althea, do have a care, my dear," Cecily said softly from the carriage where she crouched with Jemima in utter terror.

"If I shoot that fellow behind us and you aim for the one on the rock, could your driver hit the one ahead of us?" she wondered softly to the comte.

"I have my gun in hand," the comte admitted. "But you take a dreadful chance."

"They may take our gold, then shoot us anyway," Althea rapidly pointed out. The men were becoming more restive, and minutes were ticking by without her handing any *ecus* over to them.

"I will count to three and we will shoot. Will your man understand what we are about?" she added.

The comte called out something in Italian, then Althea began her count, slow, steady.

The explosion, when it came, was astounding. The man behind them fell off his horse into the dust; the one on the rocks slithered down into a stream. The forward one toppled from his steed, but fired as he went, the bullet hitting the comte's carriage.

That banditto was not killed, as were the others, and when he staggered to his feet, Althea realized she had no bullet in her gun and no chance to reload. The comte must be in the same position. Now she very much feared that she and the comte faced extinction because of her foolish plan.

"I am sorry," she whispered to him, then she begged Cecily to find her another bullet.

"He must also reload," the comte said quietly, edging around the carriage, drawing Althea with him to seek what protection they could find.

Then suddenly the banditto threw up his hands as a bullet hit him from behind. His gun dropped, and he fell to the dusty road in an ungainly heap. His bravado failed him and notions of great gold did him little good now.

"Who . . . what . . . how," Althea stammered.

"What happened?" cried Cecily, daring to peek her head out of the window of the traveling carriage.

"Give me that bullet. We do not know but what this might be another band of banditti," Althea whispered. She accepted the bullet, loaded her gun, then edged along the carriage, dashing to the forward one right behind the comte.

He also loaded his gun as silently as might be as they heard hoofbeats slowly approach.

Althea raised her pistol to a point level with a horseman. The comte followed suit. Both stood as protected as possible, guns aimed, ready as might be.

All became quiet. Somewhere a bird sang. The horses shifted uneasily, and she blessed their tired beings for not bolting as fresh creatures might have done.

Althea strained her ears, trying to guess what would happen next. The faint sound of footsteps could be heard. Her heart pounded within her chest at a pace never felt while at the target practice her father had insisted upon.

Around the bend in the road a tall man walked toward them. He looked tired and dusty, his clothing far from elegant. Well-worn pantaloons had half gaiters over them as a protection, she supposed. His jacket was some sort of odd ticking fabric that reminded her of bedpillow covering. His straw hat seemed incongruous to what else he wore, for it was crisp and looked fresh.

When he drew closer, she realized just *who* approached, *who* had been their savior.

"Oh, blast!" she muttered. "Oh, double blast," she said softly under her breath.

"You recognize the man?" the comte inquired, stepping forward from their concealment. His amazement was quite understandable.

"Indeed," the intrepid Althea declared. "It is the last man on earth I desire to see." She lowered her gun, and her shoulders slumped momentarily in defeat.

The comte frowned, as could be understandable for it seemed distinctly odd to be unwelcoming to the man who had just saved your life.

Chin up and shattered poise in hand, Althea followed the comte to greet the man who joined them on the dusty road to Chambery.

"Hullo, Lord Montmorcy. Fancy meeting you here, of all places," she said in an excruciatingly polite manner and a wave of her hand to encompass the narrow strip of road with the restricted passage.

"Good God! the Amazon again!" replied an utterly astounded Lord Montmorcy coming to a dead halt in the middle of the road, causing his horse, who had quietly trailed behind him, to bump against him.

"The same," Althea said grimly. "However, I must thank you for saving our lives, not to mention our gold and all else." Even if it killed her, she felt obligated to give praise where it was due. And she owed his lordship, much as she would rather not.

The comte gave them both a bewildered look, then made himself known to the English lord, adding that in his baggage was a message entrusted to him by the English ambassador in Paris, one that was said to be extremely important.

"We had best to go Chambery. I imagine you plan to spend

the night there?" Montmorcy said to the comte, ignoring Althea as though she were no more than a speck of dust.

She whirled about to return to her carriage, tossing an angry look at her cowardly coachman and stupid outriders who had silently trickled back to their positions. She would fire the lot of them, useless creatures. They had run for cover the moment danger had appeared. Had it not been for the comte, she and the other women would most likely be dead by now. And Lord Montmorcy, honesty compelled her to add. Drat Lord Montmorcy, she added as she wrested the door to her carriage open and climbed inside.

"What is going on?" Cecily asked. She had returned to the seat and brushed down her clothes, looking surprisingly presentable.

"The gentlemen are arranging things between them."

"The comte and who?" Jemima demanded to know.

"Lord Montmorcy, that is who," Althea said, her voice once again sounding grim.

"Oh, mercy," Cecily said with an appalled look at her cousin.

"Good, you can trust an Englishman to help us," Jemima shot back.

"The comte has been quite heroic," Althea was forced to admit to a pleased Cecily. "I intend to fire those idiots Mr. Winton hired for us. They proved quite hopeless, the lot of them. In fact, I may fire Mr. Winton as well, considering the danger he brought about by hiring such a pack of cowards."

Within minutes the two carriages set off eastward in the direction of the town of Chambery. Althea fumed all the way without making the least effort to brush off her dress or restore her appearance.

The road sank down into a plain. To either side grew mulberry trees, for the cultivation of silkworms, she supposed. It appeared peaceful and pleasant.

Why? Why, when all had seemed to be going so well did this have to happen? Had all fates turned against her? Having the men in London ridicule her was quite horrid enough, but to have her supreme humiliator confront her while she was off trying to forget the entire ordeal was beyond anything odious.

When they drew up before the attractive inn in Chambery, Althea scrambled from her carriage, informing the not-too-surprised outriders that she had no further use for their services. The chastened coachman was informed he would be retained on sufferance—after all, she didn't know if she could replace him here.

Entering the inn, she found the comte and Lord Montmorcy deep in consultation. They turned to face her, and at their combined expressions Althea felt her heart began to sink.

"What is it?" she demanded politely from the comte.

"It seems you mistook Chambery for Charmouny," Montmorcy replied instead. "You will have to travel to Geneva, then on to Charmouny if you wish to see the glaciers. Since the good comte has done me a great service, I offer mine in turn as a guide, for I know the mountains well. I will go with you, show you the way." Even in his dusty togs there was something imposing about Lord Montmorcy. With his height and manner he was one of those born to command.

Althea felt something flip inside of her. The world had suddenly become a very unstable place. Refusing to cope one moment longer, she yielded to desire and quietly slithered to the floor, for the first time in her young life giving way to a dead faint.

"What did I say wrong?" the bewildered Montmorcy asked of the comte.

"Who knows what goes on in a woman's mind," the good comte said while taking a flagon of water from a nearby table.

Chapter Four

A dousing of tepid water served to restore Althea to her senses. Comte de Bosio stood to one side, the empty container in one hand still dripping water, murmuring abject apologies to the so-brave woman who had helped defend the other ladies. If he looked a trifle disappointed that he had not single-handedly defeated the enemy, no one noticed.

"Gentlemen, I must apologize for my indisposition," Althea murmured as she leaned weakly against the detested Montmorcy. For a few moments she gazed up into Lord Montmorcy's lean, intelligent face, absently noting that his eyes were as splendidly green as ever and that he smelled of herbs and grass, and other interesting earthy scents. His arms seemed to cradle her with no effort, and she felt absurdly secure and wonderfully sheltered pressed close to his heart.

Then, annoyed with herself for yielding to an impulse to be close to him, even in distress, she struggled to sit and be free of those insulting arms. At least, *he* was insulting—fancy calling her an Amazon again, as though she were a member of some ancient Scythian female warrior tribe! She glared at the man who had tormented her thoughts so often in the last year. "Why, of all the people on this earth did it have to be you who came around that bend in the road with a pistol to hand? We might have done quite nicely without your assistance." The last was utter nonsense, but in her state she was not thinking clearly.

Her indignant reply was a trifle spoiled by her attack of quivering sensibility when she recalled that she had just shot a man. True, he would most likely have killed her given the chance, but gently bred females simply did *not* go about shooting people—even banditti. Althea passed a trembling hand over her face, at last touching her throat in consternation. She must gain control over her shaken nerves.

The gentle support and assistance from the man her father labeled tall enough to be a grenadier irked her, rather than pleased. He wrapped a strong arm about her, assisting her to stand, taking a clean towel from the innkeeper to help mop up the water that still trickled down from her face and hair. He was all that was gentle, kind, and most noble. Althea wished him miles away instead of blotting the water from her hair.

Her hair! She must look a complete and total disaster! The mental image of her dripping and tattered self was too much to tolerate. She stood in front of the tallest, most handsome man she had ever met, and she looked an utter fright. Dusty clothes, a water-streaked face, her nerves shattered, and with only a remnant of her London aplomb left in tact, Althea turned with stately grace and inquired of the innkeeper, "Could I please be shown to a room? I wish to tidy myself." And possibly have a strong case of hysterics, she added mentally.

With a minimum of fuss she bade the men good-day after politely thanking each for his concern, then followed the innkeeper to a room that was blessedly quiet, clean, and hers alone. Where Jemima and Cecily were did not concern her at the moment. All she could think of was that blasted man downstairs. In a most uncharacteristic behavior, she took one glance in the looking glass, saw her unfortunate reflection in it, and burst into tears.

In the lower hall of the pleasant inn the Comte de Bosio and Lord Montmorcy faced each other with assessing gazes. The comte gestured toward the inn's common room, and they strolled inside to sit at one of the tables.

"She held up well, considering she just shot a bandit," the comte offered in apology for Althea's words, although he certainly was not obliged to do so, and her departing words had been somewhat conciliatory.

"That she did," Montmorcy replied, recalling the soft curves he had held so close to him. The men ordered a bottle of wine, and each had sunk into retrospection while sipping.

She had trembled while nestled at his side, but whether in anger or fright, he could not say.

He could still remember holding her in his arms when they danced that waltz about a year ago. She had not said a word about his faux pas in calling her an Amazon, for it had been rude of him, and he knew it once the words had blurted out. She had felt so right in his arms—at precisely the right height so he need not feel like a giant nor acquire a dreadful crick in his neck from trying to converse. Yet she had quite terrified him. He had sensed a critical emotion stir in his heart when he had beheld her face and form that was so alien to him that once home, he had packed his bags and taken off for the Alps within days. He had not been able to shake her from his memory in all this time—she was as lovely as ever and quite as tall. And she still stirred some nameless emotion deep within him, and he found that quite terrifying.

The worst of it all was that when he laid eyes on her again, he stupidly called her an Amazon once more. She'd most likely not speak to him now or ever. Yet he felt strangely compelled to find out what that peculiar emotion was, for he'd not known it before or since. Perhaps there was some way he might atone for that slip he'd made.

But she was a delicious armful, in spite of her height, for she was perfectly proportioned—he could certainly detect *that* when the water that the Comte de Bosio poured over her splattered down the front of her gown, dampening the sheer wool as well as her face. Why, she possessed a fine bosom in addition to a lovely face. And the remainder of her was rather nice too, he reflected when he considered assisting her to her feet. Miss Ingram was quite a young lady.

Well, he could only do his best. But he sensed that he would have an uphill battle to attain her good graces. John did not probe into his reasons for wishing to gain her kind thoughts and good will.

A stir at the door brought a young man with a reddened face blundering into the room. He carried a dusty box and appeared to have been digging in the dirt, for his clothes were streaked with soil and his boots covered with gray powder.

"I say, old man, what's been happening since I left you? I heard something about an attack of banditti and a heroic woman who towers over most men like an avenging angel. I say," the slender, blond, and bespectacled man repeated, "what's been happening here?" He nervously threaded one hand through his centrally parted hair, managing to look like a nearsighted Pekinese.

"Sidney Poindexter, I'd like you to meet the Comte de Bosio. He's brought me some sort of message from England." And, John reflected, a carriage load of trouble.

"Ah, the message," the comte echoed in dismay. "I will retire to my room at once to delve into my luggage so to find it for you. I trust you will join us for dinner, gentlemen?" He bowed correctly to both, but his gaze was focused on John.

Sidney looked at John, then at the comte and nodded. "Certainly. We'll be ready." In spite of his lean frame, Sidney was always ready to eat and liked nothing better than food, other than hunting for little fossilized remains concealed in the limestone so abundant in this area.

The men watched the comte leave the room, then Sidney tugged at John's sleeve. "Well?"

" 'Twas nothing, really. I was headed toward Lyons when I met a party under ambush—banditti, you know. Two of the attackers had been shot, but the remaining one was about to do away with the two who defended the carriages, and I shot him first," John said with a simple condensation of what had occurred.

"I sense there is more to this than merely that brief statement," Sidney said after giving John an uncomfortably astute study.

"You sense too much," John replied, a trifle sharper than intended.

"I see," Sidney said, although precisely what, John couldn't guess.

In a more casual tone John continued, "Why do we not retire to our rooms to clean up? I wish to change, for if we are to have dinner, I'd not want to be seen in all my dirt."

"A woman," Sidney said softly. For all his absentminded-ness, Sidney could be bloody perceptive at times. "It must be a woman."

"Indeed, it so happens that at least one of the people in-volved is a woman," John replied dryly. "I gather there are three of that sort traveling together on some sort of Grand Tour, as it were. One of them was likely to be shot by the ban-ditti, and I rescued her from that fate. Or perhaps the comte. Hard to say who would have died first," John mused in an ef-fort to be accurate.

"English?" Sidney peered at John through those little gold-rimmed spectacles as though he were one of the blasted petri-factions Sidney liked to dig up.

"Yes, and Sidney, I'd appreciate it if you would try not to read anything into this situation." Now why had he said that? It was like sending signals that something about this was dif-ferent, and he'd not intended to do that.

"Certainly," Sidney said with a bland look at John. He picked up the small box from the table where it had been placed when he entered the room. "I found some prime bits and pieces this morning. Like to see them?" he asked with de-ceptive calm concealing his eagerness to show off his prizes. "All sea creatures, I think, although how they came to be here is beyond me. Two appear to be snails and one a clam of sorts. Another is some kind of mollusk, I'd swear to it. Come," Sid-ney urged with a trifle more enthusiasm. "See what beauties I found." He led the way into the entry hall, pausing before the foot of the stairs to wait for his friend.

John glanced about the entry and noted the approach of two women from the carriage, followed by a maid. Most likely they were the ones who had traveled with Miss Ingram, for they were burdened with parcels and other belongings of the sort women tote along when traveling. He seized Sidney's arm with more force than necessary and said, "Indeed, let us go up without delay."

Sidney also looked in the same direction and didn't object in the least when John nearly pulled him up the stairs toward their rooms.

* * *

When Althea heard the tap on her door, she hesitantly called out a summons to enter. It sounded like Cecily, and she would be most welcome. If Jemima was along with her, that would be a cross Althea must bear. Goodness, was there anything left for Jemima to fault?

Cecily peeped around the door, then whisked herself inside, shutting the door behind her with greatest care.

"I managed to elude Jemima for the moment. She *would* drag me along with her to view some shop on the other side of the street. Are you quite yourself? Why are your eyes puffy, and your hair looks dreadful. I wondered how simple short hair would be to care for, remember? Susan has no talent at all with hair." Cecily bustled about the room, tidying up the garments Althea had tossed aside before stretching out on her bed.

"Thank you for all the encouraging words, dear love," Althea said with a wry grin. "I was a trifle overcome, but shall be better directly now I have your comforting company."

"Allow me to wash your hair with this special soap I found in the little shop across the street. It smells like a bed of wildflowers. Then we will put some cucumber slices on your poor eyelids. And *then* we will join the others in the dining room of the inn for a lovely party. I found a message from the comte in my room, inviting us to be a part of the group. There is another gentleman staying here, a Mr. Poindexter. Perhaps he will interest Jemima?"

"Nothing and no one could interest Jemima, unless, perhaps, he offered her food." Althea slid from her bed and submitted to Cecily's kind offer to wash her hair in the basin of rainwater, then allowed the slices of cucumber, which somehow magically appeared upon a plate from the inn kitchen, be placed over her eyelids for a brief spell.

Sometime later, when Althea had donned a pretty blue sprig muslin and her hair had been neatly brushed into the short curls she now wore, she joined Cecily and Jemima with a feeling that perhaps she might cope rather well.

As suspected, Jemima looked at Mr. Poindexter like a worm who had invaded her garden. For his part Mr. Poindexter appeared to view Jemima with about the same degree of loathing.

Althea and Cecily shared barely perceptible shrugs, then turned their attention to the comte and Lord Montmorcy.

"You look refreshed," Lord Montmorcy said to Althea in a quiet aside. "But your hair . . . it was long, as I recall."

"I cut it so it would be easier to care for while traveling," Althea confessed, amazed that he would actually recall her hair style. "I find it most agreeable."

"Oh," Lord Montmorcy said, looking oddly disappointed. "I recollect it was drawn back and you had sparkly things in it. Looked nice," he concluded with a man's predilection for understatement.

Althea considered his words and thought, so much for diamonds. Yet she decided she much preferred his sparse praise to the fulsome—and often hollow-sounding—acclaim from a skilled charmer—not that she had been overburdened with such nonsense.

The comte broke off his conversation with Cecily when the innkeeper entered to announce their dinner was ready. The poor man looked a trifle overwhelmed at such elegance in his neat little inn, but had manfully risen to the challenge.

It was Mr. Poindexter who entertained them all through dinner, regaling them with tales of his adventures in the Alps while hunting for petrifactions of every description. His pink cheeks and sparkling eyes bespoke his enthusiasm, and his surprising wit charmed all but Jemima, who appeared to consider him a total fool.

While dessert was being served, he turned to Lord Montmorcy and said, "Forgot to tell you, I have adopted a pup. Friendly little fellow followed me home and I cannot seem to find an owner. He's a shaggy-haired creature that looks to be a comfort on cold nights."

"And most likely has a pair of speaking brown eyes you could not resist," Lord Montmorcy said with grim acceptance.

"Now, John, he shan't be a bit of trouble, I promise."

"That will be the day," Lord Montmorcy muttered so softly that Althea doubted if anyone heard him save herself.

"Is Mr. Poindexter given to difficulties?" she inquired in an equally soft voice.

"You might say that," Lord Montmorcy said, noncommittal regarding his friend's failures.

"I must thank you properly for what you did for me—for us," Althea said under cover of general laughter following one of Mr. Poindexter's tales. "It was very brave of you, and it was exceedingly ill-mannered of me to behave so earlier."

He looked so relieved that Althea decided she must truly have offended the poor man and resolved to be civil to him when she could, although it would not be easy.

"Not at all," he said with proper English modesty. "Glad I was there." He looked at Althea, and she found a peculiar constriction in her throat. No doubt it was an aftermath of nerves, for did she not detest this man?

"I still cannot fathom how I could possibly confuse Chambery for . . . what is the other town?" She moved slightly away from him, for she found his proximity unsettling.

"Chamouny," he offered obediently. "But who is your courier? And why did he not inform you of this? He ought. Your French is excellent, so it is not a matter of misunderstanding a badly spoken word. Odd, that." He frowned so deeply that the little maid who was serving the table looked quite frightened.

Althea smiled to reassure the girl, then turned to his lordship with a determined expression. "I believe I shall dismiss Mr. Winton from my employ. That is, if I ever catch up with the man. He is the most elusive creature on earth."

"Perhaps with good reason. Does he have a *carte-blanche* from your father?" He looked worried at the mere thought, and Althea hastened to assure him.

"Only a limited one, and that I should be able to cancel—if I find him, that is," she concluded, then changed the topic to discussing the wild flowers of the region and inquiring most politely what area of the country Lord Montmorcy had most enjoyed.

They all straggled to their rooms shortly after the excellent meal. Althea noted that his lordship was at the opposite end of the hall from her. What a blessing. Perhaps by tomorrow she and the others might depart while he was off on whatever business he might have and be spared his guidance. She found the notion of a trip to the glacier without his lordship satisfying, even if it left a small pang in her heart's region. For the moment she totally forgot that he had been on his way to Lyons, and if he followed his original plan, would be off there as soon as may be.

In the morning she awoke to a dreadful racket in the square outside her room. She leaped from her bed and dashed to the window to see what it might be, for it sounded as though an entire flock of sheep had gathered under her window and bleated from extreme fright—although she knew the silly animals could take offense at the slightest thing.

Pushing aside the crisp white curtains, she peered out to the view beyond the window box full of blooming geraniums. Below, more sheep than she could count milled about the marketplace, threatening the store fronts, assaulting persons who chanced to come close to them, and in general creating utter chaos.

When she searched for possible trouble, she caught sight of a dog plowing through the throng of sheep, nudging them along, running around in circles at them while barking loudly, and in general confusing the poor creatures who were not blessed with much sense to begin with.

Then she saw Mr. Poindexter. He waved his little box frantically in the air while calling, presumably to the dog, and dodging the stupid sheep all the while. Althea almost cheered when the thin blond man finally caught the elusive pup and dragged it to the side of the square.

Compelled to know more of what transpired, Althea left the window, splashed cold water on her face, dried with the soft towel to hand, then hurriedly put on her brushed and neatened traveling dress again.

In the entry she discovered Lord Montmorcy about to leave and looking as though he could easily do violence, although to whom, Althea wasn't certain.

"Best remain in here. 'Tis most likely safer by far," he counseled with a frown at her.

"Nonsense. That silly lot of sheep are not going to do me harm," she pooh-poohed.

"I gather you are not well-acquainted with the animals. Very well, come along with me, but keep to the side and for heaven's sake avoid the sheep." With that terse injunction he opened the door and moved outside without waiting to see if she followed, then plunged through the assortment of townsfolk and visitors and a stray sheep or two until he reached Mr. Poindexter, who looked so harried Althea bit back a laugh with great difficulty.

She had trailed behind his lordship with deceptive speed; he was tall and she could not possibly lose sight of him. Her height for once was an asset, for the people looked at her askance, falling back to allow her room without her having to push her way along.

She was in time to hear Lord Montmorcy demand an explanation from Mr. Poindexter. She waited with suppressed amusement, although noticing that the sheep had begun to press in on her so that it made it difficult to stay put.

"It was Hercules, you see," the tall blond stammered while adjusting his spectacles on his thin nose.

"Hercules?" his lordship inquired in a rather dangerous-sounding—to Althea—tone.

"The pup I told you about last evening. He's a good fellow, actually. Just a bit excited when he caught sight of the sheep, that's all. I am sure he will settle down given a bit of time." This last was stated with more hope than assurance by a very nervous Poindexter.

"Hercules," his lordship muttered in obvious disgust. "Trust you to find a totally inappropriate name for the animal. Best get him out of here before he does any more damage. Follow me." Lord Montmorcy turned and plowed his way through the press of people and sheep.

Althea tried to follow him and found her way blocked by a particularly obnoxious ram that smelled utterly horrid. He butted against her, nearly knocking her off her feet in the process. She attempted to get around him and succeeded in finding herself pushed out into the path of milling sheep. Refusing to panic, she searched the area for something to use as a prod.

At that moment the overgrown pup in Mr. Poindexter's grasp wiggled free and dashed madly back through the flock. He went slithering under the sheep, jumping over a few of them with utter abandon until he reached Althea's side, now helplessly trapped by the pressure of stubborn rams and ewes. He barked his apparent joy at what he deemed a rescue of sorts.

She tried to hush the dog, to no avail. The more he barked, the worse matters appeared to her. The sheep took strong objection to the pup, surging forward en masse upon Althea. Had anyone asked, she would have confessed she found her predicament most frightening. It seemed she was about to be trampled to bits and pieces by a flock of silly sheep.

When it happened, it took her quite by surprise. All at once, she was snatched off her feet, strong arms digging into her rib cage while she was dragged backward through the flock until she and her rescuer reached a safe haven, a doorway to the bakery. The heavenly aroma of fresh bread was a sharp contrast to the unpleasant odor of the sheep.

Abruptly plunked on her feet, Althea brushed her skirt down to eliminate the sight of her ankles, then turned to thank her savior. "I must thank you," she said reluctantly yet politely to Lord Montmorcy, quite aware he had saved her once again.

"I told you not to come," he pointed out in perfect logic. "You would insist upon following me. Why must women be such inquisitive creatures?" he muttered in complaint as he absorbed the somewhat bedraggled Althea before him.

"We like to know what is going on about us," she said with utmost sweetness. "And I *do* thank you for coming to my rescue, sir. I shall try to avoid you at all costs in the future, you may rest assured on that," she concluded with a snap. With an injured air she gave a sniff, then marched back to the inn without once looking behind her.

"I say, old chap, I suspect she doesn't like you by half," Mr. Poindexter observed helpfully.

John nodded; then a slow smile crept across his face. "Sidney, she has forgotten that she fired her courier—at least she intended to. I sent word on her behalf last night." At Sidney's look of horror, John said in defense, "I was merely trying to keep her from being robbed by that charlatan. Fancy a courier not revealing the difference between Chambery and Chamouny. They do not sound the least alike. I would not be surprised if the fellow intended to lure her away from the town, then steal her gold. After all, Sidney, she is but a weak female," John concluded, ignoring the strength of that self-same female when she had briefly struggled in his arms.

"And so?" Sidney prompted.

"Well, she will need a guide to the foot of the glacier," John pointed out in perfect logic. "I intend to offer her my services again. I fully intended to help her, you know."

"Hm," Sidney murmured, then stalked off bearing Hercules in his arms.

He did not reach his destination, for a delegation of shop-keepers and a man who proclaimed himself the mayor confronted poor Sidney with angry faces and a great many demands.

"They insist I must pay a fine," Sidney explained when John threaded his way to his side, deciding he could not abandon his friend to his just deserts.

"I fancy you had best appease them. Then I suggest we depart from here as soon as possible."

Sidney explained to the angry citizens that he would have to go to the inn to obtain the needed funds. They trailed behind him all the way to the door where they milled around while awaiting his return. It was clear that Sidney would not be allowed to escape without payment.

John watched him enter with the dog in his arms and a mulish expression on his face. Shaking his head over his friend's stubbornness, John turned his thoughts to his own predicament.

First of all, while he ought to confess to Miss Ingram what he had done regarding the scoundrel, Winton, John decided it best to wait with that business until later. Right now, he had to convince her that it was important to leave the town as soon as possible. Sidney might go on ahead, but John worried that he would fall into additional grief on his own. Sidney tended to do things like that.

John wove his way past the throng of harried shopkeepers and the mayor, then ran lightly up the stairs, turning to the left at the top in the direction he had seen Althea Ingram go last night.

He rapped on her door, but was unprepared for her call to enter the room. He waited.

When she opened the door, peering out with a frown, John scolded, "You ought not do that. Where is your traveling lock, and why is it not in place? Anyone might enter and do you harm."

"Thank you for the warning," she snapped back at him and made to shut the door in his face.

He stuck his foot in the opening and presented his message to her. "I trust you plan to leave for Geneva immediately? It would be best to start at once, considering the mood of the local populace."

"I did not put that dog amid the dratted sheep," she pointed out with a sweet, and false, smile.

"They might think you abetted Sidney, you know," John said blandly.

"No!" she said in horror, then considered his words. "I suppose you are right. There is no reason to postpone our departure. I shall tell the others at once."

"Allow me to help you. I should like to make up for my handling of that earlier matter."

Showing surprise, Althea Ingram slowly nodded, then agreed to a departure within the hour.

John turned and ran down the stairs to alert the innkeeper and the stables. What Althea Ingram would say when she discovered that John and Sidney, not to mention Hercules, had joined her Grand Tour didn't bear thinking.

Chapter Five

"My mother has married our old neighbor!" John replied to Sidney when his friend remembered to inquire about the important message that the comte had brought him. After arranging for their departure, John had hurried to his room to complete his packing and now chatted with his friend while tossing in the odd bits and pieces.

"*That* was the important message? Your dear old mater has snabbled herself a husband?" Sidney declared in some astonishment. "Seems a bit silly to me, marrying at that age," he grumbled while tucking the last item into his portmanteau. He glanced at the great puppy, who sat drooling over his dusty boots, making a right mess of them, and sighed. "Hercules," he muttered in a warning that was quite ignored. "At any rate, I fail to see what was so bloody important about that news."

"I expect mother thought I might like to know," John said with a wry look at his friend who now struggled with the growing and wonderfully friendly pup. "Actually, I intend to make my way down to Italy, perhaps to meet up with them. I know the earl well and look forward to greeting him as stepfather. Spent my schooldays with his son, David," John concluded with a reminiscent twinkle in his eyes.

Sidney merely nodded while coaxing the pup toward the door. The animal tilted his head in a considering way, his large brown eyes peering upward with a most soulful look in them. Then he put out his huge paw for acceptance. Sidney patiently shook the proffered paw, then straightened. "Little fellow has learned a trick," he said proudly.

"Ready to leave this fine inn?" John said while closing his portmanteau. It had proven to be an eye-opener, traveling about Switzerland this past year without benefit of a valet. He'd lived simply, going by horseback, sometimes by coach, staying at pleasant country inns. Now, returning to Geneva, he faced a different sort of society than rural shepherds and innkeepers. He'd have to see about hiring a valet while there. It wouldn't do to disgrace the family name.

"Natty, this morning, aren't you," Sidney commented before going out of the door. He surveyed his friend with a knowing grin while tugging at the leash attached to his pup.

"It is not what you think," John replied in defense of his more careful appearance. True, he had taken greater pains with his shaving and donned clean clothing with an eye to color and fit. "I should not wish to give the comte a disgust of me."

"And the queenly Althea Ingram has not the least to do with it?" Sidney gave an odious little chuckle, then tugged at Hercules' leash when the dog decided to go out of the room without him.

John had insisted Sidney acquire the length of leather less another disaster such as the sheep episode occur again. Sidney had reluctantly found one, still declaring that the puppy meant no harm and nothing untoward would happen again. At his friend's dubious look, Sidney had fixed the leash on the dog with a wry shrug of his shoulders.

When the gentlemen entered the bright common room of the inn they found the sprucely garbed comte awaiting them. The shorter and slightly stout gentleman lounged at one of the oak tables, sipping a glass of the local brew while awaiting the departure of the group.

"The ladies are across the marketplace making a few last-minute purchases. It seems Miss Greenwood desired a tin of tooth powder, and Mrs. de Lisle wished to buy a sack of comfits she observed in the window.

"And Miss Ingram?" John inquired casually.

"She wished to inspect the local cathedral before departure and assured me she would not be late."

John strolled across the room to survey the village marketplace. Beds of geraniums sat in the center of it alongside a handsome clock that proclaimed the hour with much noise. It was time they were on their way before the townspeople remembered yesterday's calamity.

Across the way he caught sight of Miss Ingram's dark blue traveling pelisse that became her so well and narrowed his gaze. What was there about the woman that disturbed him so greatly? This time he intended to remain close to her side to discover what it was about her in particular that had so upset his peace one year ago.

Crossing the cobbled street, Althea looked back at the cathedral, a soft smile on her lips at the memory of the lovely painting of the Christ with a lamb that hung over the altar. How appropriate for an area that had so many shepherds and flocks of sheep. Then she caught sight of the fanciful clock decorated with sheep and other strange figures, sitting not far away and hurried toward the inn—time to leave.

She encountered Jemima and Cecily as they left the pretty shop with its blue-and-white checked curtains and assortment of peppermint drops and curious notions.

"I bought you some tooth powder," Jemima announced. "Cecily saw me hunting through the many flavors. I vow, peppermint, cinnamon, such tastes you cannot imagine."

"I still have a bit of my own, but thank you, Jemima," Althea said, rather nonplused at her distant relative's offer. Perhaps it was a peace offering of sorts? Jemima had been her usual disagreeable self at dinner last evening. When she had left the table early, declaring the dessert uninteresting, no one had protested. Not even the courteous comte had uttered a word, and he had to be the most gracious gentleman Althea had ever met. It was a pity he was older and shorter, for she would have liked someone as kind as he for a husband. After his quick rush to defend them, she had set aside her earlier suspicions of the man. The more time spent in his company, the more she admired him.

Jemima hurried on before Cecily and Althea, claiming she had to arrange her purchases in her portmanteau, and she offered to tuck the tooth powder into the top of Althea's bag before the porter came up for their luggage.

"I believe she is trying," Althea said. She gave the departing girl a rueful look. "I try to like her, I really do, but she does make it so difficult."

"Perhaps she will grow accustomed to the foreign foods before we are to return?" Cecily said, although not with a great deal of hope in her voice.

"I shall expire of mortification if she ever again denounces a dish as being fit *only* for dogs," Althea murmured just as they entered the inn.

The traveling carriage had drawn up to the front of the inn as well as the comte's more luxurious coach. Althea ventured into the common room and came to a halt when she espied the tall figure of Lord Montmorcy by the window. The other two gentlemen were accorded a pleasant nod. Althea turned to his lordship with a request.

"May we leave immediately the carriages are loaded? I should like to proceed on our way with no more delay."

"Anxious to make Geneva? We might not arrive there today if the weather turns bad," he cautioned. "Rain has a way of turning these roads into mire."

"Then we must pray for decent weather, must we not?" Althea nodded pleasantly before leaving the room to make her way to the front of the inn where the carriage and traveling coach were now being loaded. Her heart insisted upon behaving in that peculiar manner when she drew close to *that man*, as she preferred to think of him. How providential that he could not guess his effect upon her nerves, for he would surely be amused. She had mixed feelings about his insistence upon escorting the group to Geneva. Two more armed gentlemen were a welcome addition, but she mistrusted her emotions regarding him. Perhaps it was naught but something she ate, she consoled herself.

Jemima stood by their carriage to keep an eagle eye on the servants doing the loading. With a sniff she said, "One must watch these foreign types. Cannot trust them with a thing." She gave Althea a superior look to indicate that she was willing to make the sacrifice if Althea meant to hare off in other directions.

Susan bustled up with the last of their belongings, casting a timid look at the handsome groom who assisted.

Althea was thankful that the servants most likely did not understand Jemima's words. Yet Althea suspected that Jemima's intonation and looks conveyed her intent, for the men gave sidelong looks of dislike at the plump woman in her bronze kerseymere traveling dress and frumpish bonnet with a clutch of bronze feathers stuck on one side.

Digging into her reticule, Althea found some coins, and before returning to the inn, she pressed several into the men's hands. Once back inside she smiled at Mr. Poindexter and his silly—and quite enormous—puppy. The animal sat at Mr. Poindexter's feet, wearing a look of huge satisfaction, gazing up at his new master with utter adoration in those big brown eyes.

"Does tricks, he does," Mr. Poindexter volunteered, kneeling down by his dog. He touched Hercules' paw, and the pup raised it to Althea, panting his enthusiasm for his new owner's praise.

Althea politely accepted the canine greeting and added her praise. The pup truly was rather endearing, and she was ever a soft touch for soulful brown eyes.

"I was told he is from one of the dogs that the monks of the Great Saint Bernard hospice raise," she said to Mr. Poindexter. "They use the dogs in the rescue of travelers in distress, or so I was informed," she concluded, deciding that there was a resemblance between Mr. Poindexter and the dog, which might explain why everyone felt so friendly toward Mr. Poindexter.

"See that?" Sidney said to John as he joined them on the walk to the door. "He has real hero potential."

"I would not count on that, my good fellow," his lordship murmured. "Seems to me that were he a valuable dog, someone would have come after him by now. Perhaps we shall meet up with a monk searching for his stray while we travel toward Geneva."

Hope was clear in his voice, and Althea stifled a chuckle with difficulty. Obviously Lord Montmorcy was not as enamored of Hercules as was his new owner, Mr. Poindexter.

"The only good thing about that dog is that he is keeping Sidney from hunting about for more of those dratted petrifactions he finds so fascinating," Lord Montmorcy muttered to

Althea while assisting her from the inn and into her carriage. "I thought we would end up having more of his dratted stuff than our own baggage."

"Nothing is so bad but what it does not have some redeeming factor," she murmured back to him. After a look at the sour expression on Jemima's face, Althea was not so confident about that saying, for she had yet to feel comfortable about the young woman. Although it seemed Jemima did try, witness the purchase of the tooth powder. Althea resolved to put her silly animosity aside and try to be more agreeable to her.

It was still an early hour of the day when the two carriages rumbled forth from the village. The innkeeper was likely one of the few who wore a broad smile when they left, for he had been amply rewarded for his clean rooms and good food. The other townspeople merely looked relieved to see that dog gone, the English people as well.

The drive went quite well. The road had been well kept, and even Jemima did not complain about jouncing or lurching as was her wont. The three men went ahead of them, presumably learning to know each other better.

They wound upward through woods of pine and larch, climbing ever so steadily all the while. Many little waterfalls cascaded down over the rocks that pierced the sky to either side of the road. When the sun rose high in the sky, Althea signaled to her coachman to stop. The groom blew a few gay notes on his horn, and both the carriages pulled off the road at a likely place.

Althea descended from the carriage, sniffing the clear, brisk air with appreciation. "What a lovely spot," she exclaimed to Cecily, who clearly needed convincing.

The picnic was quite different from the sort held in England. The food was simple—what the innkeeper had put up for them—plus several bottles of the wine they had bought along the road south from Paris. Althea served up little *saucissons* or Bologna sausages, fresh bread and butter, cured neat's tongue, and a dessert of fruit to the group. While it might have been simple fare, there was an atmosphere of relaxed pleasure in the meal. Even Jemima appeared to enjoy it, stuffing herself with good bread and an ample amount of the little sausages, which she proclaimed outstanding.

"This is vastly different from the sort of place I last saw you," Lord Montmorcy said in an aside to Althea while he poured her another glass of wine.

She had chosen to perch on a rock a short distance from the cloth placed on the grassy verge so no one heard his remark to her. Not quite certain what he intended by his comment, she carefully replied, "True, but enjoyable, nonetheless."

"Odd, I would have thought a beautiful young woman like you would prefer the ballrooms of the *ton* to the company of women, no matter how charming they are."

Althea cast a thoughtful look on her companions, then back at him. "They are charming, are they not?" She elected to ignore his reference to her appearance or London ballrooms. She truly did not know what to say in that regard, and she was not accustomed to receiving flattery. "Cecily, in particular, is the dearest person. It is a pity she was widowed so young. She is the sort who deserves a kind and loving husband."

"Undoubtedly there is someone who will step into that position." He cast a considering look at the pretty widow, then the comte who showered her with devoted attention.

Althea just smiled in reply, but his remark tossed about in her mind. Did he perchance view the lovely and petite Cecily as a future countess? Certainly she would fill the position most admirably. Althea could not imagine any gentleman not falling immediately in love with her fragile-looking and beautifully mannered cousin, although a person more robust and healthy Althea did not know. Even Jemima was given an occasional megrim. In spite of Cecily's delicate appearance, she was never ill for a day and most often possessed a joyous spirit.

With an inward pang she refused to acknowledge, Althea decided she would do her best to encourage a match for her dearest companion.

"Best hurry or we will be terribly late in arriving," the comte cautioned as he assisted Cecily from her cushion.

They straggled into the carriage and traveling coach with the lassitude of those who had dined well. Within minutes

Jemima had dozed off in her corner, Susan in hers, and Althea was free to chat softly with Cecily.

"What do you think of Lord Montmorcy?" Althea asked with assumed nonchalance.

"Oh, I think him an admirable man," Cecily replied promptly. "I suspect he is about to settle down and make some woman a fine husband. What do you think of him?" Cecily said with a curious look at her cousin.

"Oh, indeed. I may have been mistaken in him, for he seems all that is agreeable now," Althea said, swallowing her ire.

Cecily brightened, then happily said, "Oh, good, I hoped you would change your mind about him."

Which statement had the effect of sinking Althea's heart somewhere in the vicinity of her shoes.

The darkening sky quite reflected her change of mood, and she stared out of the carriage while convincing herself that it was for the good of all that she promote the union of her dearest cousin with the man she seemed to like and *that man* with the sweetest woman he could hope to find. Althea could always find another companion. Goodness knew that her family had two or three more widows about, ones who could use a sheltering position.

They were entering a pretty mountain village when the rain began to pour down. Heavy gray mists settled among the trees, and the road quickly became a quagmire. Even in the neatly cobbled village street puddles rapidly formed, and the poor horses, not to mention the coachmen, soon drooped with chill and wet.

Althea was not the least surprised when the leading coach pulled in before a quaint inn located in the center of the village. It was a neat two-story edifice with gay red shutters at the windows—the only spot of color to be glimpsed through the daunting downpour.

The groom, water dripping off the brim of his hat, opened the carriage door. Althea willingly dashed through the rain, keeping a firm grasp on her large oiled-silk umbrella. Going in through a small entry added on the front of the inn, she shook her garments, feeling akin to Hercules, who also shook himself before trotting off to find a cozy fire before which he obviously intended to warm himself.

Cecily had dashed through the rain right after Althea, and she shivered after shaking her pelisse and umbrella. "Rain is so chilly; I can not ever recall one that was warm," she muttered through clenched teeth.

The common room, with its pleasant fire burning in a massive grate and cheerful checked curtains at the windows, beckoned to the ladies. They entered, settling themselves before the fire as Hercules had done. Once this was accomplished, Althea was surprised to note the many decorations about the place. Flowers were placed everywhere, and small pictures of some saints Althea failed to recognize were prominently displayed.

The innkeeper bustled forward, wiping his hands on an immaculate white apron as he came. He bowed low and welcomed Althea and Cecily to his humble inn. While his English was rudimentary, his good will was obvious. Althea, not wishing to appear as so many of the English travelers she had heard about who were rude and demanding, politely requested rooms for the night. It was clear that they would go no farther this day. The innkeeper agreeably said there were rooms yet to be had.

"Lord Montmorcy was correct," she said quietly to Cecily. "When it rains up in these mountains, it is no time to be on the road."

"I wonder if there is some sort of celebration here; it seems quite festive," Cecily observed in return.

Jemima entered the inn and could be heard demanding a room, hot water for a bath, and tea brought directly to her room.

With a grimace at her dearest cousin, Althea rose from her comfortable seat to try to soften the harsh words of her other and rather tiresome traveling companion. Gently, she added a few words of her own, then smiled with gratitude as the innkeeper agreed to Jemima's request, badly though it might have been made.

When Jemima disappeared up the lovely staircase that had exquisite wood carvings on the balusters and brackets, Althea turned to the innkeeper again. "Is there a festival in the village? If so, what a pity the weather is so bad."

"Ah, yes, a festival," the innkeeper agreed. He rattled off at some length in words Althea did not quite grasp that managed to convey the festival was to be on the morrow and that excellent food and drink and music were promised. If the good ladies and the gentlemen would care to stay, they would be well entertained.

Seating herself before the fire, Althea smiled at Cecily. "I think we ought to remain for the festival. After all, it is one of the things we sought on this tour—a taste of foreign life. And this promises to be quite a taste."

"Ah, a fire and two lovely ladies," Lord Montmorcy exclaimed. "I confess that for once the fire is the greater attraction." He crossed the room in great strides, holding out his hands to the warmth of the fire while casting a jaundiced look at Hercules, who was stretched the length of the hearth.

Althea darted looks at his lordship and Cecily, trying to decide if she could detect a spark of interest flaring between them. When she saw only polite regard, she decided that perhaps she was not attuned to sniffing out romance in others. It would take practice.

"There is a festival in the village," Althea reported to the two men, Mr. Poindexter having joined them. "Our host promises good food, drink, and music. Do you suppose we may see some dancing?" she concluded with hope.

Lord Montmorcy smiled down at her. "I should be very much surprised if you did not. The local dancing is a hearty type—not the sort of tame stuff you see in a London ballroom. I have learned a few of the dances. Perhaps you would enjoy a lesson or two."

"Oh," Althea said, flustered at the teasing she glimpsed in his dark green eyes, "I am certain that both Cecily and I would like to try dancing. Would you not, Cecily?" she said, peering around the tall figure of his lordship to see how her cousin reacted to this suggestion.

"Well . . ." Cecily said doubtfully.

"Ah, all is set," the comte declared as he entered the cheerful room. Unlike Lord Montmorcy, he ran no danger of hitting the low dark-beamed ceiling with his head. He bowed elegantly to Althea, then to Cecily. "I have arranged for a splendid dinner in honor of the saints whose festival we celebrate, Saints Peter and Paul."

"How charming," Althea said with enthusiasm.

The comte turned back to Althea. "You have no doubt forgiven his lordship for sending the missive to your courier, dismissing the incompetent scoundrel for so leading you astray. It was highly improper of him to be so remiss—if indeed that is what it was, and not something more sinister."

Althea rose from her comfortable seat to face Lord Montmorcy, feeling less at a disadvantage dealing with the man when he was not towering over her. "I knew you were displeased with Mr. Winton, but had not realized that you had taken it upon yourself to interfere to that degree. I had looked forward to his guidance to the foot of the glacier." There was little point in scolding the man, for the deed had been done, but Althea knew a certain anger at his high-handed action. "Perhaps I may locate a guide in Geneva," she said with a gentle manner that well concealed her annoyance.

"But I insist upon taking his place," Lord Montmorcy said with remarkable swiftness. "I feel it incumbent upon me to assist a countrywoman in dire straits. And it would be a pleasure upon my part, I assure you," he concluded blandly.

Althea studied those unusual eyes for a hint of mockery or teasing and found neither. Before she could form a suitable reply, Cecily erupted with an enthusiastic acceptance.

"What a lovely offer. Oh, do let the gentlemen serve as our guides, for you know we have need of such and I perceive with such experience as they must have had, they would do wonderfully well." Cecily gave a happy bounce on her chair, looking for all the world like a pretty child who has been proffered a treat.

Stifling the words that longed to spring from her tongue that would refuse the assistance of so intimidating a man, Althea glanced at Cecily's eager face, then at the more closed expression worn by Lord Montmorcy. Swallowing carefully, she said, "How kind of you, sir. I vow it will be quite delightful to have such experienced guides." She turned to Mr. Poindexter and added, "I hope that you join us as well?"

Before Sidney could blurt out a word, John gave him a cautioning look and smoothly inserted, "Of course Poindexter will go along. Could you see your way to coming as well, Comte? Or are you in a hurry to return to Italy?"

Both men allowed their gazes to slide to the exquisite and delicate Cecily de Lisle before the comte replied. Meeting John's gaze, the comte said, as John had anticipated he might, "I would be honored to join you. As it chances, I am in no hurry to return to my duties at home."

"Good. We shall continue on our way, a merry group of English—with the good comte in addition," he added with a bow to the dignified Italian.

The dinner that evening was so excellent that not even Jemima could fault it—an event Althea had not thought would occur during the entire trip.

Following the meal, the gentlemen joined the ladies in the common room, which was quite unlike the common room one might find in an English inn, for it contained cozy chairs by the fire, pleasant tables with oil lamps, and the laughter of assorted guests, all in a festive mood.

When several men entered carrying musical instruments, Althea guessed that they were to be treated to an impromptu concert. Soon a music box, or accordion, held by a burly young man, exhaled a reedy tune with a flute, clarinet, and guitar of sorts joining in to create a merry sound.

Althea could not refrain from tapping her foot to the infectious rhythm of the music. She was startled when Lord Montmorcy pulled her from her comfortable chair to whirl her out to a small space that had been cleared before the musicians, creating a dance floor.

"But . . ." she sputtered, casting an appealing glance at Cecily de Lisle.

John was not having any missishness in the least and began to show the woman who haunted his sleep the simple steps involved in the country dance. It was easy and fun, and as he suspected, Althea caught on quickly.

They whirled about and stamped their feet to the beat of the music. Her cheeks were flushed an enchanting rose, and those silly curls she now affected bounced about her head in charming disarray. Hands on her hips and those long slender feet kicking out from beneath her skirts in the pattern of the dance, Althea Ingram was a far cry from the proper young woman he had seen in London. Here she looked far more approachable and definitely more appealing.

The problem as John saw it was that she still held him in deep reserve. She had clung to English politeness and propriety when the comte made the change in her plans known. But John did not need to be hit over the head to realize that she was less than pleased. Those fine gray eyes had flashed her displeasure, bringing upon him a strange desire to know what they might look like were they to be aroused in other than anger.

John intended to remain close to her. He had to find out what drew him to her side, in spite of her disdain. Once he could discover that, he could dismiss her from his mind and carry on with his life. In the interim he intended to study her character with the thoroughness of the amateur naturalists that cluttered the Swiss landscape during the summers. She was an intriguing specimen, and John grasped a glimmer of comprehension at Sidney's absorption in petrifactions.

He whirled her through a final few steps, tossing a nod at the musicians he had bribed beforehand, then he returned her to her chair. She was breathless, flushed, and looked almost good enough to eat, he decided in a moment of charity.

She curtsied politely, then gestured to her cousin as the music began anew. "Cecily next, I think."

Blast, John thought, even as he correctly drew the blushingly protesting Mrs. de Lisle out to the little dance floor. It was evident that in spite of his attempts, Althea Ingram still held him in aversion. He was more determined than ever to change that situation.

Chapter Six

The evening turned out a great success, judging by the laughter from all. Even the comte, who was somewhat dignified compared to the others, joined in the dancing. In fact, he did extremely well to Althea's way of thinking. He had twirled Cecily around the little space in a delightful adaptation of a country dance that set feet tapping and even brought a smile to Jemima's face.

Come morning the rain had cleared away, and the mists were slowly rising from the valley where the village sat at the base of the road to Geneva. They were inside the canton of Geneva, within Swiss borders, and had it not been for the downpour, would have made Geneva before nightfall.

Althea looked out of her window to see Jemima strolling away from the inn, no doubt in search of a little shop that sold sweetmeats, or whatever else she could find to nibble while in the carriage.

Deciding they might as well stay to enjoy the day and the festival, Althea quickly dressed, slipping on a warm shawl over her sensible muslin print gown. Having enjoyed a light breakfast of tea and rolls in her room, she decided to take a page from Jemima's book and wander about the village.

The inn was quiet when she ran lightly down the stairs and out of the front door. None of her party was in view when she had paused to peep into the common room, now restored to pristine neatness after the evening's festivities.

In the bright morning light she could appreciate the beauty of the area, with gay flowers about and attractive buildings decorated with painted scenes or pretty figures. How very picturesque it all was.

It did not take her long to roam about the quaint little village. It proved to be neat and clean, a distinct change from those villages they had passed through in France. Houses rose from the street with interesting overhangs decorated with fanciful corbels—some of funny old men with strange expressions. The inhabitants, who clearly had not been exposed to Hercules as yet, smiled shyly at Althea when she nodded at them.

Feeling much in charity with the world—after all, Lord Montmorcy was nowhere in sight—Althea set off to explore the terrain just beyond the edge of the settlement. She could hear the sound of falling water, and above all she enjoyed the sight of rainbows dancing in the cascading drops.

Just a short distance from the edge of the village she came on a stream tumbling and bubbling around boulders and over rocks, creating a song of sorts. Little birds darted over the water and flashed in and out of the trees. Clumps of sedge and tall grasses lined the edge of the water. A squirrel posed for a moment on a sunny rock opposite where she paused, then disappeared into a clump of wildflowers.

Althea found a tall, fat pine for a prop and plopped down on a rock, leaning against the strength of the tree to simply soak in the fresh air and sunshine. In truth the respite from the jolting of the carriage and the sharpness of Jemima's tongue was welcome. When they reached Geneva it would be necessary to figure out how to discourage the men from traveling with them to the glacier . . . and then she recalled her vow to find a nice, proper husband for dearest Cecily.

It would be worth anything, even enduring the disturbing presence of Lord Montmorcy, to make Cecily happy. And she had appeared quite delighted with Lord Montmorcy's attentions last evening.

Althea closed her eyes, insisting that there was no feeling of hurt within and what utter nonsense it was that she should know anything but happiness for Cecily when playing matchmaker.

Deciding that inactivity gave her mind too little to occupy

itself, Althea rose from her idyllic spot and began to wander along the stream.

When the sound of falling water grew louder, she hurried a trifle, eager to view a sight she enjoyed. A bend in the stream and she was rewarded with what promised to be a splendid waterfall. Running to the edge of the path and kneeling down on the grassy rim, she peered over the side for a novel view of the water as it fell, splashing, foaming mightily on the boulders far below.

Diamonds of water danced and flew about in the air currents, catching the sun and creating little rainbows in a hundred colors. The sheer beauty took her breath away, and she completely forgot all else in her captivation.

She shifted further away from the steep descent of the falls and stretched out a hand to capture a sparkling drop when she felt herself slip—or was she nudged? She struggled to regain her footing and slipped even more. A look behind her revealed no one in sight. So how could she have been pushed? It was a silly notion. Yet she had the most peculiar feeling that someone was around.

"Who is there?" she cried in concern.

Silence. Only the sound of the water, which admittedly was loud enough to cover a fair amount of noise, could be heard. She relaxed, deciding it had been her imagination. There was no one in view, only the whispering of the wind in the trees and the sound of the water.

Althea knew it was folly to linger here alone and some distance from the inn, yet she adored the beauty of the scene. But even good things must end. So she again tried to extricate herself from what seemed to be a predicament.

Instead of nimbly edging backward, she felt a thrust of pressure. It was enough to push her off balance and forward since there was naught but slick grass to grasp at. She found herself slipping and tumbling over the edge of the waterfall . . . down . . . down . . . She reached out desperate fingers, hoping to break her fall. Clawing and grasping at the wall of stones, she came to rest on a slight ledge many feet below.

Battered and somewhat bruised, damp and rapidly becoming wetter, she clung to the slippery rock with trembling fingers. Surely she must be mistaken. No one had been around. There had been utter silence! Yet she distinctly had felt the shove that propelled her over the edge.

She tried and found footing of sorts in the little niche. Then with a great deal of care she slowly edged her way downward from rock to boulder to rock until she reached the bottom of the streambed only to find she was stranded in the bottom of a ravine! It was a very pretty ravine, with ferns and grasses along the tumbling stream, but it was closed in by that steep wall of rocks.

How would she ever manage to climb out of here? It was quite one thing to manage to make her way down, but up? She craned her neck to peer at the upmost edge of the chasm and found the sight most daunting.

"I cannot believe I was so stupid and careless as to crawl so far forward." And yet the knowledge that she had *felt* a nudge, that she had sensed the presence of someone out in the woods behind her persisted. Had she not managed to reach and cling to that slight ledge, she had no doubt that at this point she would be a mangled and battered body at the foot of the lovely waterfall.

"Now, if I am to join our group and enjoy the remainder of my tour, I had best leave this delightful spot." Talking to herself did no good in the least, but it served the absurd purpose of making her feel not quite so alone.

Searching the area did not prove very helpful. Other than the curious squirrel and a few birds who totally ignored her, there was no other sign of life.

"Hullo, up there." Would someone come? "Help!"

Which brought her precisely no response.

She realized that since it was early morning she had all day to extricate herself from this dilemma, but somehow the thought was not terribly consoling. She ached from head to toe, and her hands were scratched and bleeding. Stooping down, she washed them off in the sparkling water of the stream. Drying her hands on her skirt—the once pretty gown was now reduced to a rather shredded condition, not to mention sadly soiled—she again surveyed the rock wall above her.

Feeling a bit apprehensive, she inserted a neatly half-booted foot into the first recess and found she was able to scramble up a trifle. She was attempting to locate a foothold when a voice boomed out over the sound of cascading water.

"Miss Ingram? Althea? Halloo!"

She almost sobbed in relief. Even if she recognized the voice as belonging to Lord Montmorcy, it was a welcome sound.

"Here!" she shouted back at him, hoping that handsome head would pop over the rim so she might better communicate her difficulty.

She was rewarded with just such a view. The tousled head of a worried-looking Lord Montmorcy peered down at her from above. Then he said in a voice of utter exasperation, "Egad, woman, do you not know better than to put yourself in such a fix? How do you propose to work your way out of there?"

"A stout rope and a few willing hands might help," Althea shot back at him, angry that he should think she had deliberately placed herself in this spot. "And I did not come down here on purpose!" she declared in annoyance.

"Can you not climb up?"

"Not without a bit of help, I fear." Althea returned to the level of the stream and stepped back as far as the water permitted. From here she could see that Lord Montmorcy was alone. "I suspect you had best obtain help. 'Tis clear *you* could not manage to assist me to reach the path once again. Rope, I should think," she repeated in case he had missed that earlier suggestion.

His head disappeared, and she wondered if he had heard her plea for rope and an extra hand. Now if she were as petite as Cecily, Lord Montmorcy could have pulled her up quite speedily. However, when one was ten inches above five feet and not the weight of a fairy, one did not expect to be hauled to safety by a single person.

Resigned to a wait, Althea perched on a rock, mulling over the peculiar circumstances of her fall and avoiding the consideration of what might have happened were she to have plunged to the bottom without having found that ledge. Neither presented pleasant conclusions. The sun began to dry her damp gown, and she pulled at it, wrinkling her nose in disgust at her bedraggled appearance. Was she ever to appear at advantage to Lord Montmorcy?—not that it really mattered, of course.

It seemed like an age before she heard noises again. Shortly Lord Montmorcy's head appeared, and Althea resigned herself to a scold when she saw his frown. He looked in a towering rage.

"Do you think you can manage to hang onto the rope once I let it down?" His voice did not appear to hold a great deal of confidence in her ability to follow instructions. "Notice there is a loop in the rope. Pass it over your head, then slip it under your arms. And for goodness sake, woman, hang on for dear life."

Althea ignored the sarcasm in his voice and resolutely did as instructed. Wincing when the rope cut into her tender flesh, she tugged slightly on it while calling out to those above, "Ready."

"Fine." Lord Montmorcy's head peeped over the edge again, and he studied the wall of rock up which Althea must traverse as well as possible under the circumstances. "Try to find a toehold while I bring you up. I will proceed slowly so as not to bruise you."

Althea doubted that, but again followed directions, while thinking he surely must have been mistaken when he said "I", for she just knew he'd need an assistant. Slowly, foot by foot, she worked her way up the steep wall, seeking toeholds as she climbed, relying on the steady pressure of that rope that went up and out of sight. It went rather well, all things considered. The rocks and boulders offered providential niches in which she could find purchase, and she balanced herself against the rope as she went.

Later she decided it had not really been all that long a time, but at that moment, it seemed to take an eternity to reach the flat and blessedly dry ground. For some moments she merely lay, eyes closed, exhausted by her ordeal. The earth smelled rich and pine-scented, warmed by the morning sun, and infinitely good.

Then she opened her eyes to stare up into the bewitching green ones that belonged to the dratted Lord Montmorcy. "Thank you for the rescue," she murmured past the constriction in her throat. She glanced to the side and could not see another person about. Frowning, she said, "You came alone? Where is your help?"

"I grabbed the first batch of rope I could find and dashed back here to pull you out. It did not appear to me that you were in any condition for a convention to be called." His expression was wry and self-deprecating. He was not a man who puffed his exploits, that was obvious.

"Oh, my," she exclaimed softly, overwhelmed at the significance of this information. Lord Montmorcy was no society dandy, rather a decidedly athletic man if he had the power to extract her from the ravine all on his own. She owed him a great deal.

Looking up into those unusual green eyes proved most unsettling, however, when she intended to speak her thanks. Additional words of appreciation that she planned to voice died unspoken. Butterflies did a cotillion in her stomach, and she knew the oddest desire to reach up and caress his face. Her adversary? Never!

She transferred her gaze to his arms covered in the fine cambric of his shirt and swallowed with care. Spray from the waterfall had drifted over to dampen his shirt, and his well-muscled arms were clearly revealed. Impressive strength, intimidating power barely leashed, she realized.

"Then I am doubly in your debt," she managed to say at long last. "I do thank you."

"How did it happen? Somehow you do not strike me as the sort of female who would do such a totty-headed thing as to lean over far enough to lose your balance."

"Actually, I peeped over the edge rather cautiously. It was such a lovely sight." She frowned, almost matching Lord Montmorcy in the intensity of her expression. "You will think me mad or fanciful, but I would swear that I was pushed. Yet I saw no one and heard nothing. 'Tis most peculiar."

"Hm," he murmured while bending over to inspect her face and hands. He did not respond to her charge, most likely thinking it an absurd notion. With an incredibly gentle touch, he brushed her curls away from her face, ran his hand over her head, shoulders, and arms, then with an apologetic look at her said, "Is the rest of you in one piece? I cannot check your legs and body as I might a man."

The odd trembling Althea had experienced when he had touched her faded at his words. Indeed, she almost smiled when she noted the faint reddening of his cheeks. However, her aches were making themselves painfully known so all she did was shake her head. "I am fine." Which had to be the most ridiculous lie she had ever made in her life.

"We need to bring you back to the inn. I do not suppose you can walk?" He partly rose, holding out one strong hand to her.

Considering what he asked of her, Althea almost shook her head, then she reconsidered. While she ached in every muscle, nothing was broken or sprained. She did not wish to cause undue alarm, which might result if Lord Montmorcy came back to seek a cart for her. "I can but try," she concluded with a gallant smile.

Trembling when he wrapped his arm about her to assist her in rising, Althea took a firm hold of her sensibilities and grimly rose to her feet. It was not possible she might walk to the inn without his help, but she would no doubt recall every step of the way for the rest of her life.

The path was uneven, which meant that Lord Montmorcy kept his arm most firmly about Althea, offering his other hand to provide her additional support. She had never felt so sheltered or tenderly cared for in her life—not even the time she fell from the apple tree and sprained her arm.

Near the end of the little walk, she paused to catch her breath and rest. Looking up at him again proved a mistake, for she found her gaze trapped in the warm depths of his eyes. His arm about her felt strong and comforting. She had not been so close to a man before, other than in dancing and a few hasty kisses snatched by importuning young men at various parties. This was quite different, for they stood in a piney glade, hard by a bubbling stream, and very much alone. "Ah, I . . . er . . . that is," she whispered.

John was not a man much given to words, but a man of action. He found soft trembling lips so close to his and a sweetly confused expression irresistible. He bent his head just a perfect distance and discovered a pair of lips that were inviting, delicately pliable, and utterly perfect. While knowing that he was a scoundrel for taking advantage of the delectable—and wounded—Miss Ingram in this way, he could not withdraw. This was, he argued, part and parcel of finding out the reason for this peculiar reaction he felt toward her.

Eased about and cradled in strong arms, Althea quite forgot for a few moments her earnest intentions regarding Cecily. Never had a kiss felt so wonderful, so right. His hands held her as though she were a fragile reed that might break at the slightest pressure. She felt treasured, precious, and exceedingly vulnerable.

Slipping her hands around him, she found the soft cambric of his shirt did little to conceal the strength of his muscular back. He drew her closer, and she responded until her aching muscles brought about an involuntary wince.

At once he released her, stepping away while maintaining a strong support for her with one arm.

"That ought not have happened," Althea said in what she hoped was a calm voice. A trifle breathless, she tried to attribute it to her condition.

A hooded expression slipped over his face, and he nodded by way of reply. "Come, we had best hurry you to the inn. I forgot myself and should not have taken advantage of you in such a manner. I apologize, Miss Ingram." He looked straight ahead of them to the path leading out of the woods and back to the village proper.

Such formal words, such a cold voice. Althea stiffened, and not entirely from her pain. "That is quite all right, sir. I trust it shan't happen again."

Once around the final curve in the path, they encountered Mr. Poindexter and Hercules, the latter off his leash and gamboling about in the fashion of a very large and friendly giant, if an awkward one.

"Good gad, Montmorcy, what has happened! Miss Ingram, you look as though attacked by an animal or worse." Mr.

Poindexter rushed forward to offer his arm as additional support.

Shaking her head, Althea said, "I shall be much better once I reach my room and have a little rest. I need a bath, perhaps, and a change of gowns. I fear this one is a loss."

She managed a troubled smile and allowed the conversation between the two gentlemen to flow past her while they navigated the final steps to the inn.

The innkeeper's wife bustled forth with a spate of words in her language that appeared to be sympathetic and rather curious, as well. She insisted upon ushering Althea to her tiny room on the floor above and promised to bring the longed-for hot water.

Within minutes Cecily tapped on her door, cooing words of distress and not demanding an explanation of what had happened. Her gentle manner served to remind Althea what a dear she was. It also made Althea feel outrageously guilty. She resolved to say nothing of that extraordinary kiss in the glade, for it might shock Cecily to think a gentleman could behave in such a censurable way.

Once clean and curled up in her bed, Althea said, "I shall take a bit of a nap, then I have something to discuss with you, something rather odd."

Cecily was intrigued at this sleepily offered scrap, but seeing her cousin was in no condition to talk now, she slipped from the room and down the stairs to the common room to confront Lord Montmorcy for an explanation. She found that gentleman with Mr. Poindexter, both downing pints of local ale and wearing puzzled expressions.

"Dashed peculiar, it is," Lord Montmorcy said in a quiet voice. He glanced at Cecily, then added, "She fell into a ravine just beyond a waterfall. Not the sort of thing that ought to happen if you are simply looking, y'know. She said she felt something push her, yet she saw no one about."

"Imaginings," Mr. Poindexter said dismissively.

Cecily could have done violence at that smugly spoken word. "Althea is *not* given to fanciful notions, sirrah. She is an extremely sensible girl. If she says someone pushed her, you can wager your last shilling that someone did."

"There was not a soul around when I came nor any evidence, save for a stout limb across the path," Lord Montmorcy said. "Perhaps she merely stumbled?"

"And does not wish to admit clumsiness? You cannot know Althea, 'tis plain, for she would chuckle at *that*, you may be sure. She is not one to pretend to be other than she is." The look bestowed on his lordship was censorious and perhaps a trifle accusing.

"I suspect we shan't know, then, for without any witness to the happening, we have no clue."

"Good morning, all," Jemima said upon entering the common room. "What a lot of gloomy faces. Where is Althea?"

"She fell while out walking and was badly scratched up," Cecily rushed to say before the men could offer some banal explanation.

"Oh, how perfectly dreadful," Jemima said in her usual placid way. It was difficult to know if she ever became excited about anything, for she never revealed her inner feelings in the least.

John watched the two women discuss the strange accident while musing over his own behavior. He rubbed his chin and felt not terribly proud of his actions, at least when it came to kissing the delectable Miss Ingram. She had been quite a surprise—soft and gentle in his arms, feeling so right and belonging there. The kiss disturbed him, for he'd not known that odd reaction before, that feeling of not wanting to let her go, of desiring to keep her close to him.

The peace of the common room was broken by noise from the village square. Outside the inhabitants had gathered following their church service to celebrate the festival of St. Peter and St. Paul. It was a strange mixture of solemn pride in their religious heritage and happiness in the occasion when they might have a respite from the daily tasks.

The high spire of the church stood out grandly against the distant mountain peaks. In the square just beyond the church, the musicians heard the evening before again played their jolly tunes. Couples who perhaps felt impelled to express their joy in a different way, danced a simple country dance with much laughter and swirling of skirts.

Cecily grabbed Jemima's hand, wishing it might be Althea who joined her, and with the three gentlemen—the comte had come down just as they went out the door—the group hurried out to see what had been set forth for amusement.

Booths had been erected to offer excellent cheeses and little sausages. Pretty embroidery that had been executed by the local housewives was displayed among a great many other things. Jemima immediately went to sample the variety of cheeses offered and pronounced the Emmentaler delicious when topping fresh, crusty bread.

John and Sidney—with Hercules safely leashed and tagging happily behind them—wandered about as well. John glanced back at the inn, wondering how Miss Ingram fared. She would be stiff and sore, for she had been badly bruised. That her slender body had suffered no greater damage was a miracle. Her insistence that someone had pushed her troubled him greatly, for he could not imagine anyone could wish her harm. The entire matter would bear watching, and he was glad he had insisted upon traveling along with the ladies. Unless his first assumption was correct, and it was a local person out to see if anything of value might be had, there could be danger lurking ahead for Althea Ingram.

Jemima had purchased another chunk of cheese and bread and held it out for the others to see. Unfortunately, Hercules thought she held it up for him. A simple jump against the plump, shortish woman and she was on her back in the dust of the street. Hercules happily wolfed down the bread and cheese in one gulp. Jemima squirmed and fussed, calling for help. Hercules barked for more of the treat.

"Be gone, you beast," Jemima hissed, unable to push the dog away. To Sidney she appealed, "Do something!"

The villagers gathered about, laughing at Jemima with good-natured humor and making remarks—fortunately in a dialect of French that Jemima could not possibly understand—and in general behaving as though this was a part of the festivities provided for their entertainment.

The English group had tried valiantly to refrain from laughing, for it was clear that Jemima was utterly furious. But when Hercules nosed around for more cheese and found none, thereupon howling for more while sitting on Jemima, it proved too much.

"Oh, dear me," Cecily sobbed, wiping tears of laughter from her eyes even as she proffered a helping hand to Jemima.

An infuriated Jemima scrambled to her feet and glared at the offending animal, muttering imprecations that would have curled his hair had he understood her threats. Hercules simply sat wreathed in doggy smiles, looking about for another treat. His soulful eyes begged one and all to provide him with such.

Cecily turned a troubled face to the others when Jemima stalked off toward the inn in high dudgeon. "I fear she is exceedingly angry," she said to the comte, who had come to her side.

"I cannot see you behaving in that manner, nor Miss Ingram, either," he said quietly.

"Mercy, no. Althea would have a jolly laugh, and I would take care to offer the cheese to Hercules *before* he could mow me down, you may be certain," she said with a giggle that appeared to enchant the comte.

"I suggest we repair to the inn and check to see how Miss Ingram fares," John said to Cecily and the others. "All this noise may have awakened her. I pray she had no concealed injuries."

Concerned, Cecily agreed and the four made their way through the throng of villagers and country people until they reached the inn.

When they entered, they discovered Althea at the foot of the stairs, supported by a young village maid.

"You ought not to be out of bed," Cecily scolded.

"Something woke me up. Whatever is Jemima so upset about?" she wondered, giving a clue as to what that noise most likely had been.

The episode in the square was explained, and Althea joined in soft laughter while the group went into the common room and urged Althea into a comfortable chair.

Inevitably, her fall was brought up and John leaned forward, placing an urgent hand on the arm of his chair. "I hope it may have been nothing more than an eager lad out to find a bit of loot, although what you might have brought along with you I cannot imagine. Otherwise"—he looked around the group while allowing his quiet words to sink in—"I fear Miss Ingram to be in danger for her life."

Chapter Seven

"That has to be the silliest thing I have ever heard," Althea declared, easing herself back in the chair she had chosen for comfort, taking care with her bruised hands now covered with silk gloves. "I doubt there is a soul on earth who would wish me dead. Why? I am not a great heiress; my dowry is adequate, but not astounding. I am not the sort to go about making enemies. No," she concluded firmly, "your notion is completely erroneous."

Lord Montmorcy gave her an annoyed look, then shook his head as though to dispel what he had just heard. "How do you explain that you felt someone shove you?"

"I must have imagined it," she replied with a dismissing wave of her hand. "Indeed, I am sorry I even mentioned it. I would never have done so had you not thought me a totty-headed female who would be so stupid as to bend far enough over that bank so I fell in on my own," she said with an accusing glance at Lord Montmorcy.

"So you admit that you were pushed!" he said in triumph of sorts.

"Perhaps. But it must have been a robber or the like as you suggested before. The only people I know here are all of you." She gestured to the group, and they exchanged dismayed glances. "If someone truly wished me harm, he would have pushed a bit more firmly."

"You forget Jemima," Cecily said in an undertone.

"Oh, pooh," Althea shot back. "Jemima is not capable of doing such a thing," Althea generously declared in an aside to

Cecily. Actually, although she'd not accuse the girl of it out loud, Jemima would more likely be concerned about her next meal.

"Well," Cecily declared quietly, "I will feel a good deal better when we can quit this place. It looks so charming and peaceful, and yet harbors someone who may have evil intent. Althea's poor hands and a good deal of the rest of her"—Cecily correctly refrained from mentioning other limbs or body parts—" are badly bruised. I shudder to think how close she came to an injury far more serious."

"But the lovely Miss Ingram cannot travel yet," the comte protested.

"I believe she ought to consult a doctor in Geneva," Lord Montmorcy said. Then he turned to focus those green eyes on Althea, creating a peculiar havoc within her.

Determined to foster the match between Cecily and Lord Montmorcy, Althea looked from one to the other, searching for some sign of interest or better. Sighing inwardly, she noticed little to encourage her.

"How do you feel, dearest?" Cecily asked in that sort of voice one uses to someone who is deathly ill and is not supposed to know it.

"Well, if you two believe I ought to seek medical attention in Geneva, I imagine I could travel that far." Turning slightly and wincing from the stiffness that had settled in her shoulders, Althea said to his lordship, "You did say it was not very distant, did you not?"

His features assumed a grave look and his study of Althea was most considering.

"Well?" she demanded when she could stand the suspense no longer.

"If we cushion you with pillows, I imagine it could be done. Mind you, it will not be the easiest trip you have ever made, but you seem a hardy sort."

Althea grimaced, then glanced at Cecily. There was one delicate lady his lordship would never label hardy. Attired in a pretty rose gown of sheerest wool trimmed with rows of lace, she looked like a particularly delicious comfit.

"Indeed, Miss Ingram has the constitution most brave," the comte added with a gracious nod at Althea.

"It is settled, then. As soon as the carriage and coach may be arranged, we shall proceed to Geneva," Althea declared with resolution. "I believe I will go up to my little room and pack what things I have removed. That muslin dress has already gone to the innkeeper's wife for rags, so there is that much less to put in my portmanteau." She smiled at all, then rose and stiffly made her way from the room.

She knew the most absurd desire to burst into tears, and it would not do to appear such a weakling after all the wonderful encomiums just heaped on her hardy and brave head.

While she did not precisely envy Cecily for being petite, adorable, and the very nicest person in the world, Althea would not have minded being a trifle shorter and perhaps a bit more vulnerable. It served to reaffirm her intention regarding a match between Cecily and Lord Montmorcy. Surely, he would prefer a petite and darling wife like her cousin rather than a hardy, brave, and resolute giantess. And then she wondered where that ridiculous comparison had popped up from. Her mind jumped back to the moment on the path just before Mr. Poindexter had met them.

Lord Montmorcy had taken advantage of her weakness and indulged himself at her expense, she decided. That she had quite enjoyed that stolen kiss was beside the point. It revealed a less than savory side to Lord Montmorcy. A true gentleman ought not go about stealing kisses from weakened females— even if they cooperated. Perhaps the year spent wandering through the Alps had affected his sense of propriety. Or perhaps he had been too long away from feminine companionship. She must take care to avoid being alone with him again. Perhaps she could inveigle Lord Montmorcy into tempting Cecily into his arms, for that was what was needed. All she needed for her plan to succeed was a bit of cooperation from those two.

Once she reached her room, she found that the shy Susan had packed the items that had been removed for her stay. While understanding that traveling with an entourage increased costs dramatically, she also decided that come Geneva she would hire an abigail for herself, giving Susan to Cecily. Jemima would most likely prefer to be on her own, not wishing to incur the expense. And alas, it seemed to make little difference what garb she put on, she looked frumpy no matter what.

Althea was about to inform Jemima that they would be departing as soon as may be, for they tended to forget about Jemima, and they couldn't leave her behind, when she heard a knock at the door. "Enter," she called out, thinking it was Cecily come to fetch her.

"Woman," Lord Montmorcy declared in an angry voice, "you need a keeper. Did I not tell you that is a dangerous thing to do in an inn? Particularly after that attack on your person." He shut the door behind him and advanced on Althea like a predatory cat—a very large predatory cat.

"You ought not be in here," she pointed out in a polite manner, far more polite than he deserved.

A shocked Susan backed into a corner, clutching a cloak to her thin chest. The other two ignored her.

"I came to see that you took some laudanum before we leave here. The jolting of the carriage will make the journey most difficult for you unless you have something to ease the discomfort."

"Ugh," she said before recalling that was not a very elegant reply. "I detest such potions. I should not wish to rely on them."

He took a step closer, looked about the room, then espied the glass and spoon she had used earlier. The tooth powder Jemima had given her had proven difficult to open, and she had been forced to tap the cap a great many times with the spoon before it loosened. The powder had proven to have a strange—although not unpleasant—taste with a cinnamon flavor to it. She much preferred her old sort and would look for some in Geneva, disposing of the odd powder once there without saying a word to Jemima. Since the girl had made the effort to be agreeable, Althea wished to meet her partway.

Before she could realize what he was about, Lord Montmorcy strode over to pick up the glass, removed a small bottle from his pocket, and poured in a tiny amount. When he offered the glass with the laudanum to Althea, she swiftly put her hands behind her and gave him a mutinous look.

"I know, 'tis dreadful stuff," he admitted. "However, I am concerned for you. I will not have you arriving in Geneva feeling as though you have been pulled from pillar to post. Here." He thrust the glass at her, drawing closer.

"I suppose you would pour the dratted stuff down my throat if need be," she muttered, accepting the glass and looking at the contents with undisguised loathing."

"As I remarked upon entering, you need someone to look after you. Whatever are your parents thinking of to permit you to hare off to the Continent by yourself?" He folded his arms across his chest, watching while she downed the laudanum in a gulp, grimaced, then set the glass down on the closest surface.

"I am not by myself; Cecily and Jemima are more than enough company," she snapped back once she was able to speak again. "And I also had Mr. Winton to arrange matters for me until you stepped in to fire the man. As to my parents, my father apparently has greater faith in my ability to manage than you do. Perhaps it is because he has known me longer," she said sweetly.

Lord Montmorcy had the grace to look mildly abashed when she reminded him of his interference. Then he bestowed a sharp look at Althea and said, "Your mother?"

"My mother died many years ago. Father has been quite absorbed with his new wife and infant son this past year."

"And she, no doubt, wished you to the ends of the earth." His expression was very knowing. It was a common enough circumstance that a second wife wish the children of the first to be gone.

While Althea had searched for a tactful way to say that her new stepmother was not quite like that, but undoubtedly wished Althea to another household, she suspected that Lord Montmorcy drew the wrong conclusions.

"I see."

"No, it truly is not bad. Beatrice is a very good wife to my father and a devoted mother. But having four women in the house made life a trifle unpleasant, particularly for my father.

With Jemima, Cecily, and myself out of the way, perhaps they may have a more agreeable time."

He digested this, but said nothing. Picking up her portmanteau, he glanced at the trunk that sat neatly closed not far from the door. "Come, we had best go downstairs. The carriage ought to be ready about now. How do you feel?"

"Fine," she said. While it was not a lie, she knew she stretched the truth a bit.

He did not reply, but dropped the portmanteau, then picked up one of her hands. Before she knew what he was about, he had pulled her sleeve back and stripped off her glove, thus revealing the cuts and lacerations she had sustained in her tumble down the twenty-foot bank.

"It is a good thing I remembered I had the laudanum," he said in a fierce tone with a savage look at her that prompted her to take a step back from him.

"They may look bad, but will heal quickly if kept clean, I have no doubt." She wondered why she found it necessary to reassure him. Surely he ought to be showing more interest in Cecily. Perhaps he would if Althea managed to stay out of trouble for a while.

"You *will* see a physician when we reach Geneva. I insist." He declared this with the assurance of a man who is accustomed to ordering things to his own liking.

Althea longed to ask him what right he had to demand such a personal thing, then remained silent when he again picked up her bag, lightly clasped her arm, and ushered her from the little room and down the stairs. It was a distinct novelty to be treated as though she were composed of fine porcelain. No doubt her docility had to do with the drug he had given her beginning to take effect, otherwise she might have been inclined to give him a gentle scold and remove herself from his care. After all, she had packed a small bottle of the wretched laudanum in her trunk, and had she been truly injured, would have reluctantly resorted to the stuff. However, it was nice to be looked after, even if his manner was as odious as could be. Dreadful creature.

At the bottom of the stairs he ordered a servant to see to the remaining trunks immediately in that polite manner that set people to hopping at once. They left the inn, and Althea was surprised to see all seemed in readiness.

When she entered the carriage, she gasped in surprise. She looked back at his lordship and demanded, "Wherever did you find so many pillows? I vow you must have depleted the entire supply for the village. I hate to think how many geese it took to create these!" She sank back on the puffs of down, feeling like the heroine in a novel she had read who had been captured and confined in a harem where she reclined on piles of pillows in Oriental splendor.

"It should make the trip easier for you," he said after he had inspected the interior and noted her situation.

Mr. Poindexter, with Hercules trailing reluctantly behind him, also popped a head in to wish her a good journey. Then Montmorcy called to him, and Poindexter good-naturedly went off to the comte's traveling coach, coaxing Hercules to enter the coach with some difficulty.

Jemima glared at the mounds of pillows, grumbling that they took far more space than necessary. Cecily admonished her to consider poor Althea's injuries. Susan happily settled on the front seat with the coachman and groom, seeming content to be away from the ladies for a time.

Althea sank back as she felt the carriage beginning to move. Then lulled by the unexpected luxury of the piles of down pillows, not to mention their comfort, and no doubt the effect of the laudanum, she soon dozed off to sleep.

In the forward traveling coach, John frowned while staring out of the window at nothing in particular. He truly did not like that nasty business at the stream. Could someone have used that stout limb that had lain across the path to shove at Althea Ingram? She pooh-poohed the notion, but John was not so certain. As to who might be the culprit, well, that was another matter. Most likely it was a chance thing, someone who sought gain of some sort. Had the chap intended to demand ransom? He had bungled his attempt, that was for certain.

"Odd business," Sidney said while keeping a restraining hand on Hercules, who still was not quite reconciled to the notion of traveling.

"Indeed," John murmured.

"You gentlemen appear to be very close," the comte observed, glancing from one to the other. "You seem to know what is in each other's minds, as the best of friends often do."

"Have been since we went to school together," Sidney said. "John had a way of rescuing me from my follies even then," he concluded, grimacing at the recollection.

"Your trouble is that you become so involved with your studies that you tend to forget the world around you," John said with his smile back in place once more. "Even more so now." He turned to face the comte and added, "You have no idea how many times I have caught this fellow on the verge of stepping off a cliff. He finds those petrifactions of his totally absorbing."

"Petrifactions? You mentioned them before. Precisely what are they and where do you find them?" the comte inquired of Sidney.

John groaned and leaned back against the corner, covering his face with his handkerchief so he might pretend to doze, but actually turned his thoughts in another direction. He'd kept his dealing with the gentler sex to a minimum for a good many years. For one thing, few women appealed to him—most being short, if pretty, like Mrs. de Lisle. And the other main reason he avoided the fair sex was that most women pursued him for his title and fortune, not that he could blame them for it. But he knew a strong desire to be wanted just for himself. Utter rubbish, he supposed, for he well knew what his family and society expected of him. He ought to marry, produce an heir, and settle down on his estate instead of wandering about Switzerland as though fleeing from a parcel of ghosts.

Which thought brought him back to Miss Ingram. She had haunted his dreams for the past year, true. But why? What was there about the girl that had made such a strong impact on his senses? The kiss in that pine-scented glade had been in the nature of an experiment, to see if it might offer a clue. Instead it had turned into something intriguing and raised more questions than it brought answers. It was a good thing she had winced and recalled him to what was proper, or she'd have found herself far gone down the road to impropriety with him.

As to the accident, if it was that, he would see to it that the remainder of her journey was without incident—from him or anyone else. He intended to take care of Miss Ingram, even if against her will.

This thought somehow brought him to the matter of his mother and her remarriage. He'd wager that his sister, Chloe, would not be best pleased being left with Grandmama Dancy. That old dragon would either force Chloe to flee in fright or compel her to accept the old woman's dictates.

He should have been there for his little sister and felt guilty he was not. He considered Sidney and wondered if his good friend might be interested in marrying Chloe. No, he decided upon reflection. Sidney needed a strong woman, an organizer, one who could look after him. Chloe did not fit that description.

It began to drizzle out, and Sidney poked John in the leg. "How about a game of cards?"

"Here, now, the fellow's asleep," the comte objected.

"No, he ain't," Sidney said complacently, "just pretending to sleep. John likes to think about his problems, and I'll wager with Miss Ingram he has added one or two to the list. Eh, John?"

John pulled the handkerchief from his head and bestowed a level glare on his good friend. Then he gestured to the deck of cards that had magically appeared in Sidney's hands, pulled from one of his pockets.

"Deal," John said, knowing this was the best way to solve the matter.

And so the gentlemen whiled away the hours playing whist for imaginary fortunes, as none of them carried a vast sum in their purses.

Althea stirred when the carriage bounced and jounced over the cobblestones when they entered Geneva. Sitting forward on her mound of pillows, she found herself a trifle stiff, but otherwise much improved for the inactivity and the sleep. Looking out of the window, she exclaimed in delight, "We are here."

"Yes," Jemima grumbled, "and a dull dreary trip it was, too."

"Now, Jemima," Cecily chided, "you know Althea needed

her sleep. Besides, we enjoyed a lovely game of cards while it drizzled outside." To Althea she added, "The roads coming down the mountain and into the city were excellent."

Considering how nasty it could become while traveling in England even in July, Althea was surprised the road had not turned to mire nor was the carriage freezing. Another glance outside enticed her, and she rolled down the window so to obtain a better view of the sights.

She knew Geneva was an old established city, having had a settlement in this spot for a great many years. It had been the location of the reformer, Calvin. And the industrious Genovese were famed for their fine watches and excellent banks. She needed to see a banker to present her letter of credit and receive enough *louis d'ors* and *petite ecus* for her needs. She also desired to visit a watchmaker's establishment to purchase a pretty timepiece. All in proper order, of course.

"A little conduct, please," Cecily said with none of the usual warmth in her voice when it looked as though Althea might extend her head a trifle too far out of the window.

First darting a look at Cecily, then Jemima, Althea decided that the journey had been extremely taxing for Cecily and felt dreadful. She drew away from the window and sought to make amends. "I gather the card game proved tedious," Althea commented lightly.

"Oh, look," Cecily said rather than answer that question. "What odd buildings; they appear to have great sheds high above the ground. Do you suppose it is to shield the building from snow come the winter?"

"Perhaps. I must say, there is a very solid look to the city," Althea offered, poking her head almost out of the window to gaze with wonder at the sights presented her eyes.

"There is not the least sign of elegance," Jemima said with a sniff after putting her face to the window for a look about.

Cecily and Althea were saved from searching for a reply to this unkind remark when the carriage came to a halt before the venerable Hôtel d'Angleterre.

When the door opened, Cecily and Jemima clambered out first, then Althea floundered her way through the mound of pillows until she could join them. It disconcerted her to find Lord Montmorcy offering her his hand.

"Good evening, my lord," she said properly, for the hour was drawing late and it soon would be dark.

"We made excellent time, did we not? The roads hereabout are excellent."

"I slept the entire way, so I could not say to that," Althea admitted, wishing he would let go of her hand. He obeyed her unspoken wish, then made matters far worse by slipping his arm about her, assisting her into the hotel as though she were a fragile china doll.

The manager of the refined hotel surged forward to greet the new guests. As a rule English were not very welcome when traveling, for they tended to complain a great deal, demand much, and tip rather badly. But Lord Montmorcy had already endeared himself to the community, and any people he vouched for would be made welcome.

"My lord," the manager said with dignity, "your valet, Tugwell, has arrived and will assist you as soon as we send word to him."

"Well," Lord Montmorcy muttered softly, "what a fortuitous happenstance. I wonder what brought old Tugwell here without being summoned."

"He felt you might be in need of a bit of polish, no doubt," Althea said with a twinkle lighting up her fine gray eyes.

"Be amused if you will, but yes, for Geneva is a pleasant city, and I have made a number of friends here. It will be most agreeable to see them again—and in prime twig." He gave her an admonishing look, then turned her over to Susan.

Althea subsided into total silence and followed the young maid up the stairs and around a corner to a large room. Cecily was right behind her, not wishing to go to the expense of separate rooms in the city, for it was bound to cost more, and so she explained.

"I vow, I shall welcome your company. I have found it a trifle lonely being all by myself, even if the rooms were small." Althea sank onto one of the two beds in the room, looking about her with a critical eye.

"Althea, do you see what I see? A stove," Cecily exclaimed

in delight. "A white enamel stove that looks a bit like an iced
cake, for it towers so over in the corner. However does it
work?" Cecily set down the small case that held her jewelry
and other needful items before going over to inspect this most
alien thing.

"Do not worry, for it is far from cold tonight, and pray we
leave here before winter sets in." Althea tossed her gloves on
the bed, then removed her half boots before stretching out on
the bed. "I shall test this mattress to see how well the Genovese do by their guests."

"Well, judging by the pleased look on your face it cannot be
bad."

Before Cecily could bring up anything else, a knock on their
door heralded the arrival of their traveling trunks.

Susan quickly crossed the room to see to them.

Down the hall Jemima could be heard scolding the servant
who had brought her things to her, and Althea shared a grimace with Cecily even as she tipped the man.

"I wonder what brought Lord Montmorcy's valet to
Geneva?" Cecily mused while she unpacked her clothes for a
stay of several days.

"Perhaps another message," Althea replied while she did the
same with Susan's help, wondering if Lord Montmorcy would
introduce them to his Geneva friends, for he seemed determined to take them under his wing, like it or not.

"I believe we had best find ourselves an abigail, for poor
Susan will not be able to keep up with both of us. Do you
think there might be an English one available? I would not like
to think the men will outshine us. Just look how polished the
comte is," Althea said with a sigh. "As soon as may be, I will
inquire at the desk downstairs."

At the other end of the hall on the same floor John viewed
his good valet with a smile. "Glad to see you, old man. Don't
mind telling you I can use your services. I fear I could not do
you credit with a decent cravat anymore." Then while he casually sauntered across the room, he went on, "Any news from
home of importance?"

Tugwell had begun removing his master's things from his
portmanteau, shaking his head at every item he pulled out. "In-

deed, sir. Your sister married. Did quite well for herself, I believe. A gentleman by the name of Mr. Julian St. Aubyn. Comes from an old distinguished family, or so I was reliably informed. Rumor has it that he is up for a peerage."

"Must have pots of money then. I detect a story there, one which you can fill me in on later. For the moment I need to change, and I fear you shall have to take charge of Poindexter as well. You know what a muddle he can make of his things."

Tugwell rubbed his hands together, clearly relishing the challenge of two gentlemen who could so benefit themselves from his ministrations. "Indeed, sir. Will he join you in here?"

At that precise moment the door was flung open, and a harried Sidney stumbled into the room, pulled by a determined Hercules.

"Good gracious," Tugwell pronounced in horrified accents. He gave the huge pup a wary look before returning to his duties.

"He will not have a thing to do with the stables here. I bribed the fellow downstairs into letting the dog come up here with me. What do I have to do to bribe you, John?"

"Well," John mused, "I suppose you would be willing to do the pretty with me while we escort the ladies about Geneva. I know you are wanting to hunt for more of those petrified snails, or whatever, but you must help me."

"And I suppose I must entertain Jemima Greenwood," Sidney observed in dismay. "You exact a dreadful compensation, my good friend." Sidney glared at the pup, who drooled over his best boots. "The things you drag me into, old chum," he said to the happy dog. "Very well, I will go along with the group on a tour of Geneva. Just do not expect me to enjoy it."

"All we need to do is keep Miss Ingram safe," John observed warmly. "And that should be a snap—for us."

Chapter Eight

The search for an abigail resulted in success almost at once. The portly gentleman who presided over the hotel knew just the person, he said. A young French woman had lost her position when her employer returned to England, and the girl was anxious to find a new job.

"At least she ought to understand English," Althea said quietly to Cecily.

"Giving yourself airs and graces, you are," Jemima said with her usual disdain. "*I* do not require assistance to look my best." She glared at Cecily as though blaming her for contributing to Althea's fall into decadence, then left their room in a huff. She made no mention of her plans for the day, other than a need to find a bank.

"I did feel obliged to offer her a maid," Althea said contritely. "It seems as though no matter what I do, she thinks it wrong. Before we left home, she castigated me for not bringing a retinue of servants along."

"Do not worry your head about Jemima. We shall interview this French girl, then let *us* head for the bank, after which we may browse through the shops. When I looked from our windows, I glimpsed all manner of tantalizing places. Remember, the maid who brought our breakfast mentioned furriers and milliners and jewelers and watchmakers. Oh, what a delight," Cecily exclaimed, clapping her hands.

"I had not realized you are such a city person, dearest," Althea teased. "Or is it that you wish to find a lovely sable cape to wear against the coming winter cold?"

"That would be nice," Cecily said with mock solemnity, then giggled like a schoolgirl. Her cheeks flushed a becoming rose, she strolled over to the window and stared dreamily out toward the shimmering blue of Lake Leman.

Althea gave her cousin a sharp, assessing look. Cecily was behaving like a young woman in love. Could it be that the plan to nudge her toward Lord Montmorcy was working?

Althea dutifully brushed her teeth, then a few minutes later sank down on the closest chair in dismay.

"What is it?" Cecily asked at once when she heard Althea make a soft noise.

"I do not know," Althea said, wrapping her still scratched and bruised arms about herself. "I have the most peculiar pain." She thought a few moments. "It could not be our breakfast, for we ate the same foods, served from the same dishes. Perhaps something did not agree with me—although I have never had problems in the past." She gave her cousin a puzzled look, then glanced over at the small table near the window where the remains of their morning meal still sat. Susan had been sent off to break her fast.

"It would not be surprising were you to have a minor ache or two, considering what you have endured lately—shooting bandittos, falling into a chasm. Mercy me, but this tour of yours is anything but dull. Pamper yourself the rest of the day. I feel certain you will feel better by evening," Cecily said with hope in her voice.

"Oh, are we to do something special this evening?" Althea inquired while coping with the unusual and growing discomfort in her abdomen.

"The Comte de Bosio has invited us all to be his guests for dinner. I expect it will be very elegant, as he knows a number of people in Geneva and told me it will be quite an international affair."

"Gracious, I hope that French maid can assist Susan, for our clothes are in sad need of care, and she is beset as it is," Althea managed to say. She gave in to her pain and stumbled to her bed, where she curled up like a ball and moaned. "Perhaps I ought to see a doctor after all."

"Ipecacuanha," Cecily mumbled and began rummaging

about in her trunk until she found the remedy she sought. She poured out a dose, then handed it to Althea.

Some time later Althea sank back on her bed again, feeling weak, but oddly much better after the medicine had taken its effect on her. Cecily rang for a chambermaid to clean up the room, then attended to Althea.

"I think it most curious, but perhaps it *has* been too much these past days. Maybe I am not cut out to be a traveler," Althea said with a grimace while tucking a plump down pillow beneath her head.

"Nonsense," Cecily declared, but nonetheless she perched on a chair close to Althea's bed, chatting quietly with her until there was a rap at the door.

The evidence of Althea's malaise was cleaned away by a quiet chambermaid before the meeting with the French girl took place. When the girl came, she turned out to be thin and dark, with nervous movements of her hands and eyes. Yet she wore a sweet expression and seemed eager to please.

Althea curled up quietly in a chair and watched Cecily competently handle the interview. When her cousin looked to Althea for confirmation, Althea gave her a nod of agreement. Wages were agreed upon, the maid to start at once with shy Susan as her mentor.

"Gabrielle, could you please take our gowns to press as we have a dinner engagement this evening," Althea said in her impeccable French.

The maid scurried to do as bid, then left for the laundry room somewhere on a floor below.

Once they were again alone, Althea returned to her bed on the other side of the large room. Cecily wandered about while wearing a most considering look and fiddling with anything that chanced to come to hand.

"What do you suppose was the cause?" Cecily said with a worried look. "Your reaction tells me that you ingested something poisonous, or certainly something that affected you much like a poison."

"Perhaps it was merely the result of the traveling," Althea repeated.

"Perhaps," Cecily said with a dubious note in her voice. "Somehow I doubt it."

It was decided that Althea should nap until she felt more the thing, then the women would set forth for the bank, not having any money save enough for a rather small item.

Satisfied that her cousin slept, Cecily slipped from the bedroom and down the hall until she reached the room that the chambermaid had told her was occupied by Lord Montmorcy and Mr. Poindexter.

Her hesitant rap was answered by a stranger, a very starched-looking man who had to be the valet mentioned by the manager last night.

"Tugwell? Would you be so kind as to give a message to his lordship," she whispered, not wishing to draw the slightest attention to herself standing in the hallway at the door to a gentleman's room.

Knowing it must be something serious to bring a refined lady to such a point, Tugwell nodded, assuming an even graver mien.

"I must see him at his earliest convenience. Something has happened to Miss Ingram." Not stopping to consider how this might sound to one who didn't know the complete circumstances, she retreated down the hall and after checking on the sleeping Althea again, went down the stairs. At the bottom she discovered Jemima trying to make herself understood to the manager of the hotel in her execrable French.

"May I be of assistance?" Cecily inquired in her soft, gentle manner.

Relieved to see the polite English lady again, the manager shrugged his shoulders and gestured to Jemima.

"I wish to find out where the bank is located, for I refuse to wander about this town like some looby," Jemima snapped.

"The location of the bank?" Cecily said in puzzlement. What could have been simpler?

"Ah, madam," the manager bubbled, finally grasping what was wished. He explained the direction with care, and in English so that even Jemima understood what he meant.

"Why did he not say he spoke English?" Jemima muttered to Cecily as the two walked away from the manager.

"I was told that most of the business people in Geneva speak English as well as French," Cecily informed her.

"Where is Althea?" Jemima suddenly asked, finally noticing that Cecily was alone. "Is something wrong with her? She ought not have refused the doctor's treatment."

"A trifle under the weather at the moment. I have no doubt she will come about by evening. I have a small errand to perform, then I return to her side." Cecily bid Jemima good day and watched her march off in the direction of the bank. Once alone, Cecily hurried to the nearest apothecary and asked for Althea's favorite sort of tooth powder.

When she returned to their large bedroom some time later—having indulged in a bit of window shopping—she found Althea awake and looking far better.

"I remembered what you said about that tooth powder that Jemima gave you. So"—Cecily gaily waved a small package before her—"I bought you something I think you will find more familiar—your own sort of tooth powder. That ought to cheer you up a bit."

"Best not to throw out what Jemima presented to me. I can always pretend that I have been using it in the event she asks. I shall merely dump out a trifle each day to make it appear used." Althea exchanged a rueful look with her cousin, rising from her bed to inspect the new tin of powder. She sniffed the contents of the easily opened tin with a smile of satisfaction. "That is more like it. I find the flavor of cinnamon overpowering."

"I do not see why you are careful of her feelings. She certainly makes it clear that she dislikes you," Cecily replied. She was about to stow the gift powder into the very bottom of Althea's portmanteau when they heard a sharp rap on the door.

Cecily shared a puzzled look with Althea, then walked to the door to cautiously open it.

"At least one of you shows some common sense when it comes to answering doors," Lord Montmorcy exclaimed while he strode into the room, totally disregarding the propriety of the situation. He studied Althea, then turned to Cecily. "What happened?"

"She ate something that violently disagreed with her. I had

to give her ipecacuanha, which we fortunately thought to bring along with us. As you can see, she is looking more the thing now after a nap." Cecily stood next to Lord Montmorcy while he looked Althea over with a highly assessing eye.

"You ate the same foods for breakfast?" he said while walking over to study Althea more closely.

"Indeed, we did," Althea said a bit more sharply than was her wont. She resented being discussed as though she was absent or dull-witted.

"Testy, isn't she," he murmured to Cecily, who had assumed a position at his elbow when he bent over Althea. "She must be feeling better." To Althea he said, "I should like to see your arms, if you please."

Althea took note of Cecily's proximity to his lordship, as well as his acerbic tone when he addressed herself and rolled up her sleeve. "I shall have to wear long gloves to dinner this evening," she joked.

"I ought to insist you remain in bed, but I fear it would do little good," he pronounced with a wicked sparkle in his green eyes.

"You have no right to order me about," she reminded him. Seeing the delicate and charming Cecily standing at his side brought a pain to Althea's heart, and for a moment she wondered if her earlier malaise was returning.

"Ah, but who was it that made your trip so comfortable yesterday," he countered with obvious satisfaction.

"Odious man. Had you not dosed me with laudanum, I should have enjoyed the scenery. As it is, I did not view the mountains, which I am informed are most beautiful."

"I promised to take you to see a glacier and a closer view of Mont Blanc," he reminded her. "And so I shall." He stood back and folded his arms across his chest, again studying Althea as though she were one of Mr. Poindexter's petrifactions.

"Well?" she said at last, deciding to rise from her bed and take a chair close by. Bed was not the proper place to be when around Lord Montmorcy. At least, not for her. Memories of all those alien sensations that had washed over her when he kissed her in the pine-scented glade haunted her. But the way he spoke to her, treated her, appeared to be anything but lover-like. No, 'twas clear to Althea that his interests lay in the direction of Cecily.

"Perhaps a breath of fresh air," he said, snapping his fingers. "How would you like to take a short stroll in the Bel Air, which is Geneva's town square. It is a very pretty place, and I think it might cheer you up, for you look sadly pulled, my girl." He offered Althea his hand while urging Cecily to find a bonnet and spencer for her cousin.

"I'll have you know we hired a French maid to assist us, sirrah, for poor Susan was sadly put upon," Althea said with a faint snap to her words. Looking sadly pulled, indeed. She ignored his proffered hand and rose from her chair. While she might feel slightly wobbly, she would never admit to it. Walking across the room with great care, she found her favorite green spencer and a bonnet trimmed in matching velvet riband in the wardrobe.

"Indeed, Gabrielle has taken our gowns to press them so we will look our most charming this evening," Cecily inserted in an apparent effort to be helpful.

"And I am quite looking forward to our dinner," Althea added while tying the ribands of her bonnet under her chin.

"What is this?" Lord Montmorcy said, picking the tin of tooth powder from Cecily's hands.

"That is a gift from Jemima, but Althea did not care for its taste, so I replaced it this morning," Cecily said, reaching out a hand to reclaim the tin. "Althea wants me to tuck it away; says she does not wish to hurt Jemima's feelings should she inquire how Althea likes it and does she use the stuff." It was abundantly clear from Cecily's voice what she thought of that.

"This is the cinnamon flavor you mentioned?" Lord Montmorcy asked Althea. At her answering nod, he studied the little tin again, removed the top and sniffed the contents. "Mind if I try it? I rather like the taste of cinnamon."

"But of course, with my greatest pleasure. Then I can tell Jemima that you wished to try it. At least that would give me an excuse for not having it around." Althea gave a wave of her hand, then walked to the door. "Cecily, as you still have your bonnet on, let us be off to the bank before it closes. Perhaps if we have time, we might take a stroll in the Bel Air." Althea ignored Lord Montmorcy. She might be trying to push him at Cecily, but somehow her heart was not in her effort at the moment, and she blamed that feeling on her malaise.

"Not without me along," Lord Montmorcy protested. "It is not safe for you to be alone, I believe." With that he walked past Althea, opened the door to usher them out, then turned the key—which he gave to Cecily for safekeeping, Althea noted—and guided both women along the hall and down the stairs.

When they left the hotel, they found Mr. Poindexter strolling along with a well-leashed Hercules.

"Where are you off to, Poindexter?" Lord Montmorcy inquired with a narrow look at the drooling pup, who had edged far too close to his lordship's boots for comfort. Tugwell would have a fit if John returned with his perfectly shined boots in a slather.

"The Bel Air," Sidney explained. "Plan to stop at the bank first, then off to see the posies, or whatever is there. Hercules likes being outside, y'see." The dog sat back and beamed a very drooling doggy grin at them.

Since they were headed in the same direction, they agreed it would be nice to go together.

John undertook to tuck Miss Ingram's hand close to his side so he might offer her support if need be. He was not the least insensitive to the delicacy of someone who had just lost their breakfast to a nasty spell of whatever it was that had upset her. Or had it possibly been something else? The tin of tooth powder purchased by Jemima Greenwood and given to Althea dug into his side when he adjusted his arm to Miss Ingram's height. All of a sudden the desire to sample the cinnamon-flavored tooth powder left him. He decided it might be well to have that powder tested at an apothecary shop. Not that he believed there was anything evil about Miss Greenwood, but an alien substance might have been introduced by accident before she bought it.

At the bank they all managed to obtain the monies they needed. Althea was gratified to see how well her letter of credit was received by the manager who handled such transactions. With Lord Montmorcy standing at her shoulder, it would have been horrid to experience difficulty. Then, when she considered how graciously his lordship had been welcomed to the bank, she wondered if her letter of credit had been helped along by his presence, and she fumed at the thought. *Dratted man*. She tried so hard to draw him to Cecily, and he persisted in doing as he pleased.

For some peculiar reason this seemed to cheer her, and she left the bank in good humor.

They failed to encounter Jemima on their stroll to the Bel Air. Althea wondered to the others about the whereabouts of the sullen young woman. It seemed the rest of the group neither knew nor cared.

Many of the buildings they saw did indeed have those unusual shed structures high above the walkway, looking as though they possessed great eyebrows. Althea grinned at such a notion.

"Ah, you find something amusing. At least that woeful expression has disappeared. What in the so-proper city of Geneva do you find to make you smile?" Lord Montmorcy asked.

"Those large sheds that tower high above us reminded me of giant eyebrows," Althea replied, wishing he did not insist upon holding her quite so close to his side, nor slip his arm about her when they came to a street crossing as though she were an invalid. His touch did strange things to her nervous system, and she attributed that mostly to her fragile state of health.

"They serve the same purpose—protecting the face of the building and the people below from snow or rain. Ugly things, however," he commented with an upward glance.

Althea kept their conversation confined to remarks about the buildings, observations about the displays in windows of the shops they passed, and speculation about the guests at this evening's dinner.

When they reached the parklike square in the heart of the city, they strolled along pretty squares of neatly scythed lawns and small beds of flowers. Many trees and shrubs had been planted to give a pleasing aspect.

"Earlier in the spring they have pansies here," Lord Montmorcy observed to Althea while up ahead of them Cecily chuckled at the antics of Hercules.

"You have spent a long time in this country. Did you not miss England?" Althea dared to say. It was a rather personal question, but his continued absence from his home puzzled her.

"Indeed," he said in a considering way. "Although I will have many fond memories about my stay in Switzerland, I expect it is time I return. Tugwell reported that my sister married not long ago. I did not know that she was even betrothed. And my mother remarried even before that. Distance may have advantages, but it also has drawbacks. It takes so long to receive news of importance."

"Yet they managed without you," Althea pointed out, she thought rather reasonably. "If you considered it an advantage to be far removed from London, there must have been something or someone you wished to avoid."

"True," he murmured vaguely. "There was."

Althea could see he was going to say nothing more on that account, and she was far too polite to pry. She contented herself with strolling along in the direction of the lake while tucked close to his side.

Then he looked down at her at the precise moment she chanced to peek up, and she found his face wreathed in a smile. "But not anymore," he concluded.

All of which left her quite mystified.

"Look," sang out Cecily, quite unlike a staid matron, "there are bathing machines on the beach. It is almost like Brighton, but for that silly Pavilion."

"Cecily, how can you say such a thing about the Prince's work of art," Althea said, pretending to be shocked, but spoiling the effect by chuckling.

They walked more eagerly to watch the bathing machines at work, finding them to be quite similar in appearance and operation to the ones at Brighton, with the women operating them seeming less disagreeable.

"I think you might do well to avoid using one of those. You'd probably drown," Lord Montmorcy observed to Althea.

As a regard for her safety it left a great deal to be desired, but she decided not to take him to task over it. With all that had happened to her so far, he was undoubtedly right.

A bit further along La Promenade, the street that fronted the lake, they observed the washerwomen of Geneva still at work with the laundry for the citizens of the city.

Lord Montmorcy paused, then pointed out the long ridge of mountains to one side of the city, which he said were called Mount Jura, with the Alps, the Glaciers of Savoy, and the snowy head of Mont Blanc on the other. "This is quite lovely when the horse chestnuts are in full bloom," he said.

"It is a very lovely location," Althea observed, moving away from his side so she might slowly make a turn about to see the circular view.

"I know I promised to take you to see a glacier, but I think that before we attempt anything so strenuous, you might enjoy a party on the lake," his lordship said when they continued on their way. "It is very pleasant to take a little boat to the other side for a picnic along the shore. If you like, we could stay for music and dancing before returning."

"I will consult with Cecily and Jemima to see what they wish." At his wry expression, she added, "Sir, Miss Greenwood travels with us, and I must treat her with respect, for all that she grumbles."

"It does you great credit, I'm sure," he said, sounding as though he meant quite the opposite.

At this point, when Althea decided she just might take exception to her rule against arguing in public, the Comte de Bosio rounded the corner opposite. When he caught sight of them, he immediately crossed the street to join the group.

He bowed to the ladies, greeted the gentlemen with his usual exquisite politeness, then asked if he might show them a thing or two about the city.

They strolled along the promenade planted with trees and shrubs the comte said was planned for the recreation of the citizens of Geneva until they reached a winding staircase—actually a gradual incline paved from bottom to top. He drew them to the top, then pointed out two brass plates.

"You will appreciate this one, Miss Ingram, for it commemorates the victory over the House of Savoy." At her look of puzzlement, he added, "The heroine of the battle was La Mère Royanume, who was said to have halted the initial invasion of the Savoyards by pouring a vast cooking pot of hot stew over them from the walls above. You are as brave, I believe."

"Well, I doubt I could manage a vast cooking pot, but thank you for the kind thought," Althea managed to reply. Really, was she at every turn to be reminded of her height and size? Hardy, brave, sadly pulled—these were not precisely the sort of compliments a girl desired. She glanced to where the comte led Cecily over to show her a particular vista and frowned.

"Did those kindly meant words trouble you?" his lordship inquired in that silken voice he used when he suspected he had annoyed her.

Not trusting that dulcet tone in the least, Althea shook her head. "Why should it bother me to be reminded that I am a powerful giant of a woman?" she said sweetly. "However, no one would think to tell *you* that you might serve as a weather vane at your great altitude."

"A touching point," he said with a grin.

A movement off to one side caught her eye, and she turned. "Look, there goes Jemima. I do hope she remembers that we are to dine with the comte this evening. She carries a sack that looks suspiciously like one from a bakery."

"She does enjoy her food, so perhaps she will," Lord Montmorcy said in a manner that somewhat revealed his dislike for the young woman. Then the group set off again along the walk that paralleled the lake.

The day was far along before they returned to the hotel. Althea thanked her escort, for although she had intended him to be with Cecily, truth be told, she had appreciated his strength from time to time. His strong arm had proved to be most welcome when she grew tired.

"Rest before you attempt to join us for dinner this evening. You want to look hardy and brave," Lord Montmorcy said with that wicked gleam in his eyes again.

"By all means," she said rather tartly. "What do you suggest a hardy and brave woman ought to wear, sir?"

He shut his eyes for a few moments as though considering

the matter at some length, then opened them to gaze directly at her with that gleam more pronounced than ever. "Not lace nor chiffon; leave that sort of thing to a delicate woman like Mrs. de Lisle. For you, something with substance, I think, like a stiff satin or silk damask. And no missish colors, either." He tilted his head, still studying her while Althea fumed inwardly at the effrontery of the man.

"Indeed? Pray tell, do not keep me in suspense."

"Plum, or snowy white, or vibrant blue, I believe," he replied, leaning against the wall outside her door while Cecily unlocked it to allow the ladies to enter.

"Well, as I have but what I packed, you will have to suffer through the evening in disappointment, I fear. Concentrate on your dinner, and you will not mind it in the least," she said with a sweet smile that did not quite reach her eyes.

"Why do I have the feeling that my well-intentioned offering is not appreciated?" he complained, then chuckled as the two left him, Althea shutting the door with a snap.

Gabrielle had their gowns ready for them. Susan had set out a change of petticoats and timidly offered to help Cecily with her hair.

Cecily was to wear a peach silk that floated about her like the petals of an exotic bloom. Althea would never admit that Lord Montmorcy's words had rankled, but she surveyed her simply cut gown with a pleased air. It was a plumy red Gros de Naples, the corded silk giving the gown an elegant line. It was vastly becoming in color and design.

"I believe I shall do well enough," she declared to Cecily some time later when they left their room to make their way down to where the comte awaited them.

"Lord Montmorcy has a way of bringing color to your cheeks and forcing you to rise to his challenge," Cecily observed while she walked down the stairs at Althea's side.

"That is because he is an odious toad," Althea replied under her breath, quite forgetting she was supposed to encourage an attraction between Cecily and his lordship. "One of these days I will give that man his just deserts, and what a satisfying day that will be, too." She bestowed a radiant smile on the gangly

Mr. Poindexter that prompted him to insert a finger in his cravat as though it had just shrunk.

"Oh, I hope so," Cecily murmured back. "Be careful what you wish for, my love; it might come true."

Chapter Nine

The comte had arranged to host the dinner party at the

The comte had arranged to host the dinner party at the home of dear friends, a couple from his native city in Italy. When Althea entered their glittering drawing room, she gasped with delight. A great many mirrors reflected the light of hundreds of candles above delicate French furniture of the finest woods and designs. The needlework decorating the many chairs was enough to make her sigh with envy.

"One tends to forget the powerful influence of the French in what we think of as Switzerland," she said quietly to Cecily while they perused a particularly fine painting by Fragonard.

"Napoleon was responsible for a great many changes here," a voice said from behind them and too close to Althea for her comfort.

"I trust they were to the better," Althea replied politely to Lord Montmorcy, who looked far too handsome for his own good. Considering what he had looked like when she encountered him on the road from Lyons—tired, dusty, and in the garb of a peasant—he now appeared the epitome of the correct English gentleman. Biscuit pantaloons clung to his legs above white silk stockings and black patent slippers. A coat of corbeau Bath cloth over an elegant waistcoat of exquisitely embroidered satin in refined taste was topped by a cravat of such simplicity that it bespoke a gentleman of the highest breeding.

"Tugwell has indeed performed miracles," Althea said in the softest and sweetest of manners. She bestowed a demure smile on his lordship while at her side Cecily sputtered her protest at the shocking words from her cousin to the man to whom they owed so much.

"I see that your new maid did as well," he smoothly replied. "The color reminds me of the mulberries back home. I was given mulberry syrup once when I was ill. Nasty stuff, in spite of the sugar they mixed into it." He raked Althea with a cool gaze, reducing her to a state of quivering indignation. "And you, Mrs. de Lisle, are a fairy princess come to earth, a vision of delight in your delicate peach silk. I suspected you would not disappoint me." He bowed over her hand, and it seemed to Althea that he exchanged a significant look with Cecily.

It was what Althea wanted, was it not? This absurd feeling in her heart, a sort of sick sensation, must be due to her nerves, the strain of the day. She stoutly denied that it might be anything else.

At that moment the comte bustled up to join them, and the conversation became blessedly general.

What had possessed her to speak so boldly to Lord Montmorcy? It seemed as though some imp took hold of her tongue whenever he drew near, prompting her to say the most dreadful things. Lord Montmorcy certainly had a way of bringing out the worst in her. Yet she admitted that he made her feel alive as no London dandy had ever managed to do. Not that she'd had all that much to do with London gentleman, come to think of it. But they were by and large a collection of depressing souls, gaming and whiling away their hours in the same pastimes day after day. How would those men fare had they been faced with the demands on their bodies such as Lord Montmorcy had known? At that scandalous thought, Althea murmured an excuse and wandered away to meet the honored guest of the evening, the famed botanist Augustin-Pyramus de Candolle.

Jemima had reached the gentleman's side before her and was hanging on every word he spoke. Given her interest in plants and flowers, particularly herbs, it was not surprising. What did astonish Althea was the effect he had on Jemima— the girl looked almost pretty in her enthusiasm. Her eyes sparkled, the blue of her simple gown enhancing them. Her cheeks bloomed with a pretty pink, and because of the simple line of her dress, she looked less plump.

Althea was content to listen to the flow of conversation about her, his comments on the beautiful and interesting plants to be found in the mountains around the city.

"We are to travel up to the foot of the glacier before long. Is there anything in particular that we ought to notice?" Althea finally asked.

"Ah. I believe there should still be some strawberries at the edge. Those berries are the sweetest in the world," de Candolle said with an endearing smile.

Althea had heard what a charming man Monsieur de Candolle was, that he had beguiled the citizens of Geneva to donate all that was necessary to build a botanical garden, even to construct two iron bridges across the Rhone. Listening to him speak, she could well believe it, for he charmed the eye as well as the ear.

"Persuasive, is he not?" Lord Montmorcy said from a position at her left side. How he had managed to pop up there as silently as might be, she couldn't say.

"Indeed, a most interesting gentleman," Althea said with utmost politeness.

"I shall have to remember to tell Tugwell how you appreciated his efforts. Your words will endear you to him greatly." There was a touch of irony in his voice she could not fail to miss.

"But not to you, I think. Was it not Brummell who said a man should never attract attention by what he wears?" Althea replied. She was saved from his reply—and he looked as though he might have snapped at her—by the announcement that dinner was served.

She was dismayed to discover that she was expected to eat her meal with Lord Montmorcy to her left. A French gentleman sat to her right and while exquisitely mannered, was clearly more interested in his food than in fostering a deeper acquaintance with Althea. But then, he was a man of moderate height, somewhat advanced in age, and not the least attractive to the eye, either.

"Have you had the slightest chance to shop while here as yet?" Lord Montmorcy said when she glanced his way.

"I regret that I have been otherwise occupied," she said, thinking of the wretched stomach ailment that had assailed her that morning. "However, Cecily has insisted that we are to go browsing about tomorrow. We are not on some schedule, after all."

"Why did you decide to come to Switzerland, Miss Ingram?" said the French gentleman from her other side, making her wish he had remained focused on his food.

"I wished to see some of the things my father had found so entrancing when he toured the Continent some years ago."

From her other side Lord Montmorcy offered her more wine, filled her glass, then said, "Most young women stay at home, marry, and raise a family. You wished to postpone your wedding day?"

"I doubt if I shall marry," she said with icy politeness. Then thawing slightly, she added, "One of these days Cecily will undoubtedly find herself a splendid husband, and I shall rescue another of my older cousins from a fate worse than death."

"Fate worse than death?" he asked with a puzzled look.

Althea waited for the next course to be placed in front of her and then replied, "Why, being without funds and dependent on a relative for the slightest thing is particularly noxious if one is compelled to serve in a humble capacity and daily made aware of their generosity."

He digested this while she surveyed the pretty food on her plate.

"Not to your liking?"

"Indeed, I was merely searching my mind for a cousin who might replace Cecily when she marries, which she must, as pretty and vivacious as she is."

"Indeed. Mrs. de Lisle is all that is pleasing in a woman— softly charming and with pretty manners."

Althea, in her sensitive mood, felt as though he was implying that Cecily possessed all the womanly qualities that Althea lacked. Yet was this not what she intended? That his lordship would admire Cecily, and that the dearest of cousins find happiness again? She stared down at her scarcely touched food, then pushed it about on her plate with a distinct lack of enthusiasm.

"I believe that the *boeuf en croûte* and carrots *à la Chantilly* deserve better treatment than you give them."

Althea gave a sideways glance at his lordship, discovering that his healthy appetite had made deep inroads on his food. "It is excellent," she admitted after taking a bite of the beef and discovering that it was.

"Did your nanny never tell you that you must eat all that was on your plate before you received a sweet? I have it on good authority that the dessert is little nuns—choux pastry filled with a chocolate crème and covered with icing."

"My nanny did not permit such outrageous foods as beef in pastry and creamed carrots to grace my nursery table. A bit of bread and boiled beef, with perhaps a serving of boiled potato was considered quite sufficient. Children in her estimation did not benefit from desserts. Although," Althea added wryly, "I did observe that she eagerly ate every sweet sent up on the trays."

She could feel the considering look he gave her and decided that to avoid further conversation she would apply herself to the delicious food. No lady would speak while chewing.

When the meal finally drew to a close—after the delectable pastries had been served, followed by coffee and tea—the ladies retired to the drawing room. Althea and Cecily chose a pair of delicate chairs off to one side and relaxed while a young woman played the harp.

Althea turned to Cecily and quietly said, "I am very tired. Would you mind if I leave now? You remain; I will ask for a footman to see me to the hotel. I would not for anything have you miss the evening entertainment, and all I wish to do is crawl into bed and sleep. That would prove exceedingly tedious for you."

Cecily protested, but was finally overruled by her more assertive cousin. Before the men had left the dining table, Althea had slipped from the elegant house, first bestowing her gratitude on the hostess. A footman guided her to a carriage, then accompanied her to the hotel.

In her room Althea submitted to Gabrielle's ministrations,

then propped herself up in bed, piling behind her head a number of the down pillows Lord Montmorcy had bestowed upon her.

"I am terribly clever," she announced to the four walls. "Lord Montmorcy will be able to concentrate on Cecily while not tempted to disconcert me with those nasty little barbs he so enjoys."

She could not quite convince her heart that her departure was for the best, for she found their sparring exhilarating. She snuggled into the pillows with a sigh.

The following morning found Cecily simply glowing with happiness and bubbling over with enthusiasm for the day to come.

"Come on, you slug-a-bed," she warbled when she poked Althea in the shoulder, trying to waken her.

Focusing a sleepy eye on her cousin, who was already up and wearing a luscious dressing gown, Althea mumbled something about strangling some people in their cradles. Then, truly noticing her cousin's happiness, Althea climbed from bed to slip on her wrapper and join her cousin at the little table by the window.

"Look out there," Cecily said cheerfully. "The lake shimmers in the sunshine, and we are to row across to the other side for a lovely picnic. Come, finish your rolls and chocolate so we will be ready when they call for us."

"*They* being?"

"Lord Montmorcy, Mr. Poindexter, and of course, the Comte de Bosio." Cecily hurried her way through their little meal, then rose to begin dressing in her very prettiest walking gown of lavender and purple print India muslin. "They have promised a fine day of it."

Althea, feeling a trifle out of sorts yet truly glad for her cousin's joy, finished her meal, then dressed for the day. She paid little attention to the garment Gabrielle pulled from the wardrobe. As long as she was decently covered, it really did not matter what she wore.

Properly covered from head to toe, with her largest parasol and a wide-brimmed bonnet securely tied beneath her chin,

Althea followed Cecily along the hall, pausing to collect Jemima along the way.

For once Jemima bubbled as well, chattering on about the wealth of information she had gleaned merely listening to the conversation of the great botanist last evening.

"What a pity you felt it necessary to leave so early. Do you not feel well today, either?" Jemima asked.

"I am just fine," Althea said with a firm smile glued to her lips.

"You do not appear fine, if you do not mind my saying so," Jemima insisted.

"Nonsense, Jemima," Cecily scolded. "That particular shade of deep blue becomes Althea very well, and Gabrielle has added a touch of lace at the neckline that quite improves the dress."

Then the men joined them, and they all left the hotel for the dock at the lake where a boat awaited their pleasure.

While they strolled along, Althea glanced into one of the looking glasses attached to the window frame of one of the buildings they passed. There seemed to be a great number of these odd little looking glasses about the town. She was pleased to note that she did look rather nice.

"Vanity is a besetting sin in this town, it would seem," said an all too familiar voice. "Why did you leave early last evening? I worried about you until I noticed you had left Mrs. de Lisle behind. I decided were you truly ill, she would have not allowed you to go alone."

Pleased at his assessment of her cousin, Althea merely nodded and said, "It was a trying day, and I felt an early night would be best for me."

"Such civil words," he said in his mocking manner. "I see you took my suggestion. That blue looks better on you than the chartreuse you wore the other day, which made you look jaundiced. I advise you to give that unfortunate dress to your maid."

"Such civil words, my lord," she said in an equally mocking manner.

Further sparring was prevented by their arrival at the dock in the port area of Geneva. The large rowboat was overflowing with pillows and cushions and other little accessories for their comfort. Jemima and Cecily exclaimed with delight at the thoughtfulness, and Althea eased herself back on a mound of pillows, pleased that she could trail her hand in the water and not have to talk to anyone if she so chose, for she had settled in the very rear of the boat.

She did not reckon with her view, which faced Lord Montmorcy, who removed his jacket with due apologies to the ladies and commenced rowing.

It was utterly disgraceful the way his muscles could be seen through the fine cambric of his shirt as he pulled on the oars. And the breeze tousled his dark hair into an engaging tangle, the sort that urged a woman to smooth. He crinkled his eyes—which had assumed a blue cast to the usual green, no doubt from the water all about them—against the bright sun. The effect was that he appeared to smile, and perhaps he did, if Cecily's delight gave any hint.

Althea dipped her parasol to blot out the sight of him, focusing on the distant mountains and the vista of the lake, inhaling the delicious fresh scent of water. It was truly a beautiful day.

The land rolled gently upward from the shoreline. Neat little farms, pleasant groves of trees, and rather interesting villas dotting the rim of the lake could be seen, for the distance from one side of the lake to the other was not great.

The ruffles on her parasol fluttered with the breeze, and Althea felt almost satisfied with life. She relaxed to enjoy Cecily's happy chatter and Jemima's discussion with Mr. Poindexter on the possibilities of finding any petrifactions or plants of interest on the far side of the lake. Cecily looked well on her way to acquiring the husband of her choice—if her glowing face was any clue. Jemima had failed to carp on a single thing this morning, a feat Althea had not imagined possible. And she . . . well, she had resigned herself to the fact that Lord Montmorcy would gain an admirable wife before long.

They landed on the pebble-strewn shore and sauntered along until they found a pretty parklike setting with rustic benches and a table of sorts where they might eventually have their picnic. From the looks of the area, it was a favorite site for such picnics. There was a stucco villa not far away from which a woman came out to study them. She appeared shortly after with a pitcher of lemonade and thin biscuits, for which Lord Montmorcy happily compensated her.

Jemima, with Mr. Poindexter in tow, immediately started off along the shore to hunt for plants, allowing Poindexter the delight of searching for petrifactions.

"They are unpredictable," Althea heard him say as the pair slowly walked away. "One never knows quite where they will turn up. But I should like to find a few more ammonites." His words became indistinct as the couple faded from view.

Cecily persuaded the comte to stroll along the pretty path fringed with wildflowers while under the protection of her parasol.

What an annoyance, Althea thought. Why could the comte not look elsewhere for company? It made it difficult that Althea was such a tall woman—few men displayed interest in a woman so much taller than they. While the comte was all that was polite, he had made it evident that he had but the faintest interest in conversing with Althea.

"The sight of your cousin with the comte vexes you for some reason?" Lord Montmorcy inquired.

"Not in the least," Althea said with imperfect truth. "She is a grown woman, a widow, and may do as she pleases." But Althea could not see why Cecily elected to flirt with the comte when Lord Montmorcy was there. Unless . . . Cecily sought to make him jealous. Deciding that must be the case, Althea suggested they follow the others.

"I think not," Lord Montmorcy said. "I believe I would like to stretch out on the grass with your lap for a pillow and relax."

"Sirrah!" Althea exclaimed, pretending to be even more shocked than she was. A lady permit such familiarity?

"One of the things I like about you is that you are not the missish sort. Do not fail me now," he said with a sigh.

"The rowing tired you so? Or did you have a late night of it?" she said with the virtuous air of one who had retired to bed early.

"In Geneva?" He chuckled at the very notion. "While the city fathers encourage private parties and intelligent exchange of ideas, they do not allow gaming and other such depraved pastimes to flourish. No, I enjoyed the evening very much, for the conversation was most stimulating. Pity you were so tired. Do you often require extra sleep? That could present a number of interesting problems for a husband," he concluded.

For some odd reason Althea felt her cheeks flush with warmth. A naughty gleam shone in those green eyes of his. Rather than reply to what she perceived as a question full of pitfalls, she seated herself on a rug that Lord Montmorcy had spread out, leaning against a convenient tree.

"I do not plan to marry," she reminded him.

He took advantage of her position to drop down on the soft rug and stretch out, placing his head on her lap just as he had wished to do—without her by-leave, it must be added.

"You are most persistent," she informed him, but without her intended ire. Somehow she found it difficult to be angry just now.

"It is a beautiful day with a few clouds off in the distance, enough to be poetic. Do you sketch, by the way?" he asked in a drowsy voice.

Althea brought her parasol forward so as to shade his face from the heat of the sun, then absently replied, "Of course. Every young woman must do well with a pencil or she is thought deficient."

"I should like a sketch of us now. Something to smile on in the chill of an English winter." He settled more comfortably, raising strange sensations within Althea when the warmth of his head permeated the soft fabric of her gown.

"There are lovely English summers as well," she reminded him.

"They usually last all of three days," he complained, then closed his eyes.

Althea wondered if he slept, for he was absolutely unmoving. She eyed a nearby pillow brought up from the rowboat and wondered if she might shift him to that, for although he was not heavy, the pressure of his head in her lap was most disturbing and far too intimate a sensation. His head was cradled so cozily in her lap, and while she was untutored in the intimate details of married life, she suspected it was highly improper for her to sit thus with him.

She reached out her hand for the pillow, and his eyes flew open to stare up at her with a green intensity that stopped her in midmovement, arm outstretched.

"You must think of yourself as a goddess," he said quietly. "Athena, not Juno. For if you have no interest in marriage or children, you can hardly be likened to Juno, the goddess of women, marriage, and birth. But then, Athena is the goddess of wisdom, and I think that your not marrying is the height of foolishness."

She froze at his words, for they were much as he had begun to say when she had stopped him before. "Sir, it has been brought to my attention that it is necessary to have more than one person involved to achieve a marriage."

He half sat up, leaning back on one hand and searching her face to see what might be read there. "If that is all that prevents you from joining the married state, we can solve that easily enough."

Althea leaned forward to gaze at him, meeting his green eyes with an intensity that surprised her. "I will not marry to please anyone save myself. I do not need to."

"Good," he said with obvious satisfaction. "You are your own woman. I like that."

With those words he rose in one lithe movement and loped down to the shore where he grabbed his coat from the seat of the boat. He marched back to where she sat in surprised silence, then he dug into one of his coat pockets. He fished out a small package and dropped it into Althea's lap.

"Since you have not had an opportunity to go shopping, I thought I would assist you with a trifle. The Swiss seem to excel at this work."

He joined her on the rug while she tugged at the strings tying the parcel wrapping. "You ought not do such a thing, sir. 'Tis most improper, I'll wager." But she could not prevent a pleased smile from tilting the corners of her mouth. She was not often gifted with little trinkets.

"You cannot wager in Geneva, did you forget?"

She could not answer him, for the paper had fallen away the

moment she undid the string, and in her lap sat a delightful little music box. The top was enameled with a scene of Mont Blanc as viewed from Geneva, the remainder of the little box executed in silver gilt. She lifted the lid and a lovely little tune she'd not heard before tinkled clearly in the pure mountain air.

"It is a local melody, a Swiss folk song, I believe. Pretty thing, is it not?"

"It is lovely, and I thank you very much." She thought for a moment, then confessed, "I have not been as friendly or grateful to you as I ought, and you shame me with this lovely gift. You saved my life at that pass coming from Lyons when you shot the bandit, and again when you helped me from that ravine. Do you practice to be a knight errant, kind sir?" She sparkled an amused look at him she hoped conveyed the sincerity of her feelings. She had been the veriest grouch, and he had graciously ignored her ill-temper by responding with one kind gesture after another.

She rewound the tiny key on the bottom of the box, and the melody carried across the clearing. In the distance they could also hear Jemima and Mr. Poindexter arguing about something, while in the opposite direction Cecily and the comte could be viewed strolling along the path, deep in discussion.

Ostensibly studying the music box, Althea glanced up at Lord Montmorcy to see how he reacted to Cecily's attempt to make him jealous. He looked at the couple so absorbed in conversation and then turned back to face Althea with not the least reaction on his face, much to her disappointment.

When Cecily and the comte reached them, Lord Montmorcy pointed to the sketch pad in Cecily's hands. "Do you draw tolerably well, madam?"

"Indeed, she is most talented," the comte replied, saving Cecily from any blushes.

"Then I wish a sketch of Althea and I in the shade of this tree, if you please."

Embarrassed, Althea added, "He wishes to remind himself of the pleasant Geneva summer while in the depths of an English winter."

Cecily giggled and agreed it an admirable notion. While the comte fetched her a glass of lemonade and anything else she wished, she made a rapid but accurate drawing of Lord Montmorcy with his head in Althea's lap.

With the melody of the music box going round and round in her head, Althea wished she also might have a copy of that drawing to treasure come chilly days. Lord Montmorcy had things all wrong. She'd not marry, not when she loved someone she might not have. Looking down into those beautiful green eyes, she knew she had fallen in love with the wretched man who snuggled so cozily in her lap.

Cecily had completed the drawing when Jemima stalked up to the site, looking as indignant as a hen who had found her nest raided. An unhappy Mr. Poindexter trailed behind her.

"Well, I must say I never thought to see you in such a situation, Althea. What your father will say I cannot imagine," Jemima snapped, hands on her hips and looking rather thunderous. Her expression could curdle milk.

Lord Montmorcy reluctantly rose to face Jemima and his friend. "It is a pleasant way to spend a time by the water. We all have different notions of what is enjoyable. You like to hunt plants, Poindexter, his petrifactions. Mrs. de Lisle and Comte de Bosio like to stroll along and contemplate the scene. I like to relax, as does Miss Ingram. There is nothing improper in the least."

More's the pity, Althea thought, wistfully recalling that wondrous kiss in the pine-scented glade.

"Now," Cecily inserted in an obvious effort to placate, "we shall all sit down and enjoy our picnic. Althea will wind up her music box to entertain us, and we shall all be as happy as can be."

Althea picked up the tablet and studied the drawing Cecily had done. Quite talented in her rendering, she had depicted the scene almost too well. It revealed something of Althea's feelings on her face, and Lord Montmorcy was shown at peace with the world—and not the least interested in Althea. Which is as it ought to be, Althea reminded herself.

What puzzled her was that Cecily should look jealous and she did not—not in the slightest. And it seemed to Althea that her plans were going terribly awry. Cecily and Lord Montmorcy looked no closer to an understanding, and Althea had lost her heart.

Chapter Ten

The luncheon was absolutely splendid, and Althea wished she might take up residence on the pleasant slope with its remarkable view of Mont Blanc as well as the city on the opposite shore.

"I wish Miss Greenwood and Sidney would take themselves off to do a bit more hunting," Lord Montmorcy said quietly to Althea.

She gave him a startled glance, for he had been entertaining them all with an amusing sketch of life in Geneva during the winter months. His expression was rueful, and he gave a slight shrug. "My lunch begs me to relax and digest it, and the most comfortable place I can think of is your lap. You ought to hire yourself out, you know—a cozy spot for insomniacs."

"I had no idea you found it so difficult to sleep, sirrah," she said in a mock scold. "And that is a most shocking notion, you know. I would not dream of doing something so scandalous."

"The sun is beginning to dip in the sky. Should we not return to the city?" Jemima said, gazing uneasily at the rowboat. A breeze had risen and waves lapped at the shore with more vigor than when they had departed the port of Geneva.

"I propose we remain to enjoy a meal on this side, perhaps a bit of music and dancing," Mr. Poindexter said, speaking up for the first time since the picnic had been set out. He had surpassed them all in the amount of food consumed, and Althea found it hard to credit that he could think of a meal so soon.

"Well, do not ask Althea to dance, for she is taller than you are," Jemima said with a giggle. "Indeed, Althea is so tall that there are few gentlemen who venture to partner her at a dance or ball. What good is it to be willowy if you are so tall as to qualify as a curiosity worthy of a circus." Jemima hiccuped and then giggled, revealing she had drunk a bit more wine than accustomed.

"That is quite enough, Jemima," Cecily said with a reproving look. "I believe you had best not imbibe any more of this delicious wine. For although it tastes as mild as lemonade, I suspect it is a trifle more disastrous for a young lady."

Jemima rose in a huff. "Well, I do not require you to look after me; I am not your charge, madam." She looked about her, then added, "I intend to seek out another example of that lovely plant I saw earlier and Mr. Poindexter so stupidly stepped on." She bestowed a glare on his bent head, then marched off.

Winding up the little music box, Althea gave Cecily a wistful smile. "How can I argue with what she says when it is true." Her words were spoken in a soft voice not meant to be heard by any others, but she caught a studied frown at her from Lord Montmorcy and wondered at it.

While the lowering sun painted magnificent saffrons, pinks, and lavenders on the clouded sky in the northwest, they stowed all the picnic paraphernalia into the boat once again. Why was it, Althea wondered, that you always seemed to have more going back then when you set out.

When she shortly returned, Jemima triumphantly displayed the plant, untrod by a careless foot and now neatly affixed to a paper in her portable plant press. She watched the preparations to shift their position to a site along the lake where a little inn sat in solitary splendor.

"Come along, Jemima," Cecily urged while she checked to see that nothing had been left behind.

"I should like to see Althea enter the boat first," Jemima said with a considering look at the rowboat. "It looks rather precarious to me, perched on the shore with no dock for assistance. One would have to be very scrambling to climb into that boat, I should think. Perhaps I shall walk to the inn, it would be safer." She backed away from the boat, looking intent upon doing as threatened.

"Miss Greenwood, are you doubting my ability to row that boat without disaster striking?" Lord Montmorcy demanded in apparent affront.

"He's a capital rower, Miss Greenwood. Absolutely first-rate," Mr. Poindexter offered gallantly. "Remember, we had not the least difficulty crossing over from Geneva."

Jemima appeared to doubt those words of praise and backed away.

Althea gave Jemima a disgusted look and marched down to the shoreline, assessing the boat as she neared it. She owned to a few reservations about her ability to enter the rowboat without any problems, but she refused to allow Jemima to say that Althea was scrambling.

"May I assist you, Miss Ingram?" Lord Montmorcy said in as gallant a manner as Mr. Poindexter in his support. He held out his hand, and Althea was about to accept it when she chanced to see the sneer on Jemima's face.

Ignoring his proffered hand, she studied the position of the boat, then glanced back at the group. She refused to order them to look away, and there was no help for it but to lift her skirts and clamber over.

"Gracious, Althea, how can you think to expose your limbs in such a way," Jemima said in a shrill voice. "I should never consider such a thing, I can tell you. Watch out!" she screamed. "I do believe that boat is going to tip, and you will end in the lake, sopping wet and looking for all the world like a dripping hen! Have a care, Althea."

All of which combined to unnerve Althea so that her normally graceful movements were uncoordinated and her legs did not wish to cooperate with her in the least.

The boat wobbled just enough so that her balance was shaken. She closed her eyes and waited for the chill and wet of the lake to greet her. Then the rocking ceased, and she felt as though on stable ground. Her eyes snapped open, and she turned a startled head. Lord Montmorcy had removed his shoes and stockings and had waded out to steady the boat. He gave Althea a knowing grin.

Tossing a triumphant look back at Jemima, Althea settled herself in the rear of the boat as before. "It was not so very bad, my dear, but then some people simply do not have an adventurous spirit," she said, darting a sweet look at Jemima.

"I have no qualms, as long as Lord Montmorcy does not take a chill from his assistance," Cecily said, hopping into the boat with a bit of help from the gentleman.

The comte and Lord Montmorcy hurriedly climbed into the boat. His lordship donned his stockings and shoes, revealing a shocking amount of bare skin in the process.

Althea knew she ought to have looked away, but found her eyes fixed on those strong, muscular legs. There was little about his lordship that failed to fascinate her, and she wondered if she was turning into as stupid a ninny as Jemima.

Within minutes the four of them—Poindexter bravely escorting Miss Greenwood along the shoreline to the distant inn—rowed silently away from the picnic spot.

As Jemima and Mr. Poindexter grew smaller, Althea waved a handkerchief at them, then reclined against the pillow she had tucked behind her, feeling enormously pleased with herself.

The comte and Cecily were exclaiming over a pretty chalet they espied high above the lake when Lord Montmorcy leaned forward and said, "You must not permit Miss Greenwood to disturb you with her unkind remarks. I doubt her legs would be a tenth as lovely as yours and she knows it."

Since never in her entire lifetime had she been told that she had lovely legs—nor even had them mentioned, Althea was at a total loss for a reply. It was not a subject a young lady anticipated arising when speaking with a gentleman. "Well, they suit me, I expect," she at last managed to say, then blushed when he chuckled at her response. She realized that she ought to have scolded him for so improper a remark, and she had failed. He must think her a shocking young miss.

"You are a delight, Miss Ingram." John studied her with approval, for she never failed to charm him.

"How nice that I amuse you, sir," she flashed back at John with a frigid smile.

He supposed that he had well and truly blotted his copy book with that little remark, no matter how well-intended it may have been. Indeed, Althea Ingram had not really surprised him when that hike of her skirts revealed long and shapely legs. He had suspected she would have well-formed limbs given the figure that Miss Greenwood had aptly described as willowy. Even now in the fading light of the day her form outlined against the white of the boat not only appeared supple, but perfectly proportioned. Miss Ingram was without equal.

They arrived at the little landing long before Miss Greenwood and Sidney rounded the bend of the shore. With a short dock to hand, exiting the rowboat proved no problem. John was sorry not to have another glimpse of Althea's wonderful legs again, but supposed he was most improper in his desires. He couldn't have everything, he presumed. That did not prevent him from wanting it, however.

"Delightful," Althea announced when Lord Montmorcy escorted her up to the country inn. Gaily colored lanterns danced in the breeze, now somewhat declining in strength. Cheerful red-and-white checked cloths covered little tables set out before the inn on a wooden porch. Cecily arranged herself at one of them, beckoning to the comte to join her.

"Do come here for the marvelous view, Comte. I can never recall anything remotely like it in England."

This entire day was not going as it was supposed to go, Althea thought, giving Cecily an annoyed look. While the view certainly was inspiring, it made little difference which table he sat at in order to see it.

Lord Montmorcy spoke briefly with the lady who kept the inn while her husband was off tending sheep—or whatever he did in the summer—then returned to Althea's side.

By the time a tired-looking Mr. Poindexter and wilted Jemima arrived, there was a tempting array of dishes on the tables. In the background an accordion player obliged them with tune after tune—most of them the toe-tapping sort. Althea would have loved to dance, although she didn't know what a person performed to the gay music.

When she had eaten her fill, she sat back and stared at the sky. There were far more stars in Switzerland than at home, of that she was sure. Soft night sounds filtered through the music, and she felt most contented. It was for something like this that she had left England—a romantic evening at a picturesque inn by the shore of a lovely lake, with gay music floating out over the water and lights dancing in the soft whisper of a breeze.

Then the musician began to play a waltz, and Althea sighed a trifle wistfully.

"Come, let us see how we manage," Lord Montmorcy demanded quietly. "The porch floor is uneven, but you are a sturdy girl and will have no problems with that."

Althea stiffened at his reminder of how stalwart she was. Good heavens, did the man never think of her in any other terms? In spite of her slight ire she rose from the table with impeccable manners.

She had danced with him at the inn in the mountains before coming to Geneva. This was vastly different. Then, they were in a small, noisy, crowded room, almost overwhelmed by the sound of the musicians and laughter of the group. Now, they danced by the light of the pretty colored lanterns and a rising moon that created a lacy pattern on the water. The voices of the others were muted, and the music soft and lilting. One thing remained unchanged, however. She still fit into his arms with perfect accord, as though she belonged to him.

Which had to be the silliest thought around, she decided in a fit of pique.

"Mind that post, Miss Ingram. Or am I to be allowed to call you Althea, seeing that I have performed so many valiant deeds of rescue . . . and the like," he added in an exceedingly polished manner.

She flashed him a look of warning and was rewarded by being pulled a trifle closer when he guided her around the post and into the shadows of the narrow porch that stretched around all sides of the inn. The scent of the honeysuckle draped over the porch railing teased her nose.

"You, sir, are a scoundrel," she retorted a bit unevenly, for the proximity of the man she was far too fond of seemed to take her breath away, or at the very least do peculiar things to her heart.

"I have been called worse," he admitted. He glanced back to where the others sipped coffee and sampled a berry tart, then to Althea. Before she could protest, he whisked her around the corner and had stolen a kiss of unbearable sweetness.

She could smell the spicy scent of his shaving lotion and the flowers that bloomed in abundance about the inn. The water that lapped against the pebbled shore soothed even as he stirred her with his onslaught on her fragile defenses. The sensitive tips of her fingers detected a rich texture to his finely woven coat. Every one of her senses seemed heightened, sharpened. It was exhilarating and almost frightening in intensity. She longed to wrap her arms about him to feel all those muscles and know the strength of him, to taste all he had to bestow.

"That was not well done of you sir," she said in an admittedly shaken voice when he finally withdrew. She parted her lips to give him a sound dressing down.

"I must be slipping," he murmured, then kissed her thoroughly with such expertise that Althea was certain she would melt and flow into the lake, never to be seen again.

She found herself enclosed within strong arms and cradled lovingly near his heart. Would that she knew a place therein. When he drew back once again, he fortunately retained a determined hold of her slim form.

"Now say that was better, Althea," he demanded in a whisper once he released her lips to stare through the soft darkness into her face, lit only by pale light of the rising moon. The lanterns around the corner were not the least help here, which might be just as well, for he would see the rosy blush that must cover her from head to toe.

"Sir . . . " Althea's protest faded away when he drew her close again.

"Say it," he insisted, humor clear in his voice.

"Say it was better?" she repeated, her own sense of the absurd coming to her rescue.

"Minx," he scolded with what she thought sounded like affection.

"Althea?" Cecily called. "Are you all right?"

"She has most likely demolished the poor man," Jemima added with a spiteful laugh that carried all too clearly.

Lord Montmorcy ushered Althea around the corner, waltzing her most carefully. He gave Jemima a look that Althea hoped never to know, then half bowed to Cecily.

"Mrs. de Lisle, I take great care of your charge. We have been waltzing and ran out of music."

Cecily laughed at that bit of nonsense, then turned to command in her pretty way that the musician oblige them with another waltz.

This time all joined in, whirling and stumbling a little on the uneven boards of the porch. There was much laughter, and Mr. Poindexter evened the score with Jemima by asking her if she had learned to waltz as yet.

"Thank you for another deliverance. Jemima can be a trifle uncomfortable at times," Althea said under the cover of the gaiety.

"I expect to be reimbursed, you know." While Althea sputtered at him, he pretended to consider the matter, then said, "I shall be allowed to take you shopping tomorrow."

"But I am to go with Cecily," Althea shot back with ease.

"Althea, either suffer my company, or I shall tell the world that you . . . " and he stopped.

"I what?" she demanded to know, not without a few trepidations.

He bent to whisper in her ear. "That you kiss far better than an untutored young miss ought to," he concluded with a chuckle.

Which had the effect of rendering her totally speechless.

Not long after that last romantic waltz the comte said, "I fear clouds gather; it does not look good, my friend. What say we return to Geneva? I would not wish to alarm those on the other side who expect us to return this evening."

Jemima immediately scrambled to the boat, stowing her things carelessly on one side. She was followed by the others in almost as great a haste. Lord Montmorcy and the comte settled the bills, then they pushed off for Geneva.

In the rising wind the lights from the city sparkled on the waves. It was not a sight to comfort, however.

"I just know we shall be turned out of the boat and go to a watery grave," Jemima howled, her misery evident. She clung to the side of the boat as though by that means she might keep it afloat.

"Nonsense, Jemima," Althea snapped back at her, sorely

tried to have the most romantic evening of her life spoiled by Jemima's prattling. "I have utmost confidence that Lord Montmorcy will restore us to Geneva in excellent time. Indeed, with Mr. Poindexter joining him at the second oars, we ought to do very well."

But Althea knew full well that even with two men rowing hard against the rising wind, it could be slow going and so it proved to be. The waves mounted higher against the side of the boat, sloshing over the rim at times. They all grew silent, their worry reflected on their faces. When they straggled into the port, she saw all the other boats had been battened down as though for a storm.

"At least the rain waited until we docked," Althea said loudly enough for Jemima to hear and note. "This proves that even a perfect evening may come to a misty end."

In the guise of assisting Althea from the large rowboat, Lord Montmorcy confounded her by asking, "I hope that it was perfect for you, my girl."

What could she reply to that? If she said yes, she would be admitting that she thought his kisses admirable and memorable—which of course they were. If she said no, it would be denying the pleasure she had known.

Daring to be honest, Althea gave him a direct look and said, "It was a day such as dreams are made from, sir."

"And the evening?" His voice was low and intent, his hand released hers with seeming reluctance.

Althea shivered. What could she say? Reveal how he had shattered all her self-conceptions? That he had changed her life forever with those kisses? That surely no other man could possibly effect her as he had? Dare she give him such power over her as to confess that if she had thought herself in love with him before, she had fallen into such a deep passion for him that nothing would satisfy her but completion, a life with him?

Rain suddenly poured down upon them in buckets, and she was immediately drenched to the skin. She did not have to answer his provocative question. Avoiding his gaze, she quickly grabbed all she could and dashed through the downpour to the small building at the far end of the dock. It stood close to the street where it was to be hoped they might find a carriage.

Jemima and Cecily were relatively dry, having run ahead of Althea. But then, they had not been confronted with such a momentous question.

"Here, my dear, put my shawl about your shoulders. I would not have you catch a chill," Cecily cried.

"The rain is dreadfully cold, as though it blew off the snow-topped peaks," Althea said, her teeth chattering while she wondered just how dreadful she looked.

The rain abated enough to permit the hailing of a passing carriage for hire. The ladies were thrust into the dry shelter of the carriage while the gentlemen nobly declared they would await its return, for by then they would have everything to hand.

Althea clutched to her bosom the little music box that she had thankfully rescued from the deluge.

"You may well huddle in your corner, looking like something the cat dragged through the hedge backward," Jemima said spitefully. "I am glad that no one saw *me* looking like that!"

"You are indeed fortunate, Jemima," Cecily said, her patience clearly tried at this bit of shrewishness. "You know, my dear, you sound just like my aunt—the elderly one who never married? She also is possessed of a hasty tongue."

Althea would have said Jemima was more than hasty in her speech, she was cattish and unkind. But being far too polite to give voice to her thoughts, Althea merely sat shivering in her corner of the carriage until they drew up to the entrance to the hotel. In no time at all they were back in their respective rooms.

Althea whisked off her borrowed shawl, draping it carefully across a chair before turning to check her appearance in a looking glass. It proved worse than she feared.

At her cry of dismay Cecily paused in preparing the bed for her cousin and came to stand at her side, gazing at the same reflection.

"Oh, I look horrid! Quite wretched! In fact, utterly dreadful!" Althea cried in dismay. Her hair was plastered to her skull, and her nose was all pink and pinched with cold. Her muslin gown clung too faithfully to her figure leaving absolutely nothing to the imagination. "I am mortified to think that anyone saw me like this."

Cecily gave her cousin a sympathetic pat on the shoulder, then helped Gabrielle ease Althea from the sopping gown before tucking her into a warm flannel nightdress, while Susan placed a hot brick at the foot of the bed.

It helped to dry her hair even if it took several huckaback towels to accomplish the deed. Susan whisked the wet garment from view, which served to ease Althea to a degree.

Once tucked up in bed with a tray bearing a pot of hot tea and honey on her lap, Althea sniffed her unhappiness.

"There, there," Cecily soothed, "you will feel better in the morning."

Althea downed her cup of tea with fortitude, then glared at her dearest cousin. "Can you please tell me why he always sees me at my worst?" she demanded to know.

There was no need for Cecily to inquire as to the identity of "he." Most likely she had a better notion as to the state of Althea's heart then she did herself.

"Things will seem better come morning," Cecily offered with sisterly comfort. For indeed, the two women were closer than cousins or chaperon and ward. Theirs was a bond of true friendship and affection that had nothing to do with blood ties.

"Jemima was utterly hateful," Althea sniffed, blowing her nose into a cambric square.

"Take comfort that she will one day pay for her behavior."

"She almost made me fall into the lake—but then I'd have looked no worse than I did in the rain. Oh, drat," Althea wailed in a most uncharacteristic manner. Usually stoic and accepting of the ills fate and society dealt her, it was the rare for her to yield to the dejection she occasionally knew.

"Drink your tea, dearest. I do not know what else will cheer you."

"You are right. It is foolish of me to think otherwise. It was a very lovely day," Althea concluded wistfully. She wound up her music box and listened to the happy little tune while she resolutely sipped her tea with honey.

"Indeed," Cecily whispered, her eyes shining with her own quiet joy.

The morning brought a gray day with great billowy clouds draping over the mountains, spilling into the valleys and hiding the peaks from view.

Since she always felt more cheerful come the dawn of a new day, Althea dressed with an eye to warmth and a pleasant day. After their small meal she coaxed Cecily into browsing through the shops with her.

"We shall both take our umbrellas with us, perhaps our pattens as well?" Cecily said with a raised brow.

"I suppose we must, for I cannot ruin another pair of shoes or I shall soon be in my bare feet," Althea declared with a chuckle.

"Disgraceful girl," Cecily said with a pretend frown as she locked their door after they left their room.

"Oh," Jemima sang out, "what did Althea do now?"

"It was merely a jest, Jemima," Cecily admonished, exchanging a look of forbearance with her cousin.

There was nothing to do but to invite Jemima along with them, and although Althea knew she ought to have patience and forgiveness in her heart, it was not easy.

The young women slowly sauntered down the stairs until they reached the entry where they encountered Mr. Poindexter and Hercules.

"I am having to atone for leaving him at the hotel yesterday while we took our excursion. He was not best pleased to have the hotel groom walk him, for the fellow has not the least understanding of Hercules' wants."

"We intend to stroll along the main street. Why do you not join us? I feel sure that Hercules will be able to offer his sage wisdom on anything we might see in the windows," Cecily said with good humor.

"Going somewhere?" Lord Montmorcy said after running lightly down the stairs to join them. "Shopping, perhaps?" he added with a very direct look at Althea.

She willed herself not to blush and bowed slightly in his direction. "As you can see, none of us suffered any ill effects from the rain last evening. We had planned to do a bit of shopping this morning."

"Ah, yes, I believe you mentioned it yesterday," he replied with an odd glance at Althea. "May I join you? There is little else to do on a dreary day, and the company of three charming ladies will brighten the day considerably."

"With such an enchanting request we could scarcely deny you pleasure of our company," Althea said dryly.

"I should hope not," he said quietly so that she alone heard him. They left the hotel only to encounter the comte outside, and of course he begged to join them, falling in beside Mrs. de Lisle, while Jemima flounced along beside Hercules, avoiding the slightest contact or speech with Mr. Poindexter.

"I thought we had an agreement," Lord Montmorcy said.

"And I thought it was no more than a jest, sir," Althea thought to toss back at him. She concentrated on her speech with him, for it was beyond her to even look in the windows while he absorbed her attention. They came to a corner, and he reached out to assist her when a carriage came dashing along the street.

"Watch out!" Jemima cried out, pushing at Althea in alarm.

At the same time Althea felt a tug from another direction. Turning her head, she saw that she was in danger of being run over by the exceedingly large horses that pulled a fast racing carriage.

Cecily darted back and threw herself against Althea who had frozen, unable to move, bringing Althea to the walk again.

The danger passed in moments. They milled about, with Althea giving her cousin a hug of appreciation.

"How silly of me," Althea murmured.

"You must be in need of a restorative," the comte declared in concern.

Althea smiled and waved off the offers to return to the hotel. "Nonsense, I am fine." But inwardly she vividly remembered the touch of Lord Montmorcy's hand on her arm, and she would have sworn he had pulled her into the path of the oncoming carriage, not away from it.

Chapter Eleven

Badly shaken, but determined not to reveal her inward feelings, Althea bravely smiled at the others, avoiding Lord Montmorcy. How could she look him in the eyes, suspecting what he had done?

"My, but you are careless, Althea," Jemima scolded in a high, shrill voice that could be heard some distance, Althea was certain. "Why, you might have caused those poor horses to bolt and think what might have happened then? But then, you are always so awkward."

"Miss Ingram always appears to be graceful, Miss Greenwood," the comte said with a small bow to Althea.

"Come, let us cease causing speculation among the citizens of Geneva and continue on our way," his lordship said, urging Althea to at last cross the street and pause before a shop while waiting for the others to join them. "I believe Miss Ingram wanted to look at a furrier's shop—or was it Mrs. de Lisle?"

Cecily smiled her sweetest at the gentlemen and tucked her arm into the crook of Althea's. "We both wish to look. Perhaps Jemima will want a pretty muff to keep her hands warm this coming winter?"

"I scarcely think it proper for the gentlemen to accompany us to the furrier," Althea said quietly, for she did not wish to sound as shrewish or sulky as Jemima did so often.

"I will confess I do not know all that much about furs," Cecily replied softly. "I think it might be wise on our part to have their advice. After all, they may have bought such items before."

The thought of Lord Montmorcy purchasing furs for a mistress or anyone else dismayed Althea, but she realized that a gentleman led a much broader life than a lady.

The comte paused before the modest entrance to a shop that had a simple display of a fur muff in its window. "I propose we enter here, for when I inquired of one of my Geneva friends I was told this is the best furrier in the city."

"That is comforting," Cecily said with a grateful smile to the comte. "How nice to have such good and kind friends."

"Well, friend I might be, but I think Hercules might object to the place—all the fur, you know," Mr. Poindexter said with a shrug. "I believe we will continue on along to the Promenade for our stroll." He gave the dog a reassuring pat, then strode off.

The others entered the shop. Jemima immediately went to the window to examine the beautiful muff of white spotted ermine. Within minutes she had determined the price and decided to purchase it without consulting the others, particularly the men.

"I shall see you later," she said in her high-pitched voice. "I have other errands this morning. When do we leave for Chamouny?" She paused before the door, asking the question of Althea, but darting a glance at Lord Montmorcy.

Since his lordship had promised to lead them on the trip, Althea turned to him, her brows raised in inquiry.

"Shall we say on the morrow?" he replied without looking at Jemima.

"Will that allow us sufficient time to pack?" Cecily wondered aloud.

"Gabrielle and Susan will take care of things, and I believe we can leave them in charge of the belongings we do not wish to bring along," Althea said. "Perhaps we might persuade Tugwell to oversee them while we are gone?"

"Certainly," Lord Montmorcy replied, looking extremely satisfied that he'd had his way. At least, Althea decided he looked smug about something.

With the departure agreed upon, Jemima left the shop and the others turned their attention to the beautiful fur pelisses and other items brought out for the ladies' approval.

Cecily decided that she wanted a fur muff more than a pelisse and selected a soft gray chinchilla one of great size, then bought a pretty hat to match.

"I imagine you will want something to keep you warm when you return to the countryside and face a snowy winter. Why not try this cloak of chinchilla?" Lord Montmorcy took the cloak from the hands of the shop owner to slip it over Althea's shoulders.

The fur had been placed on the inside, as was most practical. When it settled around her it felt luxurious, silken, and soft as a whisper on her skin. While not heavy, it caressed her with its warmth. The outside of the cloak was an exquisite deep blue woolen cloth of tight weave that would wear well. Yet, she could always have that changed if she tired of it. Half decided to purchase it, she jumped when his lordship placed a close-fitting bonnet with a small brim created in the same fur atop her head, then handed her a muff to match.

"A trifle much, I should think," she said quietly to him, with a questioning look at Cecily, who stood off to one side by the comte.

"Your hands and head are worthy of warmth as well, Althea," he said softly.

She studied her reflection, noting that his lordship hovered at her shoulders, his hands still resting there.

Had he pushed her? She looked at those beautifully gloved hands that she knew were strong and powerful. He had pulled her up the rock wall after she had fallen. It made no sense for him to have pushed her now. He would not do such a thing. Or would he? But why? No, she refused to believe it. He might say the most annoying things about her, but there was no motive for him to harm her. Yet a trace of doubt lingered in the back of her mind.

"It is breathtaking, my dearest Althea," Cecily cried with enthusiasm. "And you could take the cloak along in case you become chilled while at the glacier. It seems most practical to me."

"Practical?" Althea gave the gorgeous fur a dubious look, then nodded her head. "I shall arrange payment for these," she said to the shop owner. With the comte's recommendation and

Lord Montmorcy's added suggestions it was not long before the sale was concluded and they left the shop, the promise that the items would immediately be delivered ringing in their ears.

"Now, what else is there to see," Cecily demanded in her pretty way, with a smile directed at the comte. Althea decided she'd had quite enough of Cecily trying to make Lord Montmorcy jealous—or whatever she was attempting to do by her behavior—and subtly maneuvered herself so that within minutes she had consulted the comte on an Italian picture she had seen and strolled along at his side while Cecily fell back to walk beside Lord Montmorcy.

Not really in the mood to purchase anything else, Althea watched while Cecily pondered over a pretty timepiece in a little shop the comte suggested.

"I thought you also wished to buy one of the excellent timepieces made here?" his lordship said, coming up behind her from where he had observed Cecily inspecting the various things on display. The comte had eased over to take his lordship's place next to Cecily. It seemed that both men found her desirable company.

"I had considered it." Althea turned away to stroll over to a case where other pretty timepieces rested on velvet beds.

"I trust the furs did not empty your purse," his lordship said in a reflective manner.

"Not quite," she said absently. "While Papa gave me a generous amount for the Tour, I also have sums from my own inheritance from which to draw. I believe I scandalized our banker when I requested a considerable amount be placed at my disposal. But since this is most likely the only trip of this sort that I shall ever take, I wish to have no regrets."

She glanced sideways at him, noticing that the twinkle had returned to those remarkable green eyes again. He looked immensely pleased about something. Maybe he found her little story amusing.

"May I suggest this little locket watch?" He gestured to a pretty little timepiece of gold, set with tiny diamonds and garnets in a lovely design.

"I do not know," Althea said, wishing for some reason to be difficult. Actually, it was the sort of thing she'd had in the

back of her mind. In the end she bought it, and they all left the
shop in smiles, for the comte had found just the pocket watch
he'd been wanting.

Lord Montmorcy surprised Althea when he requested they
go on to the hotel without him, for he had to stop at the
apothecary's for just a moment.

The group strolled on at a leisurely pace. Althea was surprised when his lordship caught up with them a short time
later. Apparently his pause had not been made to avoid their—
or her—company.

He placed her hand on his arm, earning a frown from
Althea.

"Now, be still," he urged in a low voice. "I wish to tell you
what I just learned."

"And that was?" she inquired while noticing all the while
the strength in his arm, the muscles beneath the Bath cloth of
his finely tailored coat.

"I was suspicious of that tooth powder so I brought it to the
apothecary to have the fellow test it. Althea, there was poison
in it!" He said the last in a whisper, looking about to make
sure none other heard what he had to say.

"I cannot credit that, sir," Althea said, utterly aghast at this
information and the implications.

"I have his results here," he waved a paper in the air before
them. "Arsenic. True, it was a very small amount, but in time
it could have killed you. Who knows when it was placed there.
I recall you said something about the top being difficult to
open. That precludes Miss Greenwood tampering with it, for
she does not look strong. Perhaps it was but an accident."

"Perhaps," Althea agreed. "There appear to have been quite
a few of those on this trip," she mused in a chilled voice.

"Come, let us catch up to the others, then we shall have a
splendid cup of tea when we reach the hotel."

His words were bracing, but did not serve to reassure
Althea. Until they had met up with Lord Montmorcy nothing
of a dire nature had happened to her. Since that moment it had
been one thing after another. Then she brightened, for if he
told her of the results, that meant he wouldn't have put the poison in the tooth powder, did it not?

Nothing was said to the others about the poison in the tooth powder. Certainly Althea had no accusations to make. But she resolved to be more careful in the future and less trusting of everyone—including Lord Montmorcy for another reason altogether.

Dinner that evening was lively and gay. Even Jemima was in good spirits. And the others, who dined together most meals now, joined in the laughter with determination, it seemed to Althea. She wondered if his lordship had confided the information about the poison to the comte.

"We shall leave here early in the morning, so our evening will be cut short," Lord Montmorcy informed the group while tiny pastries were being served.

"You mean you do not intend to go off to some gaming club as in London?" Cecily asked with laughter in her voice.

"No gaming clubs in Geneva. The city fathers would frown on such," the comte said. "However we might find a private game if we wished. There are always ways around city fathers, you know."

"I am off to bed," Althea announced, rising from the table with regret, for it had been a leisurely dinner and much enjoyed. She feared that once alone she would fall into a blue-deviled mood, wondering if the poison was intentional or merely the accident Lord Montmorcy insisted.

Cecily drained her teacup and also rose from the table. "Jemima? Will you join us?" Since there was no drawing room to which they might retire, the ladies had enjoyed the company of the gentlemen following their dinners. It had proved to be a delightful change.

They all decided to retire for the night and straggled up the stairs and along to their rooms. Lord Montmorcy paused in the hall, placing a hand on Cecily's arm.

"Do you know if Althea has proper riding gear? She might enjoy riding part of the way." Along the hallway Althea could be seen walking rapidly toward her room.

"Indeed, would you like to see if she intends to ride?" Cecily turned to see that Althea had entered their room, so the two walked along to the open doorway.

Turning to face the pair who looked so elegant together,

Althea realized she might have succeeded better than she had hoped. "You wish to tell me something?" she inquired with sinking heart.

"I merely wish to know what your riding gear is. You brought it along?" Lord Montmorcy said, standing with his hand on the doorknob.

"Indeed, I shall be comfortable, thank you."

"You are *not* going to wear that divided skirt, are you?" Cecily demanded in dawning horror.

"Of course. Why else did I have it made, if not to wear when deemed practical?" Althea said with an expressive shrug of her shoulders. "It looks excessively proper. Indeed, one can scarcely tell it is a divided skirt."

"Ever the practical girl, I see," his lordship said with amusement clear in his tone.

"Practical, sturdy, brave, there is no end to my sterling qualities," Althea said dryly. After all, she strove to push these two together, and if his lordship found Cecily to be worthy of notice, it ought to please.

"In the morning, then," Lord Montmorcy said with a melting smile at Cecily, who dimpled a smile back at him before gently closing the door. She affixed the traveling lock in place, then turned to face her cousin.

Althea had turned aside from this display and consulted Gabrielle about the packing. Assured it was complete and that the maids would take care of the belongings they did not wish to drag along with them, Althea quickly undressed and popped into her bed while Cecily drifted about the room, humming and sighing and smiling to herself like a schoolgirl in the throes of her first romance.

"Morning will be here before you know it," Althea reminded politely.

"You like your furs? Your little locket watch? Do you intend to take them along?" Cecily demanded.

"Yes to the first two queries, but I do not think I shall bring my cloak with us. I suspect the wind from the glacier could be very chilling and yet it is summer."

"I do not know if I care to climb very far up," Cecily said

with a dubious frown. "Perhaps I shall find a nice flat rock and watch everyone."

"Well, I made sure that Gabrielle packed woolen socks, linen tapes so we might hike our skirts up if necessary, and every bit of warm clothing we possess." Althea gave a prodigious yawn, then settled beneath her covers with a hope she might find sleep.

"Do you like the tooth powder I found for you?" Cecily said while she clambered into her bed across from Althea. "I had it specially compounded for you."

"It is fine, dear," Althea mumbled. But in spite of her desire for sleep, she stared into the darkness of the room, wondering who it was that had put arsenic into that tooth powder. The obvious one was Jemima. But it might have been compounded for someone else and bought by mistake, or it could have been someone who entered her room—like Lord Montmorcy.

The very notion that someone she knew might have committed such a terrible crime upset Althea so much that it took her a long time to fall asleep.

Their hot coffee and rolls arrived very early in the morning. Althea struggled to rise. "I would much prefer to sleep another hour or two," she admitted to Cecily.

Gabrielle shook out the simple black wool divided skirt that looked for all the world like an ordinary riding habit skirt, with fullness, but without the sweep of fabric that usually fell to one side.

Althea stepped into it, then turned to show Cecily once the maid had fastened the closings. "See? It ought to be ever so much easier to ride and hike without the narrow dress skirt to hamper movement or that awkward bundle of wool in a riding habit to drape over the arm. Now, agree with me," she demanded with a laugh.

"You said you brought along linen tape. What for?" Cecily asked while sipping the last of the strong coffee guaranteed to wake the sleepiest of persons.

"If you wish to venture onto the glacier, you may need to tie your skirts up, and there is a paper of pins and tape for fastening in our case so it ought to be no great problem. Come now, hurry. We do not wish the gentlemen to think us a pair of slug-abeds." Althea gave her cousin a pat on the shoulder. She crossed the room to have Gabrielle assist her with her riding jacket.

"Best call Jemima," she urged Susan.

Before long the women gathered in the entryway to the hotel with their parcels and baggage around their feet.

"Well," Jemima crowed, "I do believe we are the early birds and they are tardy." There was enormous satisfaction in her voice, and Althea wondered if Jemima had long harbored this resentment of the male half of the species.

Then her smug face drooped when Lord Montmorcy and the comte entered the building, bringing with them a hint of brisk, early morning air. Outside a traveling coach awaited them, and a groom collected the baggage in a trice to be loaded into the capacious boot of the coach.

"Ready?" his lordship inquired as he studied the women, nodding pleasantly to all.

"Let us be off, for I vow if I stand here very long I shall fall asleep," Cecily said with a merry chuckle.

The hotel staff paused in their duties to see the group hurry into the coach and depart. Jemima had fussed over her baggage, insisting she inspect the boot to see if everything was just so, causing the staff to exchange amused looks.

Althea rode in the coach for the first part of the journey, not wishing to scandalize the staid people of Geneva by riding astride.

They were not long from the city when they began to climb through the hills. Steep mountains crowned with deep forests rose on either side of the surprisingly good road.

Althea waited impatiently for the coach to reach a place where they might pause so she could leave the stuffy confines of the coach and join the men on horseback. When the coach rolled to a halt on a wide verge, she was out in a flash as soon as the groom opened her door.

Approaching them was a flock of sheep with their shepherd, bleating a mournful tune. Althea froze, well recalling the incident in the village when Hercules had tried his skill at herding and failed badly.

Having seen the sheep in the distance, Sidney had tied Hercules to a tree, then stood guard by his pup.

Only when the noise of the herd with its tinkling bells and nervous bleats had faded did they set about having a light repast. Once that was done, Althea mounted the fine horse arranged for her use, and the ladies returned to their carriage, Jemima for once taking the forward facing seat with Cecily.

Cottages were scattered here and there along the way, with only a few of the inhabitants to be viewed. Around a bend in the road ruins of an ancient castle rose dramatically, silhouetted against low hanging clouds. It gave rise to thoughts of Mrs. Radcliffe's tales of gothic ruins and ghosts.

"Very picturesque," Althea called out to the other riders, feeling her words were horribly inadequate. How wonderful to be out of the coach, able to look in all directions without any obstructions. The air, while yet brisk, felt fresh and pure.

Lord Montmorcy fell back to ride next to her. "I wonder, Miss Ingram, since we are in such confined company, if we might dispense with formality and use our given names?"

"I suppose so," she said in a considering way, as though it was something that required great thought.

"Good. Did I tell you we will have to hire a guide when we leave Chamouny for the glacier and Mont Blanc?" he said while riding easily beside her.

She glanced over to him, then turned her gaze ahead once more. "I thought *you* would be our guide."

"Well," he countered, "although I have been there before, I'd not wish to go without some chap who is familiar with the area and route. Why, an avalanche can wipe out a trail, then a new one must be cut and all looks different."

"I suppose the trees are bent and rocks carried down the mountain. Is there much danger that we might encounter an avalanche this time of year?" She glanced back at the coach, thinking of how she had assured Cecily they would be in no great danger.

"I doubt it," he said with a confidence that was catching and Althea relaxed.

They crested a hill, then made a sharp turn and began their descent into a pretty valley. Now walnut trees, oaks, and chestnuts grew in profusion along the road, and the air became milder. Althea wished she might unbutton her riding jacket.

"You find the riding easier?" with a gesture to her sitting astride.

"Yes," she said with amusement at his expression. "Do you find my attire scandalous?"

He snorted with derision. "How could I? There is so much fabric I doubt if there are any legs beneath it all. Or," he said with that twinkle in his eyes again, "do I offend you with such bold words?"

"I believe you are a great tease, sir," she said.

He ignored her, turning to look ahead of them. "Chamouny is a charming village. I trust we will be able to find adequate housing, for there are two excellent inns."

"How nice to know we shall have a good bed," Althea said, feeling the effects of being in the saddle for much of the day. She suspected she'd be stiff tomorrow. "It's a pity there are no hot baths here as in Geneva. Have you ever sought them out?"

"No," he said, not inquiring as to the reason for the non sequitur. "I suggest you request a hot tub when we arrive. They are accustomed to English people demanding peculiar things."

"And a bath is odd?" Althea said with a chuckle.

"They will bathe once a week, perhaps once a year as it suits them. There are other things deemed more important."

"Well," Althea promised, "I will make my request in heartfelt tones and most politely. Perhaps they will see my riding gear and guess my difficulty?"

He said nothing, merely looked at her skirt. Althea wondered what went on in his mind that he would have such an expression on his face. They rode on in silence, watching Hercules gambol along the edge of the road now that he had been freed from the confines of the coach.

Then he added, "You ought to have some of the excellent liniment Tugwell makes up for me. It would soothe your aches in no time." She made no reply, but entered the inn.

She obtained her hot water and a slipper bath of small proportions that required the barest amount of water.

"I feel as though I am sliding into a shoe," Althea complained from behind her sheltering screen to Cecily, who had come in to help her. Since the rooms were quite small, each of the women had her own.

"Well, the coach was excessively dusty, and I intend to wash well before supper, you may be sure," Cecily said. "Jemima hardly complained the entire trip, which you must admit is a blessing."

"She is definitely a puzzle," Althea admitted. "I believe it might be more pleasant without her, but she does give us a bit more respectability."

"We are rather daring, I expect. Do you think Lady Jersey would speak to us ever again should she know our exploits on our Grand Tour?" Althea asked with an arch note in her voice.

"I doubt if Princess Lieven would, for she is the highest stickler, you know. But, I thought you cared not the least for their opinion." Cecily offered a stack of towels, then waited by the window while Althea dried herself off after extracting herself from the confines of the tub.

"I suppose I do in a way," Althea replied thoughtfully. "Who knows, if you were to marry, I'd need a decent reputation to acquire another companion."

"What makes you think I'd marry again?" Cecily demanded with pink cheeks and lashes that dipped to conceal the expression in her eyes.

"I have eyes in my head," Althea replied dryly. "You are a very pretty woman, with lovely manners and a sweet disposition that any man in his right mind would adore." She had not forgotten that melting look Lord Montmorcy bestowed on her cousin the night before they left Geneva.

"Thank you, Althea, that was very nicely done of you," Cecily said.

Her words brought back to Althea the scene at the little inn across the lake from Geneva when Lord Montmorcy had whisked her around the corner to dally with her. At least, she now considered his attentions in that light considering his interest in Cecily. But she would say nothing to her dear cousin about his perfidy, for doubtless Althea had in some way encouraged him. It certainly showed most eloquently the reason why young women were guarded diligently by a chaperon. It was clear that were they not, there would be all manner of trouble for them.

Once dressed in comfortable, if not stylish, clothes, the women went down to the main room of the little inn, where they found the gentlemen awaiting them.

"Did your soak in hot water improve your aches?" Lord Montmorcy asked in an aside while they walked along to the dining room where the guests at the inn were to eat.

Ignoring the impropriety of his question, Althea simply answered him. "Yes, and Cecily said she has some lotion that will help."

"Tomorrow will require difficult riding. It is some forty miles from Chamouny to the glacier."

"But that is not so very long," Althea said with a puzzled look.

"The other women will not be able to proceed by carriage. I have arranged for *chaises-à-porteurs* for Mrs. de Lisle and Miss Greenwood. They are used for those who cannot walk or ride a horse or mule. There will be eight porters per chair, four used at time."

"What's that I hear?" Jemima demanded. "Chairs? Whatever for? I do not think I would be easy in a chair going over some mountain pass from what I have seen so far."

"Rest easy, Miss Greenwood. If you are uneasy about the steepness, sit with your back to the abyss or the worst part of the road. The lively songs of the porters are bound to inspire your confidence."

"Mercy," Cecily whispered and hastily sat down. "How ever will we manage to cope with this? I am not fainthearted as a rule, but the thought of traversing above an abyss does give me a chill."

"They rarely lose a chair," Lord Montmorcy comforted. "Only rarely?" Jemima whispered, for once stilled into stunned silence. She too sank down onto a chair, contemplating the trip on the morrow with a distinctly unsettled expression.

Chapter Twelve

Following an interesting meal during which Althea was served a fried egg with baby asparagus, she slipped away from the others. Taking a warm shawl along, she ventured out of the inn to an area up and behind where she could breathe the pure air of the summer alpine night. Crisp, still air made her aware of the snow not so very far above where she stood.

Around her towered craggy peaks crowned white with snow that glistened in the light of the moon with an unearthly glitter. The impressive sight stirred a feeling of awe within. Upon finding a wooden bench, she sat down to contemplate her Grand Tour. Where would she go from here? To Austria as originally planned? Or perhaps to a warmer clime, such as Rome?

The silence wrapped itself around her like the soft wool shawl she had picked up—comforting, welcoming after the noise of the inn, incredibly peaceful. Here she could allow the worries that plagued her to fade away.

"There are no frogs or crickets here," John said quietly. "Did you notice the silence, how total it is?" His footsteps on the carpet of pine needles had been unheard.

"Indeed," she said in an equally hushed voice. If he noticed her startled jump of surprise, he said nothing. She wrapped her shawl more tightly about her, glancing up to see his shadowed face and wondering why he had sought her out.

"It is a tranquil spot," he said in a low, relaxed voice, followed by a sigh. He came closer, yet she could not hear his steps.

"Not even a night bird, or is that an owl I hear?" she said softly.

"Could be," he agreed. "Are you troubled by the trek tomorrow? Miss Greenwood seems closer to a panic than I have yet seen her. And Mrs. de Lisle has the comte hovering over her to assure her that he will personally see to it that she remains safe at all times."

"You could not do that? You left it to him?" Althea blurted forth. Then, realizing the impropriety of her questions, she added, "Forgive me, it is none of my affair what you do."

He joined her on the bench, taking more than his share of space so that she had to shift to accommodate him.

After a time he said, "No, I suppose not."

As to what he meant by that—that it was not her affair, or that he could not see to Cecily—Althea didn't venture to guess.

They sat in oddly comfortable silence for a time, Althea acutely aware of the arm he placed behind her—to brace himself, she supposed. Tall men seemed to use an inordinate amount of space.

"What do you plan to do after we leave here and return to Geneva?" he inquired after another spell of silence which was becoming less tranquil by the minute.

"I have not decided," she admitted. "We had planned to travel to Vienna, but I think Cecily is inclined to head south to Italy."

"And you? What if Cecily decides to remain in Italy? Or if she decides to marry?"

His voice held a curious note in it that she could not quite interpret. She looked at him and wished she might see his face. The darkness concealed so much, especially his expression. She could make out the shadows of his eyes below his brows, his aristocratic nose, the flop of his hair over his forehead, but no details. She found it frustrating, not to know his facial cast.

"She does not need my permission, you know," Althea chided. "I should continue on my way, with Jemima as a companion until I returned home." That was a depressing thought—Jemima as her sole companion. "And you?"

"I have plans," he said in an intriguing way that made Althea long to shake him. His hand strayed from the wood of the bench to touch her shoulder, absently caressing it—at least that was what it seemed to her, that it was an absentminded gesture. That he could think of plans for his future, which apparently included Cecily, while sitting on a bench caressing Althea's shoulder was beyond acceptable—at least to Althea's way of thinking. She pulled away from his hand and the attraction to him that disturbed her.

"Forgive me, I did not wish to intrude on your privacy," she said in a starched little voice that did not sound the least like her own. "Although to be fair, I was sitting here first," she pointed out with a sweep of her hand. She rose in a huff from the little bench where he had chosen to join her. Her peace shattered, her poise suddenly in tatters, she knew it time to retreat to her little room under the eaves of the inn.

He also rose from the bench, clasping her arm to halt her steps away from him. "The journey to the glacier will not be the easiest thing you have done. A proper night's sleep would not come amiss."

"That is precisely what I intend to do," she said, refusing to look into those magical green eyes. Even in the dark she could sense the perception in his eyes. She suspected he saw too much, even in this pale light. The feel of his hand on her arm brought back not only the memory of that waltz at the inn by the lake, but the incident at the street crossing in Geneva when she had not been able to decide if he pulled or pushed her. Consequently, she fled down the hill as though pursued by ghosts from one of Mrs. Radcliffe's haunted castles, passing Mr. Poindexter and Hercules in a flurry of skirts.

"Well," Sidney said with a thoughtful look at the rapidly disappearing Miss Ingram, "I suppose you blotted your copy book again."

"Oh, I fancy I do that more often than you'd expect. How's the pup?" John did not want to discuss his chat with Althea Ingram. He supposed he ought to make his desires known to her, but he wished to return to Geneva before he said anything. He wanted to clear up the matter of the attempted poisoning first.

"You frighten the daylights out of Miss Ingram—and not for the first time, I might add—and you want me to keep my nose out of it." Sidney allowed Hercules to wander off, his leash trailing behind him. The pup could be heard sniffing about the trees, but his padded steps were hushed by the pine needles just as John's had been earlier.

John sighed and returned to the bench. "Join me?"

"Gladly," Sidney said.

John guessed his old friend deserved some manner of explanation, but he scarce knew what to say. Could he reveal his suspicions about the poison and his fear that something else more deadly might occur while on this trip to the glacier?

"If you don't want to confide in me, I quite understand," Sidney said in the understanding way of an old friend who is clearly puzzled but will respect a reluctance to speak.

"It is not that, precisely. I guess I do not want you to think me a fool," John confessed.

"Because you care for Althea Ingram? That is wise, my friend, not foolish." Sidney leaned back against the bench to contemplate the glimmer of distant white peaks.

"I did not think myself so obvious," John said with a rueful grin lost on his companion.

"You forget, I know you of old. Since it cannot be that alone, what else troubles you?" Sidney snapped his fingers and Hercules came loping back to him. The dog flopped down by the bench, then placed his large head atop Sidney's boots. This was followed by a sigh from Sidney.

"I suspect there is a person trying to do away with Althea. Somewhat inept, it is true, but even a stupid effort can be deadly."

Sidney didn't appear too startled by this revelation. "I've wondered about the fall in that ravine. She dismissed it too lightly, as though she might be trying to protect someone she knew. And that tooth powder, well, that seemed a bit havey-cavey to me as well. I mean, why would a shopkeeper put poison into a tin of tooth powder, I ask you."

"She nearly tumbled into the lake. If you cannot swim a stroke, that could be fatal," John added.

"No one pushed her. We were all present," Sidney reminded his friend. "The girl has a dashed fine pair of legs," he inserted into his summation, clearly recalling the sight of those long slim legs in their pink silk stockings.

"As I said, the person attempting to do away with Althea is inept. Efficiency would have resulted in a death before now. But why? I think I know who, but why?"

"If you have a suspect, why not denounce the criminal and have done with it?" Sidney leaned down to scratch the pup's head.

"Not good enough. It would be merely speculation," John said glumly. "I'd like to set a trap. The thing is, I need to use Althea as bait, and I am loath to endanger her life more than it might be otherwise."

"I shall be glad to help, old man," Sidney said in an encouraging voice.

John rose from the bench, pausing to consider his friend's offer. "We shall see how it goes," he said at last. "You plan to leave Hercules here, do you not?"

At Sidney's mumbled "I should hope so," John set forth his plan.

"You must watch everyone, particularly the other women. The comte will be close to Mrs. de Lisle, but Miss Greenwood as well must be observed. To tell the truth, I do not trust anyone. Mrs. de Lisle could have a motive—wishing to be free of her cousin while absconding with the money Althea brought along and has left in Geneva, although she does seem innocent."

"Is that Miss Greenwood's motive as well?" Sidney asked in a worried voice while they slowly returned to the inn.

"Perhaps. However, I have observed the looks of malice directed by Miss Greenwood at Althea when no one seemed to be watching her. There is no love lost between those two."

"At least you don't suspect the comte," Sidney said with relief.

"He might do it in order to whisk his love away from her cousin."

"Noticed that, did you? I must admit that for a time I thought you had an interest in the fair Cecily."

"Althea seems to as well. I'll not disabuse her of that notion until we solve the riddle of the attempted murder. The more remote we are, the more dangerous it will be for Althea."

"And yet you don't stop her from going?" Sidney said when they paused by the door before entering.

"Could I? I doubt it. She is a very determined young woman with rare courage. If anyone can handle this danger, it will be Althea," John declared with confidence.

"I notice you ain't said what your intentions are toward her," Sidney said before parting at the top of the stairs.

"That," John said with a grin, "would be telling."

The party that set out from Chamouny early the following morning was blessed with good weather. That is to say, great clouds swollen with water hovered over the snow-capped peaks, but no rain fell to mar their traveling. Water dripped from the boughs of the pines, witness to a nighttime shower.

The path twisted up from the village, beginning at the side of a river, then rising steadily every mile they rode. This meant that the slope down to the river grew steeper as they traveled. Althea tried to put the memories of her tumble near the waterfall from her mind, but was not totally successful. Every now and again she would give the abyss an uneasy glance, for the road—if one could call it that—wound very close to the edge at times.

They went along silently through the deep green of the forest, where even the sound of the carriage was hushed by the carpet of pine needles. When they emerged into the relative light of the day, it was to the sight of low-growing plants and boulders and herds of goats here and there. Cottages were ever fewer here.

Althea had slept fitfully, with a great many thoughts plaguing her. Come morning she had upon arising peered into the looking glass with dismay, then decided that Lord Montmorcy would ignore her anyway, so why concern herself? Pride was such a bothersome thing. She glanced at the man who rode so effortlessly not far from her side and decided he had not only slept well, but did extremely well without the attentions of his valet.

He wore garb similar to the sort in which she had seen him the day he rescued her from the bandittos—dark pantaloons to his calf with half gaiters, a gray jacket of a sort of ticking fabric with a sensible shirt and simple cravat. From his saddle hung a pair of shoes with spikes attached to the soles. She noted he wore a straw hat with a wide brim much as she had purchased in Geneva. On the mule that carried their supplies were several umbrellas and cloaks of oiled silk plus stout walking sticks or poles.

They wound up and around the rutted and narrow excuse for a road for what seemed like hours, yet the hands on Althea's locket watch moved very slowly. The rain-dampened earth sent up a pungent scent, and the breeze carried hints of wild animals and distant flowers. Everywhere about them rose splendid peaks with lush valleys below—hushed and desolate, yet giving a sense of welcome peace.

"Magnificent scenery, is it not?" Lord Montmorcy said, sidling up to her closely given the nature of their beasts and the road.

"I could not have imagined anything like this." She gestured with a wave of her hand to the incredible landscape before them. "I can see why my father speaks of his Grand Tour with nostalgic fondness. I shall as well," Althea replied, easing her horse along a narrow place in the road. She pointed to the region ahead of them. "That peculiar red porphyry and that marvelous granite cannot be viewed on a jaunt in England. At least not in such spectacular outcroppings. Is this what so appeals to you about this country?" She gestured with her hand. "The wildness? The remoteness from the strictures of society? Or is it merely the beauty of the place?"

"All of that and more," he admitted. "But since all good things must come to an end, after I meet my mother and her new husband, I will return to my estate to tend matters left too long to a steward."

It did not sound as though he intended to bring a bride or bride-to-be along with him. She gave him a curious look, then said, "And nothing more? With all due respect, I believe you said something about tending to an heir."

"Oh, yes. I must find me a wife, I suppose."

That gleam had returned to his eyes again, and she suspected he was teasing her. He seemed to take great delight in teasing her.

"I believe we are to stop for a bite of lunch," Mr. Poindexter announced as he joined them. The carriage had rumbled to a halt, and the women scrambled from it, looking as though they had been tumbled pillar to post.

Instead of taking himself off to hunt for petrifications, Poindexter maintained vigilance over the women, seeing to their comfort. John, that is Lord Montmorcy, consulted with the driver and the other men in his excellent French.

All was relatively quiet until something frightened the mule who carried provisions for the expedition. He sidled and backed and nervously jumped about until he went over the edge of the road and tumbled, sliding down into the ravine. His braying was most pitiful, touching Althea's heart.

She rode her horse to the edge of the abyss, staring down at the animal who had somehow managed to survive the descent, scrambling and sliding to the very bottom. He stood, dazed and unmoving near the river.

"We cannot leave it there, you know. Someone must fetch the poor thing up here," she said to John when he joined her to study the situation.

"Are you game?" he quizzed. "I fear the men will simply let it find its way back to Chamouny, unwilling to risk their necks. It does not seemed badly harmed, does it?" John leaned forward in his saddle to better study the situation.

"How do you propose to bring it back up the slope? 'Tis not a gentle walk, you know," she reminded him while also continuing to study the animal. They could well need those supplies even if the men might not agree.

"You are not thinking of going down there, are you Althea?" Cecily cried in alarm while hurrying across to join them.

With a glance at John, Althea brought one leg over her horse, then slid to the ground. In moments she stood at the edge of the abyss, fighting back her recollections. Could she? Then with a firming of her chin and a cool look at his handsome lordship, she marched over to a great flat rock, plunked herself down on it and pushed off down the hill. She had wrapped her divided skirt tightly around her and now blessed the riband that held her straw hat snugly to her head. Her jacket was partly undone, allowing her arms freedom of movement to grasp the rock with both hands.

With shouts from all who had assembled on the rim trailing behind her, she rode the rock down the slope, bumping and pounding, fearing her fate yet oddly thrilled. She had heard of others doing this when faced with rock slides or blocked roads. It was quite another thing to attempt it—but it worked. She bounced and slid to a halt, then sat, a trifle shaken and certainly dusty. Once she ascertained that she was in one piece and unharmed, she stood and surveyed the mule.

Within seconds she had managed to traverse the slope that would have taken her some time to climb down. It would be another matter to persuade the sometimes stubborn animal to climb up the hill.

"That was a damn fool thing to do," John said breathlessly after he had bounded and jumped down the slope behind her. "Took years off my life when I saw you sail down that hill," his lordship scolded with an intensity that amazed Althea. He must have run madly behind her, for he was panting and disheveled, his brow damp from his exertion.

"I only did what seemed necessary," she snapped.

"You could have killed yourself," he argued.

"I doubt that bothers anyone unduly," she said crisply, looking away from his frowning gaze. "Now let us see if we can convince this mule that it must make an effort to climb. Do you happen to have a carrot handy?"

"Althea," John said in a voice that ought to have warned her he was not pleased with her.

"Do not be tedious," she cautioned. "This is neither the time nor the place to give me a scold." She did not wish to admit how shaken she was inside.

"Later," he promised, then grabbed the mule's halter and

pulled. Althea searched the area beside the water, snatching handfuls of grass to use as persuasion.

The hike back up the hill was slow, hot work. The sun had come out, making the climb worse. She blessed her divided skirt more than once, for it allowed her the freedom to find a good footing on the loose soil and rocks. Perspiration trickled down her back, dampened her brow, and rivulets ran between her breasts. Hot, dusty, tired and shaken, she also felt victorious. She had overcome her fears of the chasm and survived. And, they were bringing up the beast with its precious load of supplies.

With Althea feeding the succulent grass and John tugging on the rope halter, they managed to half-drag the mule to the top where the others awaited them. Even the coachman shook his head in obvious amazement at the tall Englishwoman who had so madly charged down the hill.

"If there is a bit of water around, I'd appreciate a drink. I imagine Lord Montmorcy would as well." Althea gasped when she gained a foothold on the top. She wiped her hands on her divided skirt and wondered if the trembling in her limbs would cease if she sat down. The babble of voices failed to really reach her ears, and she felt oddly weak.

"Here, drink this."

She obediently took a swallow and nearly choked on the brandy as it burned its way down her throat. "Of all the . . ." she sputtered, unable to say another word.

"Good, your color is better." John joined her in a drink of the bracing liquor, then held the great silk umbrella over her head. She felt blessedly cooler.

"I think we should have our luncheon, then be on our way. This sunshine cannot last much longer, given the gathering clouds," Sidney reported when he joined them.

The group, oddly subdued now that Althea and John were quietly seated among them, quickly ate the food set out. Before long the men and Althea were back in their saddles, the ladies returned to the dusty old coach, and they set off up the trail.

When they at last reached the tiny village where they were to spend one night on the way to the glacier, Althea found she was a trifle stiff and had sustained a few bruises, but was actually none the worse for her adventure.

The simple meal placed before them disappeared rapidly, and Cecily joked that the appetite increased the higher one went.

Desiring to exercise before finding the cot where she'd sleep this night, Althea left the small inn and wandered out to stare off into the distance. She heard steps behind her and said, "Look at the mountain peaks. What a beautiful shade of purple they are at sunset where the sun has broken through the clouds to shine on them. 'Tis pure magic. I'd not have expected that."

"I promised that I would chastise you later for your foolhardy stunt," John growled.

"You sound most menacing," she said, feeling not the least threatened.

"What is one to do with you, Althea?" he said, less threatening now.

"Why, nothing," she exclaimed, turning to face him. "It was . . . great fun, if you must know," she said with more than a hint of bravado. "Though I doubt I would do it again. It served to drive away my fear of precipices."

He shook his head at that defiant statement and laughed. "That is my hardy, brave girl."

"Perhaps hardy and brave *if* you insist, but scarcely yours, sir." She backed away from him, frightened more of her feelings toward him than anything he might do to her.

"Althea," he said, then paused as though searching for the right words.

Unwilling to hear him tell her that he had decided to make the delicate and unhardy Cecily his wife, Althea abruptly fled down the little path, disappearing into the little inn while he called out to her—quite in vain.

The road had continued to deteriorate until this small settlement was reached. Althea knew that come morning the coach would be left behind. Jemima and Cecily must transfer to the *chaises-à-porteurs*. She hoped the pair would not make a great to-do about the journey.

Althea went to her little cot, giving thanks that she had chosen to ride. And she also blessed the strength that saw her from the proximity of John, Lord Montmorcy, and into the inn, when she had so wanted to throw herself into his arms and know the comfort she might have there.

She felt better come morning. Today would be the final push to the glacier. They ought to reach it in a little over an hour or so. That would give them time to spend climbing around before they had to return for the night. She had no desire to camp in a tent as John had mentioned that some did. Spending a night grouped together beneath a canvas roof seemed too hazardous to her.

Before the inn stood the poled chairs along with the porters who were to carry them. Althea decided it was most likely the sum total of the male population of the settlement, at least the able ones.

The sun was rising over the peaks when they set off along the narrow, rocky trail. Jemima and Cecily had opted to face backward, both declaring themselves cowards, unable to look ahead.

Althea sat effortlessly in her saddle, thinking that riding in this fashion was a great deal easier than sidesaddle. With her straw hat at a jaunty angle and her green-tinted spectacles in the pocket of her jacket, she looked forward to this final thrust up into the mountains.

Fitful sunlight streamed around the clouds that still paraded across the sky, although not as threatening as the day before. The valley below them was lush and green, fed by countless little streams that ultimately combined to make the rushing creek that sped down to Geneva and the Rhone.

John joined Althea behind the pair of chairs with their jolly chairmen singing the songs of the mountains in excellent harmony. Jemima and Cecily alternated between peering around the chairs to see the scenery and retreating to shudder at the narrowness of the trail. The comte rode close to Cecily, reassuring her all the while.

"You quite enjoy all this, don't you," John said in a musing tone. "I saw you just after dawn, out communing with nature."

She inhaled deeply, then smiled. "Actually, I was walking about to ease the stiffness from my back," she admitted with a short laugh. "But yes, I enjoy all this. I confess that London will be exceedingly tame when I must return. I believe I shall take some of the money my grandmother left me to set up my own house somewhere off in the country."

"Unusual for a young woman to do," he commented while shading his eyes to look off into the distance.

She contemplated an answer which she fortunately never had to offer.

"Look," he said quietly, pointing to a site across the valley. "There is a herd of chamois over there. See them? High above that cluster of goats?"

"I do," she breathed, impressed with the sight of the nimble animals bounding over the steep terrain.

A change in porters stopped them briefly, then they went on. When they made a sharp turn in the trail, Althea exhaled an awed sigh.

"Oh, my goodness. I suppose you have seen this before, but you must admit that glacier is incredible . . . awesome . . . magnificent." She searched for more words with which to express her feelings while his lordship merely smiled at her enthusiasm. "I cannot wait for the chairs. Come, let us fly ahead." She set her horse to a trot, which was about the fastest she dare go given the rocks and roughness of the terrain.

Leaving the others far behind, Althea and John rode up to the edge of the glacier. The sun came out, and its rays felt more powerful than she had ever known before. Without thinking, she pulled her green-tinted glasses from her pocket and plopped them on her nose. The change was remarkable for the glacier stood out in sharp relief, with the snow not quite so blinding.

She was off her horse in a flash and advanced upon the snow. "*La mer de glace*," she murmured. "I intend to walk on the snow, that river of ice."

Balmat, their guide, had ridden up behind them and from somewhere he pulled forth a ladder to assist in the climb.

"First you must put on a pair of crampons, such as I have affixed to my shoes," John urged. "And remember, there is frozen snow between the ridges of ice, often concealed, and more often quite dangerous. That snow is of uncertain strength, as I have seen. Should you fall through it, there might be a chasm of untold depth beneath. Come, let me tie a rope to your waist, so that in the event you fall I will be able to stop you."

Althea, her mouth far too dry to answer him, allowed John to tie a length of rope about her waist and attach the spiked crampons to her half boots, then she set forth to the glacier right behind him.

Chapter Thirteen

"Stop!" Jemima tumbled from her chair, ignoring the stares of the chair men. She began hurrying across to the foot of the glacier.

Althea turned back from the tantalizing frozen slope to give Jemima a puzzled look. "My goodness Jemima, you look very queer all green." Althea reached up, removed her green-tinted spectacles, then awkwardly walked a few steps toward the agitated woman who ran madly across the rock strewn earth. "These crampons are not intended for use on ordinary ground, I suspect," Althea said to Lord Montmorcy while she waited for Jemima to cross the remaining distance.

"No, they will serve you better once on the snow," he replied, watching the approaching Jemima with curiosity.

"You do not intend to actually go out on the snow and ice," Jemima cried when she arrived at Althea's side, panting and out of breath. "Oh, please say no."

"That has been my intention from the moment I decided to come to Chamouny," Althea said, perplexed at Jemima's seemingly stupid question. "This *is* a guided excursion to see the snow and ice. Surely you heard me speak of it?"

"You must not go. I fear something dreadful will happen to you." Jemima placed her hands together before her, giving Althea a pleading look that would have melted her heart—ordinarily. Something about Jemima's to-do bothered Althea. Jemima had known quite fully of the plans and had insisted upon joining them for the trek. It seemed highly peculiar that she would try to bring the expedition to a halt at the foot of the glacier.

Cecily had by this time left her chair to join the pair. She looked at Jemima with an uncertain frown. "I thought you intended to attempt the ice as well? It seems a silly thing to insist on at this point."

"I had a dream . . . a nightmare, actually," Jemima said with an anxious gesture. "The notion that someone would be hurt, fall into a chasm, overpowered me."

"You might have said something about this before we left the village this morning," Althea said impatiently. Lord Montmorcy—whom she found it most difficult to call John, although he appeared to have not the least trouble referring to her as Althea—joined the trio of women. Since he was united to Althea by the rope, there was little chance she might go very far from his side.

"Jemima had a nightmare and believes one of us will be hurt or fall into a chasm," Althea explained, trying to sound logical and fair in her report.

"And she waited until now to tell us of her qualms?" He gave Jemima a quelling look that ought to have daunted her clear into next Tuesday. "I wondered what all the bother was back here. Seems a bit silly at this point."

"Precisely what I said," Althea said.

"I beg you not to go," Jemima wailed. "Tell her, Cecily," she begged as Cecily joined them. "Tell her she ought to stay here."

"Nonsense," Althea cut in on the frantic, although possibly well-intentioned plea. "I intend to begin my ascent at once. Lord Montmorcy has secured a rope at my waist. Should you wish to join us, I feel certain we can attach another rope to encircle your waist and Cecily as well. In fact, I suspect we should all be joined together by ropes. Think how much safer we would feel." She gave Jemima a pat on the arm, then turned to his lordship.

"I suppose you want me to produce some rope at this point?" he said, resignation clear in his voice. "As a matter of fact, it has already been planned and would have been done had you not hared off toward the glacier at such a pace."

Althea avoided meeting his gaze, for truth to tell the feel of his arms about her waist when he tied the rope around her, his very closeness to her, must have scrambled her brains to a degree. However, that was a feeling she'd not share with anyone, especially the man who caused it.

"Yes, well, I am eager to proceed," she admitted with a longing look at the entrancing snow and ice that had flowed down through the gorge for heaven knew how many years. "But I have no intention of giving up my climb, and I cannot leave these dear ladies here to fret. Best tie the rope on immediately, then. *Is* there a great danger?" she whispered. Althea searched his face for any sign of evasion. She had not traveled all this distance, endured hardships, only to be thwarted now.

"It will hamper *you*, I fancy," he muttered while hunting through the supply bags hanging on the mule.

"I say, look at this absolutely superb petrification I just found. Why, the place is littered with them!" Sidney suddenly shouted. Leaving his horse in the care of one of the chair men, he totally ignored the others and began prowling about the area, nose nearly to ground. He picked up another small piece of what looked to Althea like a chunk of rock and beamed a smile at them.

"Sidney, do you not wish to join us?" John called patiently.

"Ammonites, crinoids, crustacea, cephalopods! I cannot think of leaving here." And that was the last intelligible remark they had from Sidney. He began wandering across the exposed ground at the foot of the glacier, popping bits and pieces of stone into the knapsack he had toted with him this morning.

"He promised," Lord Montmorcy said with evident disgust.

"But Mr. Balmat will be with us," Althea said, puzzled, as she could not think why it would be necessary for Sidney to go with them. "Surely you do not think we will come to harm?" she concluded in a soft voice that the others could not possibly hear.

"Just stay near me," he murmured as Jemima drew closer, as though to hear what they discussed.

"I am thirsty," Jemima complained. "I feel as though I could drink a sea of water."

"I confess that I am thirsty as well," Cecily added with an apologetic look at Althea.

"It's a normal reaction," John quickly said, pulling a bottle of water from the supply bag. "I suppose it's due to the altitude, or so I have heard it explained. I will set one of the men to thawing snow for us. At this rate we will exhaust the supply we brought with us in no time." He untied himself from Althea and walked over to speak with one of the chair men.

"Althea, I think it disgraceful that you even think of tying yourself to that man," Jemima said in a low voice, confronting Althea with a hostile glare.

"Jemima, 'tis the way it is done. Please listen to those who know about climbing on the ice. Lord Montmorcy did not mean to frighten you last evening, but I do feel we ought to be sensible."

"Well, 'tis easy for you to say, a great girl like you," Jemima said with a hint of spite. "I believe he called you an Amazon? How apt."

Althea firmed her lips and turned away, determined not to allow Jemima to goad her into an equally bad-tempered reply. It would have been disgracefully simple to have remarked that Jemima would most likely stick at the top of a chasm were she to tumble into one, so she need not worry.

"If you plan to go with us, you ought to put on these green spectacles. I brought an extra pair with me, just in case I lost or broke them." Althea held out her spare pair to the antagonistic Jemima and waited. "Mr. Balmat said they are helpful."

"I'll not wear those dreadful-looking things," Jemima said with scorn.

"I think they are delightful," Cecily inserted, donning her green-tinted spectacles and turning to the comte, who had also put on his eye protection. "You all look so amusing," Cecily said with a charming laugh. "The whole world has turned a peculiar shade of green."

The comte chatted quietly with her while adjusting a length of rope around her waist.

Althea surveyed the pair with a glum feeling. No matter what she did, nothing seemed to go as she planned. She refused to allow the incidents that had occurred to deter her from the promised excitement of the glacier exploration. Why Jemima thought she would suffer injury . . . or would it be someone else? She'd not thought of that. Turning a considering gaze toward Lord Montmorcy, Althea studied him. It would be utterly dreadful were something to happen to him. When he returned to her side, she wiped from her face the concern she feared showed on it.

"I have enough rope for all. And the men will begin melting snow at once. They also feel the dry air. Now, permit me to tie you to me again."

Althea refrained from a tart remark, nor could she tease as Cecily would surely do if a gentleman made such an offer to her. Instead she stood tongue-tied, silent, when she longed to beg him to hold her and soothe her fears. She was acutely aware of his hands going about her, looping the rope and making a firm knot. At this proximity she could see the flecks in his green eyes, which were as green as though she gazed at him through her fancy spectacles.

How could she have tumbled into love with such an impossible man? Why did she not utterly detest him? He teased her, called her a hardy, brave girl, and worse—an Amazon. He had seen her looking frayed and dirty, wet and bedraggled, sweaty and frazzled. What hope did she have of him ever seeing her in a better view? No matter how she tried, she managed to find a way of turning a situation into disaster when he was around. It was a sheer wonder that she hadn't fallen into the lake when they went boating, and she'd almost done that.

So, *why* had the dratted man kissed her with such intensity? *Why* had he insisted upon serving as a guide of sorts, for of course they had a hired guide, Mr. Balmat. Experienced as he might be, Lord Montmorcy was scarcely a native. Yet he chose to join them at his own expense. It must be that he wished to be near Cecily.

"Althea?" the man in question said. "Come back from wherever you are. I believe we are ready to go." He touched her gently on the arm with a questioning look in his eyes that brought her to her senses.

"Right," she said with her former brisk air. She followed

Mr. Balmat, only looking back once to see if the others trailed behind.

While the walking was awkward on the ground, once on the snow her steps became easier. There was an odd exhilaration to clambering over the rough, grainy ice. Some of the surface ice was melting in the sunshine, rivulets of translucent water making their whitish green path to the ground below where they joined to form tiny streams. She paused to look ahead at the unusual sight of brilliant sun on the ice and the ragged path of the water, so clear, and undoubtedly very cold.

"Come, we shall go this way," John said, looking back to ascertain the others followed at a proper space. They were an odd-assorted group. He knew of one woman who had actually climbed Mont Blanc to the top, but few women dared to risk such an ascent, nor would he encourage it. A climb on the snow and ice was quite sufficient.

The comte wore a top hat with a wide brim, and Cecily de Lisle looked most fashionable in her gown of kersymere with her straw hat tied firmly beneath her chin. One hand held her oiled silk parasol aloft to protect her skin from the effects of the sun, the other hand held her pole. He only hoped that she wore woolen petticoats.

Althea had felt more bulky than usual, and he suspected she had donned woolen vests and extra wool petticoats as suggested by the guide. About her face she had tied a length of veiling that Balmat had given her and also carried a stout pole in one hand. She was an amusing sight, but he wouldn't dream of smiling, for he suspected she was a trifle incensed with him yet. She had been aloof this morning and held herself rigid when he tied the rope about her waist.

That he had deliberately lingered at the job, enjoying the feel of his arms around her, his hands at her waist, she seemed not to recognize. Could she still be so oblivious to him? He reflected wryly that any pretensions he might have had to being a gentleman who attracted women were far and away off.

Jemima Greenwood squinted at the snow, refusing a parasol to protect her, clinging to her stout walking stick with determination. Her rather ugly bonnet failed to protect her face as well as the excellent straw hats did. John feared she would be too exposed to the sun the way she went on. He noticed that Balmat had not offered her veiling, or had she rejected that as well? Was she merely foolish or simply as stubborn as their mule?

Looking back, he could see Sidney on his hands and knees, probing the ground for more of his blasted petrifications. So much for his promise to help watch the two women. Yet with the comte close to hand by the pretty Cecily de Lisle, perhaps all that was needed was to keep an eye on Jemima Greenwood. Now, that was a daunting task, he decided when he again checked to see how she progressed. If there was anything that she might do incorrectly, she managed to do it.

A gust of wind tugged at Althea's skirts, and she glanced up at the sky to see a few clouds approaching on the horizon. They did not appear as menacing as yesterday, so she dampened her worries on that score. She did not relish the notion of a soaking rain while traversing the snow and ice. Large the umbrella might be, it could not compensate for wind. Although there were oiled silk cloaks in one of the bags, one had to return to the mule in time to put a cloak on to prevent a wetting, which was apt to occur while bound for it—providing the stupid mule stood still. Althea had no great amount of confidence in the animal after its tumble into the ravine.

On the low side of the valley a shepherd could be heard playing his pipe. It was a sweet tune, and Althea envied the sheep that heard such melody every day. She paused to listen. It must be a lonely occupation, herding the sheep high in the mountains. She said as much to Lord Montmorcy when he turned to check on her progress.

"They are stout fellows and do not seem to mind it overmuch. I doubt they'd enjoy a throng of people. How do you like this snow? Is it what you expected?" He gestured to the expanse of white, far more varied in terrain and texture than she had anticipated.

"I thought it would be colder and more slippery. But it is fascinating, truly it is." She could not hide her enthusiasm from him, even if she had wished to appear sophisticated— which she really didn't think mattered in the least to the dratted man. Cecily could flutter her lashes and gurgle out some delicious phrase. If Althea tried that, his lordship would likely ask her if she had something in her eye and offer his handkerchief in that dampening manner he could use when put upon.

Jemima stopped, poking about with her pole.

"Did you find something of interest?" Althea called out.

"No," Jemima said glumly. "I thought I saw some plant life, but that cannot be. Nothing could live in snow."

"Actually," Lord Montmorcy said, "there is a red snow late in June, early July. 'Tis past time for it now, but it is peculiar. I have seen it and cannot imagine what might cause it. Some say it is a tiny animal, others say a plant, the seed of which was dropped by passing birds and somehow survived here."

"How odd," Althea said, looking about her more carefully to see if she might catch a glimpse of the red snow he described.

"Oh, see, what charming waterfalls!" Cecily exclaimed to the comte, waving her pole wildly about in the air.

Althea turned to see the collection of little falls and lost her balance. She flayed the air with her arms in an attempt to regain it and instead tumbled to the ice. She would have slid down the glacier but for the restraining hand of Lord Montmorcy. Her pole flew away and her spectacles went down her nose, restrained only by the veiling. She felt the complete frump as often the case when he was about.

"That is why it is good to be tied together," his lordship pointed out when he helped Althea to her feet. He picked up the long pole Balmat had provided and returned it to her, then lifted the veiling to push her spectacles up on her nose.

"Confidentially, I would much enjoy a slide on the snow and ice. It looks jolly fun," Althea said with a chuckle. If she could not be graceful and charming, she might as well develop a sense of humor.

He glanced behind them to take note of Jemima's rosy face and muttered, "Perhaps you might have the opportunity of another trek to the ice tomorrow."

"You do not think she will take ill, do you?" Althea said with concern for her relative, however distant, as she followed the direction of his gaze.

"I have seen a serious condition result from being in the

snow and sun in my travels through the mountains. The individual reacts badly; it can be serious. I wish she would use the parasol at the very least." He frowned at the stubborn Jemima, then turned back to check on Althea.

"You must not blame yourself for her neglect. You can scarcely command her, you know." Althea favored him with a friendly grin, then brushed her skirts down, sending bits of snow and ice flying. When she glanced at Jemima again, it was to see that impossible woman undoing the rope that held her to the others. Althea was appalled.

"Jemima, please . . ." Without stopping to think about herself, she quickly undid the rope that attached her to Lord Montmorcy and clumped over to Jemima's side. "Oh, do be sensible, Jemima," Althea urged.

"I just saw what happened to you," Jemima charged angrily. "You were tied to his lordship and still fell down. It was a humiliating sight, for a woman to fall at a man's feet like that. Disgraceful."

"Well, it is not as though I was worshiping at his feet," Althea said with a wry chuckle. "That is a dim likelihood."

"Well, I am ashamed to think we are related," Jemima stubbornly concluded. She dropped the rope, then set off across the expanse of snow at a far too rapid pace, given the conditions.

The sun had warmed the snow so that it was quite granular and almost slushy in places. Althea shook her head in disgust, then she started after Jemima—although a trifle more careful in her speed. The spikes in her crampons had less purchase here.

"Wait," she called to the rapidly distancing woman.

"Althea," John called out. "You forgot your rope." He followed her, rope in hand, carrying the pole that Jemima had tossed aside in his other hand. It was as well that Cecily de Lisle had chosen to be tied to the comte, for it would have proven difficult to hare after Althea, not to mention Jemima Greenwood and be tied to the others. John wondered what Jemima was about. He tried to hurry, dropped both poles and had to dash to prevent them from sliding across the ice and down the slope to the bottom.

When he looked up after rescuing the poles and regaining

his footing, it was to see Althea and Jemima near the far side of the glacier, close to the other side of the glacial valley. Jemima must have crossed at a near running pace. He set out after them, hoping he might prevent possible disaster. If ever there was a woman who seemed to attract danger, it was the Honorable Althea Ingram. Perhaps that was one of the things he found intriguing about her—her penchant for the dangerous, even if it was accidental.

"Wait, Jemima," Althea gasped, clutching her side.

"I fail to see why we need that rope. We have traversed nearly the entire valley with nary a misstep," Jemima pointed out. "And how interesting it all is, I must admit. Why, look at those needles of rock piercing the sky, and the pyramids of ice up there that look almost sea green in color, when you would expect them to be white. Of course, *you* can scarcely detect the color when looking through those hideous spectacles you persist in wearing. Foolishness, pure silly foolishness. I would wager," she added with an additional note of spite in her voice, "that you put them on merely to please his lordship. I have seen the way you look at him when you think no one is watching. And he is interested in Cecily, is he not? He fusses over her like a mother hen." Jemima gave the innocent Cecily a hostile look.

"Please," Althea said when she could speak again, "we must return to the others. It is foolishness to go off on your own when on an excursion such as this. Come," she said persuasively. "Please, Jemima."

"No, I wish to explore this side before I return. As you said, we might not see this again. I might as well obtain my money's worth." Jemima turned and resumed her exploration, poking at the snow with her pole, studying anything she chanced to note that appeared odd.

At this jibe Althea fell silent. It was true that Jemima paid her own way, and Althea had done all the planning. But in fairness, the dratted woman had insisted she join them, had insisted she take part in everything even if she apparently hated what they did. It was as though she did not trust them to go on without her presence.

Althea hurried after Jemima, unwilling to see her come to

any harm. Even if she might not care for her, Jemima must have a redeeming quality somewhere. It just needed finding.

"Be careful, Jemima. Lord Montmorcy warned me that there are areas where a fall of snow conceals a crevasse. You would not wish to plunge into one." Althea breathlessly dashed up to where Jemima had paused in her trek.

"It would be no more than I feared after that nightmare I had," said the gloomy Miss Greenwood while contemplating the whiteness before her.

"Please return," Althea said, noting that Lord Montmorcy now crossed the snow to join them. It made her feel much safer to know he was not far away.

"I shall go just a trifle farther. Look over there—what do you suppose that is?" Jemima pointed a gloved hand to the left, to a shadowed area.

"I do not know," Althea admitted. Neither did she particularly care. All she could think about was to rejoin the others. Jemima seemed intent upon spoiling the day for Althea, and it was making her beyond all things cross.

"You look for your *parfaite santé* to rescue you?'" Jemima sneered softly.

"I am not in need of rescuing," Althea pointed out.

Jemima said nothing more, just hurried off toward the patch of shadowed snow.

Above them the clouds gathered, and Althea wondered which would do her in first, the rain or Jemima. She hastened behind her stubborn and thankfully distant relative with the hope that she might be persuaded to behave in a sensible manner. Corkbrained would aptly describe her behavior at the moment.

Then the worst happened. As Lord Montmorcy had explained, snow often covered a gap in the earth. Jemima stepped into the shadowed area and plunged downward, stopping herself with her hands—and her girth, as Althea had so unkindly predicted.

"Oh, help!" Jemima cried. Her eyes wide with terror, and rightly so, she struggled to extricate herself from the widening split in the ice.

"I ought to wait for his lordship," Althea said. Then, at

Jemima's pleading look and more cries of terror, she edged over to the chasm. Forcing herself to crawl on her hands and knees until she could touch Jemima, she offered her pole. "Now push against the wall of ice with your feet and try to come toward me," Althea instructed.

Instead of taking the pole, Jemima grabbed Althea's hand and jerked her toward the chasm. She sped across the remaining ice with frightening speed, and before she knew what had happened, she stared down into the depths of a split in the ice that continued for only God knows how far.

There was an ominous creaking and what was almost like a groan from the ice. Althea thought her heart might just stop its beating. "That was foolish beyond permission," she muttered through gritted teeth.

"Oh, Althea, please help me out of here," Jemima cried more piteously than before.

Althea was greatly tempted to tell her that she could jolly well wiggle out of her predicament on her own. Althea worried about edging herself to safety. "Use the pole," she managed to say.

As bid, Jemima grabbed the pole, then pried herself from the chasm, popping forth somewhat like a cork from a jug. She crawled some distance, then rose to her feet. "Well, I expect all you have to do is roll away from there. I shall rejoin the others." And with that she took off across the glacier with no word of thanks and nary a backward look, passing a confused and very worried Lord Montmorcy on the way.

"Oh blast!" Althea cried. "That woman will be the death of me yet." By edging her body first one way then the other, Althea managed to grasp the pole. With that in hand she dug in her toes and used the pole to push away from the crumbling edge of the split in the ice, a split that grew wider by the moment.

"Woman, will you never learn?" Lord Montmorcy said.

She felt his firm clasp on her ankles, then he gently and steadily pulled until she reached a safe distance from the gap. She sat up, pushing her straw hat to the back of her head, ignoring it when it slipped down her back, the veil as well.

"Thank you very much. It would have taken me some time

to make it to this point." She glanced up at his dear face, then added, "But I could have made it."

"What happened?" He sat down beside her and offered her his flask.

She accepted the proffered drink, not caring what the contents might be. She again coughed when the brandy slid down her throat, but it brought welcome warmth. "Jemima fell into a split in the snow. It turned out to be far deeper than either of us guessed. She used my pole to pop herself out."

He glared at the now-distant Jemima. "And left you on your own. You might have fallen in, you know."

"But I did not," she pointed out with perfect truth.

"We had better go back at once. The clouds appear more threatening all the time."

"That would be all I need," she said with resignation.

Feeling as though it took her last reserve of strength to make it, they crossed to join the others near the edge of the glacier.

"My," Jemima said in a malevolent tone, "you certainly took your time."

"Miss Ingram is with us no thanks to you, Miss Greenwood. After a look at your face, I suggest we hurry back to the village as fast as possible."

Cecily took off her green spectacles and gasped. "Jemima! Your face! 'Tis all swollen, and very, very red. You look utterly dreadful."

For once Jemima said nothing in reply. She appeared somewhat dazed and silently stumbled to the chair she had ridden in from the village.

"How perfectly dreadful," Althea said to no one in particular while she removed the crampons from her half boots.

Lord Montmorcy ushered Althea to her mount, then assisted her. When she settled in her saddle, he looked up at her and said, "I told you that you might see the glacier tomorrow. We shall return on our own. I vow you will enjoy it far more."

Althea stared after his retreating figure feeling as dazed as Jemima had looked. What did he mean by that, pray tell?

Chapter Fourteen

With the clouds drooping over the mountains in an ever more threatening manner, Althea elected to accept an oiled silk cloak from Mr. Balmat. She tied it over her habit, relishing the added warmth for the ride back to the village behind Lord Montmorcy.

"I suggest we go ahead to make preparations for Miss Greenwood," John said urgently. "I expect she will feel far worse by the time she arrives there," he added when he also accepted an oiled silk cloak from Balmat. John swiftly mounted and began to race back with Althea following closely behind. Within minutes they had galloped far ahead of the chair men.

Althea worried about Jemima. She did not wish her ill even if she did not care much for her. In addition, she was a responsibility. By accepting her as a member of her Grand Tour, Althea also took on an obligation to see to her comfort and safety—although how anyone could make Jemima have a care for herself was beyond Althea.

Without the more leisurely paced chair men, Althea and John made excellent time. They thundered across the mountain trail in an exhilarating ride, scattering a flock of sheep as their horses flew over the ground. The thought crossed Althea's mind that a ride in the confines of Hyde Park would be dreadfully tame after the unrestrained freedom of the Swiss mountains. And she could never dream of riding astride in her divided skirt among Society! The mere thought of the reaction from all those starched London matrons brought a bemused smile to her face.

Midway a mist began to fall. How good they had thought to put on the oiled silk cloaks. With her veil and the ribands holding the straw hat firmly in place Althea was still reasonably dry when they raced into the tiny village.

In his excellent French John explained what had happened, and the innkeeper's wife knew enough of that language so she could understand the problem. Apparently, she had experienced something of this sort in the past, for she nodded her head, then set about fixing a posset for the unfortunate Jemima.

"It is going to be difficult to care for her should she be very ill," Althea fretted, pacing back and forth in the confines of what passed for a common room in the little inn. "The room holds but a cot and small dresser, with that little stove in the corner, and is not the sort you'd wish to spend much time in while ill or otherwise."

"We can only do so much." John walked over to sit down by the fitful fire, picking up a poker to prod a pine log into flame.

"I feel a responsibility for her," Althea explained, echoing the sentiment that had struck her while riding to the inn.

"I repeat, you cannot force her to do what she does not wish to do. Perhaps she is unhappy?"

"Jemima?" Althea stopped her pacing and stared at Lord Montmorcy. "I have never thought her to be what you would call a happy woman. Now, Cecily is a happy person; she fairly radiates liveliness and vitality." Althea watched his face closely while she spoke, wondering what went on in his mind. If he was attracted to the fair Cecily, he gave little clue to his feelings.

"Well, if Jemima can be nursed through this coming night and tomorrow, perhaps we can take her by carriage to Chamouny the following day." He rose and crossed the room to stare out of the window beneath the low-hanging eaves. Water dripped from the roof at a steady rate, and dark clouds enveloped the distant mountain tops. Pale misty clouds hung suspended in the valley, almost transparent and quite ethereal.

"And tomorrow? Did you mean what you said about returning to the glacier?" Althea took several steps in his direction, her hands clasped lightly before her.

"I did, but knowing how responsible you feel about Miss Greenwood, I shan't push you to leave here—unless Mrs. de Lisle insists you take a rest from your nursing duties. I warn you now, Jemima will most likely be quite ill."

His voice contained a grim note in it, and Althea wondered just *how* ill Jemima would be. She joined him at the window, contemplating a night of nursing a fractious Jemima. The knowledge of what lay ahead of her made her shudder.

"You look very graceful in that skirt," John said with a distinct change of subject, surprising Althea from her sober reflections. "I had not expected to approve such a garb, but it looks well on you. It does not seem so terribly improper—to look at you now."

"Thank you," she said with modest grace and a wry expression. "It is exceedingly comfortable. The thought has crossed my mind that I could not have this freedom while in Hyde Park." She sighed, gave him a bemused smile, then turned her gaze out of the window again.

"You enjoy a bit of freedom?"

"Of course," she replied, startled he should even ask such a question. "You must know how restricted life is for most unmarried girls. When I return to London, it will be the same again. Life and manners will not change while we are away. That is why I contemplate a cottage in the country. I believe I should like to become a lady gardener and plan beautiful gardens. I like flowers," she concluded.

"Well, tomorrow, should circumstances allow, we will ride back to the glacier and explore on our own. We never did find those strawberries, did we?" A smile crinkled up his eyes in a delightful way, catching Althea off guard. He was a wretchedly attractive man and doubtless knew the power and appeal he possessed.

"No, I fear that between my eagerness to inspect the glacier and then chasing after Jemima there was little time to spare for such a search." She tore her gaze away from his potent charm with difficulty, then glanced back when he spoke.

"We shall take a picnic and bring along a bit of cream for the berries," he said with that lazy grin and a gleam in those green eyes that sent a thrill of warning through her. She should be cautious, but she had not the least inclination for such prudence. She again looked out of the window, thinking she heard a noise.

"There they are," she exclaimed when the chairs came into view. She was thankful she had the diversion so she could avoid any comment on his proposal for the morrow.

She hurried from the inn with her umbrella in hand, assisted a complaining Jemima from her chair, then supported her into the inn, ignoring Cecily, the comte, and Sidney Poindexter, who all fussed about in the background.

Once inside she gently removed the ugly bonnet and surveyed the swollen face before her with dismay. It was clear that Jemima could scarcely see out of her eyes and that with her face so terribly reddened she suffered great pain.

"Distillation of willow bark, I think," Cecily said quietly when she joined Althea to inspect the poor Jemima.

"Bed, at once!" Althea said. Assisting Jemima up the narrow stairs was not a simple matter, for the girl was bulky and becoming more fretful by the minute.

"I can barely see," she complained. "I feel burning hot on my face. What is the matter, Althea? I insist you do something about it."

"Had you worn a properly wide hat, carried a parasol, and used that pair of green glasses, you'd not be feeling so ill, I'd wager," Althea snapped, goaded into the reply by Jemima's unfair demand.

"Here, Jemima," Cecily said when she scurried into the tiny bedroom a little later. "I have some soothing lotion for your skin."

"I do not want anything from you, madam," Jemima whined while Althea worked to remove Jemima's bulky garments.

Althea and Cecily exchanged worried looks, then helped Jemima from her ill-fitting clothing and into a voluminous nightrail. Once in bed, with a cool cloth on her forehead and the willowbark potion drunk, Jemima soon fell asleep.

"How perfectly dreadful of her," Althea whispered to Cecily

while conferring in the hall outside the bedroom as there was certainly no space inside.

"I noticed that you used the lotion anyway," Cecily said with a shrug.

"She is not rational, I fear. If you could take her nursing for a few hours, I will sit with her through the night. I believe— from what Lord Montmorcy said—that she will be more than fretful. This is a serious ailment. Her skin looks to be burned, most likely by the sun, for it is terribly red. And her inflamed eyes are probably the result of not wearing those green-tinted glasses. I am guessing, mind you, but it would seem logical."

"If she is burned, would you not wish ointment?" Cecily said while they walked along to her room where the little chest of medicine had been placed.

"If I were burned, I think I would like nothing more than to be bathed in ice water," Althea said with a wry face. "I have never heard of such a treatment and it might not be good for one, but how cooling."

"We have no doctor here. You must do as you think best," Cecily said. "I'll take care of her for now. You had better try to sleep."

Cecily checked the medicine chest before returning to sit by the thankless Jemima.

Before she took the needed nap, Althea sought out John in the inn's tiny common room. "Sir, what think you of ice for Jemima's face? I know 'tis not what we do at home, but there we do not have ice. She complains of her burning face."

"I do not know. I have never heard of such a treatment, but I confess I believe it would feel welcome." He rubbed his chin, studying Althea with a most disconcerting look. "I could procure some for you, if you have a mind to try it on her."

"Later, perhaps. Cecily is sitting with her now. I intend to try for a nap, then I shall take the night watch. It seems to me that people are always worse during the hours of the night."

"You seem young to have learned that," he said with a frown and a searching look.

"I may have been young when my mother went aloft, but I well recall that the night was her worst time. She had a cough and nothing seemed to help her. She did not live long after she became ill. Had she had sunshine and warmth, she might have survived, I think." Althea turned to leave the room, pausing at the door to add, "I will see you at dinner. We can but try the ice to see if it will help her. When I see someone in great pain, I think it most frustrating. I want to ease it, and there seems so little one can do."

"Jemima Greenwood is not overly fond of you," he stated with a curious expression on his face.

"What has that to do with it?" Althea said with a shake of her head. "When there is someone in pain, little else matters." With that, she turned and marched up the stairs to her room and some sleep.

John watched her leave, then considered what she had said. Did all women feel compelled to nurse those in pain? He doubted it. Cecily de Lisle most likely did. She was a very pretty armful, but he had no doubt that were he to look more than twice in her direction he'd be answering to the comte. He wondered if Althea knew how deep that attachment continued to grow.

Althea Ingram was another matter entirely. While his first reaction to her had been most puzzling, urging him to flee London as though hounded by a plague, he now felt a strange desire to possess her for himself. She had an admirable spirit, a lovely figure, a most charming manner, and she pleased him. The latter sentiment was the strongest of all. She pleased him . . . in many ways. In fact, there had been moments today when he wondered if his attraction for her had turned to something deeper. He'd never fancied himself in love, could not define it, but he suspected he might be infected with the emotion.

He found her invading his thoughts at all hours of the day and night. In fact, she gave him little peace. Did she and Cecily confide in one another? And if they did, what could Althea have said regarding her feelings for him?

The front door of the inn slammed shut. The comte and Sidney came in from the shed where they had looked after the animals. They shook off the drops of water from their coats, stamped their feet, then joined John by the fire, now blazing nicely thanks to his efforts.

"How is the not-so-very-pleasant Miss Greenwood," the comte inquired politely.

"Not well, I fear. Mrs. de Lisle is taking a turn with her now. Althea will spend the night at her side." He said nothing about arranging for ice to be brought, thinking the men might not approve. He wanted Althea to have a chance to try out her idea without interference.

"She is a hard one to understand," Sidney said. "I doubt Miss Ingram will receive a word of thanks from the woman for all her concern and care."

Silence met that truism, for none could refute it, based on their slim knowledge of Jemima Greenwood's character. The men turned their conversation to the day's events, skirting around the scene when Jemima had stalked off to leave Althea on her own by the crevasse.

Dinner proved to be a subdued meal, such as it was. A humble but tasty stew with dark bread, followed by a dish of pudding was the fare for the evening. No one seemed to care. Althea ate her food hastily, then announced she would be off to tend Jemima.

John left the table at the same time, exchanging a significant look with Althea, to let her know he had not forgotten about the ice. Shortly after she had switched places with Cecily and settled by the bedside, a gentle tap on the door brought John with a bowl full of ice.

"Since the room is not very warm, it should not melt rapidly," she whispered after thanking him for his efforts.

"I hope it helps keep her quiet. Goodness knows she deserves to suffer a bit after all she has done to you."

"I doubt anyone really deserves to suffer," Althea said compassionately.

Giving her an odd look, he left and Althea turned to applying the ice she wrapped up in a linen towel to Jemima's swollen face. It was slow, tedious work, and Jemima became fretful, complaining first about the cold, then the burning. It took every bit of Althea's considerable patience to deal with her.

Never had a night seemed so long. But by morning Jemima slept in peace, her face looking far better and less swollen. The marsh mallow cream Cecily had brought soothed Jemima's skin; the ice had worked marvelously well to lessen the sensation of burning.

When Cecily peeked in the room after an early breakfast of coffee and bread, she found Althea nodding on her chair.

"Off to bed with you," she whispered with a guarded look at Jemima. "You need sleep more than she does at this point."

With no argument Althea stumbled to her room where she fell onto her cot, not even bothering to change her garments. In seconds she was asleep, dreaming of strawberries and cream on a mountainside.

Some hours later a noise in the hall woke her from her sound sleep and she sat up, then peeked from her small window. The sun beamed down on the mountains, providing a breathtaking sight. Gone were the clouds, and sheep dotted the grassy slopes between the patches of deep forest.

Unable to return to her bed and possible sleep, she hastily dressed in her divided skirt, the white linen shirt, and her jacket. She looked in on Jemima, exchanging a sympathetic glance with Cecily when the girl complained about a draft. It was not difficult to leave that room for a bite to eat.

At the bottom of the stairs she ran into John. "Good morning, I think," she said, still feeling a trifle sleepy, but much improved. He looked different today, dressed in a neat bottle green coat over dark gray breeches. His tan waistcoat looked quite natty with its gold buttons.

"Have a cup of tea and your bread before we leave," he suggested in his autocratic way.

"You plan to take me off for the afternoon? I had thought we would need more time." She must have looked confused at his abrupt, quiet speech, for he gave her an impatient glance.

"We ride without the chair men to hamper us. Sidney has gone off petrifaction hunting again, and the comte is content to assist Mrs. de Lisle should she need help. We will be just ourselves."

Althea decided that if she had any brains—which she very much doubted she did at this point—she would thank him for the invitation and retreat. "Very well," she said with a conspiratorial twinkle entering her eyes, "I will do precisely that. I should not be above thirty minutes."

"Make it twenty and I will await you in front of the inn," he ordered, then turned on his heel and left the building, headed for the stables.

"Twenty minutes, indeed," she muttered to herself as she sought out the beleaguered wife of the innkeeper who was clearly not accustomed to housing so many English under her roof for so long, especially one who was ill.

Althea didn't mean to hurry, but in twenty minutes she found herself in front of the inn. His fine lordship assisted her into her saddle, then before she could demand an explanation for his high-handed tactics, he was mounted and led off in the direction they had gone yesterday.

The gallop was a joyous romp. Fresh air made her feel alive again after hours spent cooped in with Jemima and her fretful whining. Poor woman likely could not help herself, but it had not been an easy time.

They slowed after a time, not wanting to overtire the horses. John dropped back to ride at Althea's side.

"Feeling better now you rid yourself of the cobwebs? I always find that sleeping during the day makes me crabby and my head all stuffy."

Althea could not help but laugh at the image of his elegant lordship all crabby and out of sorts with a stuffy head. When he looked affronted, she said, "I do not mean to laugh at you, but I cannot imagine you as crabby. I suspect you would be more apt to have a glass of wine to clear your head and march out of the door."

"Your father does that, I suppose. I cannot imagine where else you come by your wisdom regarding men."

Taken aback by his sharp words, Althea decided that he possessed more than a touch of male pride within him.

They rode on in silence for a few moments before they turned to each other and began to both speak at once.

"I have no brothers, but I do have eyes," Althea began.

"Forgive my hasty tongue," he inserted. "This business with Miss Greenwood has quite annoyed me, for I see her take advantage of your generosity and kindness. Although I suppose I ought to be grateful to her for giving us our strawberry afternoon."

"Did you remember to bring cream?" she teased, foregoing an explanation regarding her limited knowledge of men, mainly derived from observing a good many cousins. Since she more or less agreed about Jemima's imposition, she ignored that topic as well.

"That I did," he said, apparently restored to good humor at the thought of berries and cream. "A bit of bread and cheese as well," he added with relish.

Their fast and furious ride brought them to the edge of the glacier much faster than the slow pace of the day before. Althea slid from her mount and hunted about for a place to tether the animal.

"Allow me. 'Tis the least I can do for being a crab," John said with that gleam in his eyes again.

Althea watched while he walked the horses to a fir tree some distance away, rubbed them down with a cloth that had been tucked behind his saddle, then looped the reins over a branch so they might have access to the abundant grass and a stream that meandered close by.

"Strawberries?" she inquired with an impish gleam of her own. The thought of ripe, wild berries made her mouth simply water with anticipated pleasure.

He said nothing, but took her hand lightly in his, and they strolled along a short distance from the edge of the glacier. She joined him in the hunt, searching everywhere for the telltale leaves and bright red of the fruit. At last they found their quarry. Tiny berries peeped from beneath equally small leaves. They set to work, picking the fruit and dropping it into a wooden bowl John had brought forth from his knapsack.

"It will take a great number if you insist on tasting them first," he complained.

"They are difficult to resist," she said with a gleaming look at him, running her tongue over a berry sweet mouth. At the arrested look in his eyes she paused in her efforts, wondering again what it was he thought when he studied her so. Deciding it was best to ignore anything that might prove to be dangerous

ground, she returned to picking berries until they had a respectable amount.

"First we shall enjoy our fresh bread and cheese, then our
treat."

She agreed, but not without a longing glance at the bowl of
red fruit. The cheese was sharp and tangy, blending well with
the rich dark bread.

"A little wine, perhaps?" he said, whisking a small bottle of
white wine from the knapsack that appeared to have no end of
delights within.

They shared the bottle, enjoyed the bread and cheese, and
then after restoring the green tinted spectacles to their noses,
leaned back against a fir tree at the edge of the meadow with a
sigh. The sun warmed them even as a cool breeze wafted
across the snow and ice.

Althea thought she might easily fall asleep were it not for a
persistent fly and the knowledge that the most disturbing man
in the world sat next to her.

He brought forth another wooden bowl and divided the
berries, then pulled a small glass bottle full of thick cream
from the depths of his knapsack along with two spoons.

"You have thought of everything," she cried with delight.

"I'm afraid so," he murmured with a provoking note in his
voice.

Deciding that it might be more prudent not to pursue whatever he had in mind at the moment, Althea daintily nibbled her
berries and cream, relishing every morsel of the delicious treat.
She sighed with regret when the last berry disappeared. "That
was a feast," she pronounced with a happy smile.

He opened his mouth to say something, then snapped it
shut, apparently thinking better of it.

Althea picked at the reedy grass at her feet, suddenly terribly aware that they were very much alone, miles from others.
She looked about her at the mountains, sharply defined today
in the clear air. Crisp and clear, fresh and bright, it was definitely a day to remember always.

In the following moments of silence Althea could feel an
odd sort of tension building between them. It was almost solid
and real, a tangible thing. What would happen were she to

touch it, grasp it, whatever *it* might be? Part of her wanted to reach out, turn to him. Oh, she was so very drawn to him. Did he know it? Could he detect her foolish desire to fling herself into his arms and plead with him to love her?

That dangerous thought brought the need for sensible action. Althea softly giggled to herself, then simply rolled down the bumpy hill toward the bottom of the sunlit meadow into the grass dotted with tiny wildflowers. She propped herself on her elbows and laughed at his expression of affront. "It was wonderful!" she cried. "You should try it, for it's jolly fun." Never had she felt so alive, so free.

Before she knew it, he had rolled down the slope to join her, stopping just short of where she had settled. He looked down at her and smiled, the green of his eyes as intense as the meadow beneath them.

"Enough," he whispered. Her spectacles were slowly removed.

She was utterly bereft of words; not one came to her rescue. Instead, she listened to her heart and allowed the dratted man to sweetly kiss her. He tasted of wine and strawberries and warm sun and cool alpine winds.

His touch was as gentle as a flower petal and as pleasing as the scent of the sun-warmed crushed grasses under them. She felt tenderly cherished.

When he drew away from her, she wanted to pull him back, for surely there could be nothing more delicious, more fitting on earth than the two of them together.

"I suspect this is more than a little dangerous," he admitted in a strangely husky voice. He reached out one hand to thread his fingers into her curls, now free of the bonnet and veiling that had protected her on their wild ride through the mountains.

"Touching my hair?" she said, pretending she did not know of what he spoke. He had felt it too, this sensual, overwhelming desire.

"No, not simply touching your glorious hair. Come," he said with a reluctant sigh, "I had best be noble and behave like a gentleman. I'll admit I scarcely feel like it at the moment." He quickly bent down, placed a light but exquisitely precious kiss on her lips, then sat up, pulling her with him. He replaced the spectacles with a gentle touch.

"I feel rather warm," she naively confessed. "Let us slide on the snow as you promised."

He shook his head at her, then gallantly escorted her to the glacier where they climbed up through the granular snow until they had gone a fair distance. He had taken the poles with them and now handed one to her.

"Here, use this to propel you. I shall go first to show you how. Follow me," he instructed.

She would, she knew. She had the absurd notion to tell that blasted man that she would follow him to the ends of the earth if he wished. Only she could not do it.

Instead, she watched him slip and slide down the slope, using his pole to assist when he reached a slow patch of snow and steer around boulders and rocks in his path. It looked wondrously fun and within minutes she followed him—down the slope, nothing more.

A cloud came up and cast a shadow over the meadow. She looked up at it with a frown, adjusting her spectacles on her nose.

"Time to leave," he said when he joined her. He tied her straw hat under her chin, then wrapped the veiling over her face with what appeared to be regret. "Come."

And she followed.

Chapter Fifteen

They tramped across the icy snow toward the meadow, laughing and slipping all the way. Althea shrieked when she almost fell to the ice, narrowly preventing a tumble with the aid of her pole and a helping hand from her companion. Her green-tinted spectacles slid down her nose, threatening to fall off completely. John reached over to push them up into place, and Althea shot him a disconcerted look. He seemed to expect her to be self-sufficient, then would turn around and at times look after her like a child.

He clambered down the lower edge of the glacier, offering her a hand now and again until they neared the meadow. John gallantly assisted her, although she suspected that as tall and sturdy as he had proclaimed her to be, he simply performed the deed as an ingrained courtesy. Anyone less likely to be in need of help than the hardy, capable female he thought her, she couldn't imagine.

She paused at the edge of the glacier, gazing down at his tanned face, memorizing the crinkle lines around his wonderfully green eyes where he laughed and it showed, and the tilt of his mouth, the touch of which had thrilled her. He gave her a quizzical look while extending his hand to her. Then she jumped to the ground and the spell shattered.

Rills and streamlets rambled here and there, and they skirted them with care. The grasses were for the most part damp as far as the higher ground. In the distance clouds continued to gather, looming like gothic castles in the air.

Althea glanced down at her divided skirt; bits of snow and

ice clung to the black wool. She brushed herself off and found the back of her skirt to be exceedingly damp. She wondered if that was from the snow, or was it the interlude on the grassy meadow? No matter, that was part of the past. She had experienced the delight of a lifetime these recent days, something to appreciate for a long time to come.

He studied the sky and the position of the sun, then began stowing away the poles and other things they had used. "Even if the weather does not look like rain, it is time to head for the village. There are a few clouds gathering on the horizon. With any luck at all Miss Greenwood will have improved sufficiently to make a return to Chamouny soon."

"Of course," Althea agreed, growing subdued at his remark. Did not people say that all good things must come to an end? Why should she think that he had nothing better to do than to gambol about in an alpine meadow with a tall, passably pretty, not to mention—what was it he had called her? Oh, yes, sturdy, hardy, determined, and healthy. By all means she had best remember that. Why could he not have murmured a word or phrase to console her, something about her that included delicate, or exquisite, or delectable? The clouds on her horizon were of a different sort, she suspected.

She set her hat firmly in place, then wound the sheer veiling about her head to keep the hat from flying away. It was but a few steps to where he had tethered the horses.

Accepting that she was destined to ever remain in his eyes the resolute Miss Ingram, that Amazon of women, she mounted her horse, watching while he tucked the remnants of their picnic into his knapsack.

Strawberries and cream followed by delicate wine while breathing in the crisp pure alpine air, surrounded by nothing more than birds, pines, and cascading creeks was a memory to cherish. She decided she would record in her journal for the days to come the mental treasures she had enjoyed this trip.

That all these treasures involved John, Lord Montmorcy, must be endured. He would of necessity be a part of all those memories. And *that* was a reality she must face.

They cantered along what passed for a trail in seeming amiability until they reached the tiny village. Here they were met by Sidney Poindexter, who wore a grin almost as large as the one Hercules habitually sported.

"Found some jolly good petrifactions," he reported in greatest good humor. "I daresay I shall have something to show those scientific fellows when we return to London." He glanced at the pair who dismounted. "Have a nice ride?" he inquired without sounding terribly curious.

They chatted about the ride and finding the strawberries, which Sidney viewed with mixed enthusiasm. It was clear that while he enjoyed strawberries and cream, he felt his precious petrifaction discoveries of far greater importance.

When they entered the little inn, they found Cecily coming down the stairs.

"Thank goodness you are back," she said with a grimace. "If I must spend another hour with Jemima, I swear I shall do violence!"

"How dreadful! Was there no pleasing her?" Althea murmured while she stripped off her gloves, then unwound the veil and removed her hat.

"Perhaps you will have better luck." Cecily drew Althea along with her to the kitchen of the inn where a broth had been brewed especially for the invalid.

It was over, Althea suddenly knew. Her special time had passed. Now she must return to the petty worries of day-to-day living, which did not include John. She tilted up her chin and accepted the tray with the broth and a bit of bread from the kitchenmaid, who was clearly in awe of the Englishwoman who towered over her.

When Althea returned to the stairway, there was no one in sight. Once upstairs she entered Jemima's room, prepared for the worst.

"I do not see why you had to go haring off across the countryside on a pleasure jaunt," Jemima complained. "I might have died for all you cared."

Wanting to be considerate of the ailing woman, yet quite fed up with Jemima's eternally churlish behavior, Althea set the tray down with care, then said, "Rubbish. Cecily took excellent care of you. After nursing you through the night, I felt the need of a bit of fresh air."

"I scarcely think you ought to have gone off by yourself," Jemima said sullenly.

"I did not go by myself. Lord Montmorcy saw to my safety. Mr. Poindexter collected his petrifactions and preferred them to the berries and cream we feasted on." That the three of them had not gone together was not mentioned. Althea had no desire to hand Jemima a means with which to make trouble.

"Oh." Jemima digested this news along with the broth then said, "You might have brought me some berries. I am quite fond of them."

"I am sorry, indeed, Jemima," Althea said with genuine contrition. "It went quite out of my head, although to be honest I had no bowl in which to put any if I had remembered."

The young woman on the cot studied Althea with a narrowed gaze, but made no further comment.

Of course it was hard to tell if that was indeed a narrowed gaze or simply her eyes still puffed and swollen, Althea decided. Since Jemima was exceedingly plump to begin with, it complicated the matter of assessing her condition.

By that evening it was clear that Jemima could tolerate the trip to Chamouny. Plans were drawn up to leave at first light.

Althea had little patience for the complaints that followed when Jemima was given the news.

"But we fear for you, Jemima," Althea said. "We all decided it is of utmost urgency to have a competent doctor examine and treat you. Skin burning like yours is not to be taken lightly, nor is the damage to your eyes. Who knows what may have happened? I was most careful yesterday and again today, to wear my tinted spectacles. I wish you had been less willful. You'd not be in this pickle if you heeded the advice given you by those who patently know more on the subject."

"I'll have no lectures," Jemima whined, then turned over, apparently to sleep.

Since Jemima was much improved, it was decided it was not necessary for anyone to sit up with her that night. A bell such as the ones tied to the sheep was left on the tiny chair by her bed so that if a problem came up in the night she could call Althea from the room next door.

A still-sleepy group assembled before the inn the following

morning. Jemima climbed into the chair with difficulty, exhorting the men to treat her with great care.

Since Althea doubted the chair men could understand a word of Jemima's terrible French, she pleasantly added her own injunctions, promising that the men would receive extra pay for a cautious journey.

It proved scarcely the joyous romp of the day before when Althea and John had raced over the mountain trail. Rather, they plodded along at a sedate trot, inquiring frequently as to Jemima's condition and Cecily's comfort. The comte in particular took the latter task as his own.

After observing one of these solicitous inquiries, Althea impulsively turned to John and said, "It does not bother you that he is so attentive to Cecily?"

"It did at first," John admitted, "but no more."

Althea felt his green gaze study her with disconcerting intensity and wished she had kept her mouth shut. So, Lord Montmorcy confessed that the comte's attentions bothered him at first. Well, it seemed that her plan had worked after all. For in order for one to be bothered, one had to care. For example, it bothered Althea greatly that Lord Montmorcy was bothered by the comte, which silliness made her smile.

They paused at the same place as on the way up the mountain when it came time for a rest and a spot of food.

"Gracious, I hope that mule does not take it in its head to plunge over the side again," Cecily exclaimed, darting a worried look at the placid animal.

"It did not precisely go without a bit of help, Mrs. de Lisle," John said quietly.

Overhearing this comment, Althea edged closer and, under the guise of offering him a plate of bread and cheese, she said, "Explain that if you please."

"Someone tucked a burr under his load. It had to be done here, but as burrs are not to be found locally, it had to be planned, and the burr brought along. Stupid thing to do, actually. Whoever tried the thing had no idea what might happen. He . . . or she could well have been hurt."

With that Cecily shrugged, then wandered back to answer a question from the comte and Sidney Poindexter.

Althea watched them a moment, then turned back to his lordship and what troubled her the most.

"There was no notion that I might be the one involved in the rescue, was there?" she asked in an undertone that Jemima or the others could not overhear.

"Unless the person knew you well enough to suspect you would take it upon your capable self to salvage the animal and its load."

So she was capable now. Oddly enough that did not rankle, largely because of the admiring tone in his voice and the glint in those green eyes when he spoke.

Althea said nothing of this to Jemima or Cecily, not wishing to cause any additional discussion or problems. It seemed that with Jemima along there were sufficient burdens without adding any.

Chamouny was a welcome sight. As before, Althea and John dashed on ahead to warn the inn that there was an invalid arriving who would need extra consideration.

Jemima appeared highly gratified at her reception. The innkeeper's wife and the chambermaid joined the host in ushering her into the spotless inn and up the stairs to a room. She was assured a doctor had been summoned at once and was fussed over and coddled to her heart's content.

"Another day of this and perhaps she may be ready to return to Geneva," John said to the others when they assembled in the common room of the inn.

"All because of her foolish stubbornness," the comte said with a fond look at Cecily.

"Althea enjoyed an extra day on the snow. It must have been nice to slip and slide without having to worry that Jemima would try to push her into a crevasse," John said. "I believe that once that young woman is better she must answer to a few charges."

"You mean you believe it is Jemima who has been responsible for all the things that have happened to Althea?" Sidney asked wryly.

"Impossible," Althea declared. "I believe I mentioned before that there is no reason for her to wish me ill."

"And I recall saying that she has a number of reasons," John countered.

"Miss Ingram is beautiful in a queenly way," the comte said thoughtfully. "Perhaps Miss Greenwood resents that beauty."

Althea held her breath, wondering what John would say to *that* remark. While she was under no illusions about her looks, it would be nice to hear a polite lie or a blatant compliment.

"Althea's unique appearance could well be a source of discontent to Miss Greenwood," was the fulsome reply from John.

So now he bestowed the blessing of a unique appearance on her? Althea wished she might pick up a vase or something equally breakable to crack over his miserable head. Never in her life had she been so given to such violent thoughts as while on this trip. It was all because of his eminent lordship, this exceedingly tall, wickedly handsome, and dashing gentleman who had the romantic soul of a slug. She quite ignored the episode of strawberries and cream in the alpine meadow and the waltz by the lake in the soft moonlight.

Since Jemima could not join them for dinner to spoil their pleasure, the five of them had a jolly evening. Once again Sidney Poindexter had them laughing with his dry wit and amusing tales through dinner and following until it was time to go up to their rooms.

John drew Althea to one side while the others straggled up the stairs to their rooms. "You will be exceedingly careful in all you do, will you not?" he urged. "If it is Miss Greenwood who has been behind all these peculiar happenings—as I strongly suspect it is—she may be inept, but she could also succeed in her attempts one of these times. We do not want such a thing to take place."

"I shall be as usual," Althea said with a calm she could not feel. At his frown she added, "I decided some time ago that it was useless to be overly considerate of Jemima's sensitivities in regard to anything she does to or for me. In other words, I shall be extremely wary. No gifts," she concluded. "Not that I expect any."

"She may claim to be grateful—and she rightly ought to be, offering you some little thing in recompense," he cautioned.

"Beware a Greek bearing gifts, Lord Montmorcy?" she said dryly.

"I thought we agreed on John. My title is a bit of a mouthful," he admonished.

"But exceedingly correct," she said with a smile, edging toward the stairway and sanity. They were alone save for the lingering attention of a maidservant in the back of the hall. Dim light and soft shadows—along with the unknown threat—made her uneasy.

"When we return to Geneva, there are a number of things that require our attention," he said, slowly drawing her along with him and up the stairs.

She cast a look behind them, then at him, wondering if he could sense any of her inner emotions, her longings. Had all they shared been nothing but mist, like the clouds in the valleys—transparent vapor that faded to nothing?

At the top of the stairs he bid her good night, marching along to his room with no apparent difficulty in their separation.

She hurried to her room, closing the door, then leaning against it with a sigh. Perhaps it would take time, but she would learn to live with her feeling for John Maitland, now Lord Montmorcy. After all, she'd been attracted to him for a long time. She could jolly well remain in that state, but from afar, of course. Unless—and she stepped away from the door, hands clasped before her—she did something utterly outrageous, completely daring, and totally unladylike. A purposeful gleam lit her eyes. It would take a bit of consideration, but she would not be like so many other women she had met who docilely accepted fate.

Then she recalled Cecily, her dearest cousin and best of friends. Althea had pushed John and Cecily together at every turn. Now John declared it no longer bothered him that the comte showered attention on the lovely blonde. Which had to mean, of course, that John was confident his interest was returned.

"Blast and double drat," Althea fumed, picking up a pillow and firing it across the room to land in a soft thud against the door.

She almost failed to hear the gentle scratching at her door. Retrieving the pillow, then opening the door a crack, she admitted an obviously concerned Cecily. It would take all her acting skill to cope with an enraptured Cecily, were that the case.

"Oh, Althea, I feel dreadful," Cecily whispered.

"Oh, my dear, tell me," Althea demanded softly. Alarmed, she drew her cousin to a small chair, urging her to sit, then perched on the edge of the bed, waiting for what was to follow.

Cecily was unable to sit still and popped up to pace back and forth in the little room. "You will hate me. I know it," she almost sobbed in her distress.

A growing sensation of dismay filled Althea at these words. "What is it?" she repeated, willing the words to be said so she might numb her heart.

"I have fallen in love—something I thought never to know again," Cecily said, her fact lit up with a joy that was lovely to behold.

"I see," Althea said quietly.

"He wishes me to marry him, and I have agreed," Cecily exclaimed, bringing her hands up to her face to peep coyly over them at Althea. "But it is dreadful, for it means I must leave you for him. You have been so kind to me, and I repay you thus." She paused to study Althea's face, then continued, "I have asked him, and he graciously agreed that you may make your life with us if you so choose. I would not send you back to that unpleasant household with Beatrice and Jemima unless it was your desire."

"You want me to live with you?" Althea said, thinking that it would be the harshest of circumstances, far worse than enduring Jemima's barbs and Beatrice's complaints.

"It would please me very much. Who knows, perhaps we may find you a nice gentleman who is worthy of you and appreciates you for your wonderful self."

"Thank you, but no," Althea said, ignoring the gesture of distress Cecily made with her dainty hands. "I suspected something of the sort was brewing and have made my plans accordingly. I feel certain I will be able to find another companion—although no one could be as dear as you, Cecily. I wish you happy."

With those words Cecily burst into tears of joy, dabbing her cheeks with a scrap of sheer linen and looking utterly lovely in the process.

Once again alone, Althea plunked down on her bed, staring off into space for a few moments while she contemplated the prospect of another companion. She could not tolerate Jemima, especially if she was the one responsible for the stupid attempts to harm Althea. But there ought to be someone, she decided with rising optimism. Surely there would be a woman in straightened circumstances who needed help, much like Gabrielle. With that cheering thought, Althea made herself ready for bed and tried to sleep.

The doctor proclaimed Jemima would be ready to travel back to Geneva by the end of the week. This meant that they must amuse themselves for several days. Althea did not relish the notion of watching Cecily and John together.

The next morning she set out to find something to occupy her hands, if not her mind.

"Going shopping?" John said, turning from where he conversed with Sidney Poindexter, who stood with an impatient Hercules at his side outside the inn.

"I fear there is little to see here and even less to do. I hoped to unearth something of interest."

"You go alone?" he said with a frown.

"Cecily is keeping Jemima company for the moment. I shall take over later. If I find some needlework, it will be more agreeable." Althea nodded pleasantly, then began to edge away from the men.

"I can imagine," John said with a flash of his old grin. "We shall join you if we may. Sidney needs to walk that dog, and I could do with a bit of fresh air."

There appeared no way to avoid their company without being utterly rude. They made their way from the charming inn and along what passed for a walkway to the few shops.

Althea was delighted to find one of those excellent little shops that carried nearly everything one could want, just as in

English villages. Sidney excused himself, declaring Hercules in need of a run. The dog was growing at an incredible rate and soon would be nearly as large as his master, it seemed.

"Needlework is universal," John commented.

"Long evenings and a desire for occupied hands," Althea murmured while she examined a pretty design of local wild-flowers in Berlin work. She bought it and sufficient yarn, then left the shop with his lordship at her heels.

"Cecily told me her news last evening," Althea ventured to say, figuring it was well to bring the matter out into the open.

"And how do you feel about it?"

"I am quite happy for my dear cousin," Althea said in a voice she suspected sounded a trifle frozen. She excused herself and hurried back to the inn as though Hercules chased her, leaving John to his puzzled thoughts.

With the needlework to occupy her hours, Althea sent a de-lighted Cecily off to spend time with her betrothed. That was a sight that Althea could miss with no qualms. Jemima's acerbic tongue and incessant demands served as a diversion. However, by the end of the week Althea eagerly awaited the trip to Geneva.

Jemima, who had been prowling about her room, made her way to the coach, demanding that she ride facing forward. Having anticipated this turn, Althea sweetly informed her that it was quite all right, taking the wind from Jemima's nasty sails.

They wound their way along the sweeping valley of Chamouny, across the river, then along the edge of the deep green wooded slopes. Above them the snow-capped mountains looked down in brooding silence, for no avalanches had been heard while they were in the area. In the distance one of the several glaciers could be seen trailing a twisted path down the slope, appearing, disappearing.

Althea leaned back, finding the sight of the glacier to be bit-tersweet, for she thought of strawberries and cream, a romp at the glacier hand in hand with John, sunlit laughter and breath-less joy. And then there was the kiss to consider. She glanced uneasily at Cecily, deciding it might be better not to mention that, for it could only distress her, and obviously it had meant nothing to John . . . Lord Montmorcy. She had best remember to think of him in the more formal manner from now on. The casualness of the journey was past, as was a good deal else.

While the journey to Chamouny seemed to have taken ages, the trip to Geneva appeared to fly. Before she could believe it, they were entering the city and within a short time pulled up before the Hôtel d'Angleterre. It was like coming home, Althea decided, and said as much to Cecily as they marched up the steps.

"Well, our rooms are clean and comfortable, but then, the inns were pleasant as well. I believe they serve travelers very well here. Better than France," she added as Jemima approached once inside.

"I should like Gabrielle to attend me," she announced.

Tired of Jemima's continual demands that had become more and more strident, Althea gave her a cool look and shook her head. "I have given her to Cecily, who will certainly have need of a maid now that she plans her wedding," Althea concluded with as much composure as possible. "However, I will share Susan's services with you on occasion if it is possible."

"I will tell your father about you if you do not do as I say," Jemima hissed, drawing close to Althea in a menacing way.

"What is there to tell him that could not be revealed in any drawing room in London?" Althea said with a look of puzzlement shared with Cecily.

"You have behaved like a hoyden, riding astride, going off with men on picnics, in general acting most scandalously," Jemima declared.

Not wishing to offer entertainment to anyone who chanced to pass through the entryway, Althea said, "I suggest we discuss your charges upstairs in my room."

Jemima gave a virtuous nod, then barged ahead of the others like a very fat queen. When they had reached the security of Althea's room, Jemima rounded on the other women with a venomous look. "Your father will cut you off without a penny when he learns of your behavior. Then my dearest Beatrice will have everything you possess for her son, William, the heir. You deserve nothing and should have nothing," Jemima concluded.

"Is that why you tried so hard to do away with Miss Ingram?" came a familiar voice from the doorway. None had heard the door open, and the three were surprised to see the comte and Lord Montmorcy standing just inside, listening.

"What if I did? I came along with that express purpose in mind," Jemima snapped.

"You failed to do away with her at the waterfall, underestimating her strength. The tooth powder made her so ill she immediately ceased using it. It contained poison, enough to make Althea ill but not dead. You were not very clever when it came to the boat, for it achieved nothing—she didn't fall into the lake. That burr was a stupid notion, for it might have done *you* in. And as to the glacier, even there you failed to nudge her over the side of the crevasse. You are a rather bumbling villainess. You failed in every count. We shall refute anything you might say, and when we are finished with you, my girl, you will wish you had not conceived such a stupid notion."

"I cannot tolerate the thought of her company any longer," Althea said quietly.

"She will have to go," Lord Montmorcy said in a voice that sent chills down Althea's spine.

Chapter Sixteen

"You'll not touch me," Jemima cried, her voice rising to a shriek. She drew herself up as though to fend off an attack, looking very much like a pouty hen defending her nest.

Althea backed away from Jemima, fearing the mad gleam in her eyes. Cecily sidled up to Althea, clutching her arm with trembling fingers and staring silently at the impassioned Jemima, possessed of an insane scheme to help her cousin Beatrice.

"As soon as we arrived, I spoke with the manager," John said sternly, taking a step from the doorway. "There is a respectable family departing Geneva for England the end of this week. I immediately sought them out, and Mr. Ebblewhite has agreed to take you with their party. I told him that you have been severely ill and cannot continue with the tour as originally planned."

"I shall not go with just anyone," Jemima said with her customary contrariness. She primmed her mouth into a thin line and looked as though she smelled something horrid.

"I said they are respectable, and you have no choice in the matter. It is arranged." He spoke as a man of power, the eminent John Maitland, Earl of Montmorcy.

Althea felt a sense of his lineage, one of the oldest families of England, certainly among the wealthier. Who was plain Jemima Greenwood to argue with him?

It appeared that Jemima experienced much the same feeling, for she seemed to shrink and her face crumpled into an expression of disappointment mingled with malice. "I hate you, Althea Ingram," she hissed at Althea while edging toward the door.

"I must confess that I am not exactly fond of you, Jemima," Althea replied in a somewhat unsteady voice.

"That is neither here nor there," John inserted. "You had best seek your bed and some rest, Miss Greenwood. You obviously are not yourself. If you were, you would be gracious enough to thank Miss Ingram for her generosity thus far, not to mention her forbearance. Few women would be as magnanimous to one who had attempted, however clumsily, to kill them."

Althea frowned thoughtfully, then said, "Wherever did you arrive at the conclusion that little William would inherit my fortune if I died? Nearly all of my money comes from my mother's family, with the greatest sum from my grandmother. Were I to die without issue, the money would go to some distant female relative. William would not receive so much as a penny, other than the modest amount father gives me—as is only proper."

Jemima turned seven different shades of green before crying, "You lie!" She advanced on Althea, shaking her fist in frustration. The effect was a trifle ludicrous as Althea towered about the plump Jemima like a goddess on a pedestal.

"I fear not," Althea said serenely. "What a pity you did not learn this before we left England. It would have saved a great deal of bother and expense."

"Oh, I really do hate you, Althea. I shan't forget this, you may be sure." Jemima stormed past the two men by the door and along the hall to her room.

"Oh dear," Cecily murmured, placing a comforting arm about Althea. "She really is not quite right in her head."

"I must say, it is a novel experience to be informed of such violent hatred," Althea said, firming a lip that had an unfortunate tendency to tremble. She clasped her hands before her lest she reveal the extent of her distress.

"Do not allow it to overset you," John said with a bracing smile. "You have held up extremely well to date; it would be a shame to spoil your record."

"Indeed." Althea turned from the three who stared at her, their sympathy almost too much to endure. "If you do not mind, I would like to be alone for a time. I have a great deal to plan and consider. I shall see you all at dinner?" She glanced back at Cecily, who had drawn close to John and the comte. The three women had separate rooms now, for which Althea was profoundly grateful.

It was agreed that they would meet before dinner in the entry and a time arranged before the three left the room.

Cecily paused by the door. "Althea, are you certain you wish to be alone? I should be happy to help in any way I may."

Bestowing a forgiving smile on her dearest cousin, Althea nodded. "I shall be fine."

Once alone, Althea crossed to the dainty desk placed so as to have a view of the lovely lake. She sank down on the chair before it, then fiddled with the fine quill pen for some time while sorting her thoughts aloud.

"First I must find a new companion. Perhaps I ought to consult the manager of the hotel? He certainly obliged Lord Montmorcy with a family traveling to England just when we needed one. Then I shall buy a fitting wedding present for Cecily and her new husband." Althea could not bring herself to verbally unite Cecily and John. It was simply too painful.

Pulling out a small sheet of paper, Althea began her list. How different she felt now while drawing up these plans than when she was in England, preparing to embark on her Grand Tour. But even with setbacks, she would not retreat.

She dipped her pen into the inkwell and continued jotting down her intentions. Perhaps she might give a farewell dinner at the end of the week? When Jemima left for England, Althea intended to set off for Vienna. Later on she would visit Venice and from there go to Rome.

She leaned back on her chair, staring out at the shimmering lake with bemused eyes. For all she had said of Lady Hester Stanhope, perhaps Althea would become the traveling Miss Ingram. And hadn't Maria Edgeworth visited Geneva some years ago? She appeared to jaunt hither and yon, meeting interesting people and conducting a huge correspondence, if what Althea had heard was correct. It sounded perfectly ideal, traveling, seeing beautiful places, and meeting fascinating people. With her money Althea had no doubt that she would be able to fit into almost any society, even if she was tall. Maybe she could even find a place where everyone was tall, and she would be merely another person. The thought amused her as she set about turning her plans into reality at once.

No one she knew was about when she went down to interview the manager. He was flattered that the elegant Miss Ingram—or so he phrased it—would seek his help, and he intended to do his utmost to find her just the right companion. As to the dinner for her friends, he would arrange every detail for her; all would be the very finest.

Suspecting her bill would be enormous, she thanked him, then left the hotel after summoning Susan to accompany her. It was but a few minutes walk to the same clock shop where she had found her pretty locket watch. She debated on a gift until the owner pointed out an exquisite clock with a dainty Cupid swinging back and forth in perfect time beneath his glass cover.

After arranging for payment, she ordered the clock be delivered to Cecily. But she could not quite bring herself to add Lord Montmorcy's name to the card. It was utterly foolish, this refusal to accept what was so evident. But how did one argue with the heart?

Upon her return to the hotel, she surprised Lord Montmorcy and Cecily in the entry. They were in deep conversation, and at first Althea thought she might slip past them undetected. However, his lordship caught sight of her and broke off their discussion.

"I thought you were going to take a needed rest," he scolded, taking a step in her direction.

"I had an errand, and now I shall dress for dinner." She gave softly voiced instructions to Susan, then waited to see what would happen next.

"Lord Montmorcy . . . that is, John"—Cecily blushed prettily—"was offering his advice, Althea. I wish to obtain a wedding dress, and he inquired for me as to where I might go for the best quality. Was that not kind of him?"

"Indeed. I am very happy for you both."

Cecily exchanged a puzzled glance with Lord Montmorcy, then said, "I shall go up with you now, for the dinner hour fast approaches."

Althea, her poise still wrapped carefully around her, nodded, then walked slowly up the stairs with Cecily at her side. She was terribly conscious of a green-eyed gaze watching them and hoped that he could not know that her knees were weak and her eyes beginning to water. But then, he would be intent upon Cecily, not that tall Amazon at her side.

"Althea," Cecily said, placing a gentle hand on Althea's arm, "something seems to be wrong. I can feel it in my bones. After dinner we must have a talk."

"Oh, pooh," Althea said with a dismissing wave of her hand, "with Jemima out of my hair I am as right as rain. Speaking of which, I see it is beginning to mist again." She turned to go into her room, then stopped, "By the way, the manager of the hotel said he will assist me in locating someone to travel with me. He did well for Jemima."

"I wish you would reconsider going with us." Cecily gave Althea a troubled look.

"On your honeymoon? No, silly girl. I am not one of those females who believe that a newly married couple needs company." She made an amused face, then opened her door.

"I suppose you are right. John," and Cecily blushed again, "remarked that you have been most understanding, and I do appreciate all you have done for me."

Althea gave her cousin a fond, if somewhat sad, smile and murmured something about rushing to dress for dinner, then entered her room, shutting her door with a click.

Wanting to appear her very best, Althea turned to Susan and said, "I wish to look special this evening. What do you suggest?"

The maid smiled broadly, then removed a lovely, simply cut satin gown from the wardrobe. It was in an odd shade of green, a misty color that recalled the clouds in the pines. Tiny pearls decorated the low-cut bodice in a delicate design with rich embroidery enhancing their luster. The sleeves, slashed with white satin, puffed out rather prettily. The maid gestured to slim slippers of the same green with white satin insets.

"There is a white satin reticule with green embroidery that Miss can use," Susan pointed out while draping the gown carefully across the bed.

"That will do nicely," Althea said with commendable restraint. She sighed with satisfaction, for she would look her best this evening. Oddly enough, she wanted very badly to appear absolutely stunning.

Once dressed and her gloves drawn up her arms, a string of pearls at her neck, and a white silken shawl draped loosely over her shoulders, she stared at her reflection in the cheval mirror. She would do.

She joined Cecily as soon as she heard a tap on the door. "How lovely you look," Althea exclaimed in all truth, for Cecily was a vision in pink and silver and looked years younger.

"You also look extremely well," Cecily said with a sedate nod while walking down the stairs to where the men in dignified garb awaited them.

"What visions of loveliness," the comte exclaimed, stepping forward to claim Cecily as his partner. She beamed a smile up at him while Althea frowned at the pair.

"I thought you approved your cousin's decision, Miss Ingram," Lord Montmorcy said from a point too close to Althea for her comfort.

"Of course I do. I should think you might object, however. Or are you one of those terribly modern men who take a broad-minded view of life?" Althea allowed him to place her hand upon his arm and walked stiffly at his side until they reached a small private dining room where Sidney Poindexter awaited them.

"Ah, we are to be spared the deadly presence of Miss Greenwood forever," he said with a dramatic sweep of his arm. "How delightful."

Althea was surprised to catch a frown cross Lord Montmorcy's face, although what difference it might make to him she did not know.

"A bit too deadly for Althea's comfort, I fear," his lordship said with an acerbic cut to his tone. "At least you can eat in peace this evening, my dear." He ushered her to the table, seating her with polished ease, then joined her—again a trifle too close for her comfort.

She opened her mouth to remind him that she was scarcely his dear when she caught sight of a charming ring gracing Cecily's now-ungloved hand. The ring had a sapphire as blue as her eyes, surrounded by a delicate gold tracery setting.

Cecily again beamed up a smile at the comte and patted his arm. "What a dear man you are. Is he not, Althea? See how he indulges me with such extravagance."

The comte, seated as close to Cecily as John was to Althea, took the dainty hand, raising it to his lips in a caressing kiss that brought a pink glow to Cecily's cheeks. She gazed into his eyes as though he was all that mattered on this earth, and perhaps he was.

Althea could not have spoken had her life depended on it— nor could she have moved one inch.

"They make an admirable couple, do they not?" John murmured in her ear.

"A toast!" Sidney declared. "May you know many happy years together and all your troubles be little ones." He chuckled at Cecily's gasp and the comte's wry gin.

Althea knew something was expected of her, but what could she say? She was stunned. She raised her glass of wine in a salute, but made no sound. Cecily and the comte? Turning to John, Althea impulsively put out her hand to lightly touch his arm. "I am sorry," she whispered. Then she faced Cecily and blinked a tear away. "I am very, very pleased for you both. You acquire a fine lady, sir," she added fiercely to the comte. "I trust you will appreciate all her lovely qualities."

Lord Montmorcy cleared his throat, then said, "I believe they are about to serve our dinner." To Althea he murmured, "What maggoty notion have you squirreled away in your brain, my girl?"

"I have not the slightest idea what you are talking about, my lord," Althea said primly. She turned to the servant who waited on the table to nod her acceptance of the soup, a delectable concoction of mushrooms and cream.

"Very well," he replied. "We will discuss this later, however. Do not think I will allow you to fob me off with some poor excuse."

"I will be very busy, sir. I must find that new companion, if you recall. I intend to leave for Vienna by the end of the week," Althea said with firm conviction.

This latter comment reached Cecily's ears, and she exclaimed, "You will not go before our wedding, surely!"

"Of course not. We are family, after all." Althea bestowed a delighted grin on her cousin. How wonderful that Cecily was marrying the perfect man for her, and not Lord Montmorcy. She ignored her past reservations about the comte in her happiness for her cousin.

"Althea is quite dutiful. You are fortunate to have such a devoted relative," his lordship pronounced.

Althea felt something explode within her. Dutiful, he called her now. She added this to the list of attributes she had compiled during his time with the group. Of course they were all admirable—if you were discussing some noble creature who spent her life devoted to the good of mankind.

Had there ever been a more infuriating man in all the world? It took every ounce of self-possession she claimed to sit quietly at his side, seeming to enjoy the dinner—which she assumed was excellent given Sidney Poindexter's praise of it—and not pour the wine over his head, or dump the *gratin savoyard* into his lap. She smiled grimly, wondering how he would cope with a lap full of potatoes and onions baked in cream. That brought to mind the episode on the shores of the lake when he insisted her lap was made for such delights as cradling his head, and she pressed her lips together to keep from bursting at the seams with indignation at the wretchedly handsome and incredibly aggravating male.

Somehow she managed to survive the dinner, escaping from Lord Montmorcy with the excuse that she must seek her pillow early, tired from the day.

"Most sensible, for you have the beginnings of circles beneath your eyes, my dear. I am concerned for your health," he added judiciously.

"Oh," Althea exclaimed, before whirling about and sailing from the room in utter fury. It was one thing to sympathize, it was quite another matter to tell her that she looked simply worn to a frazzle!

Sidney strolled up to join his friend. With his hair flying wildly about his face, Sidney looked more like a Pekinese than ever. He pushed up his spectacles, then said, "I say, John, will you never stop blotting your copybook with the queenly Althea? 'Tis a wonder she don't do violence to you. If ever I saw an angry woman, it was Althea Ingram when she left here a few moments ago." He shook his head at his friend.

"That's just it, Sid." John scratched his head in frustration. "I never have pretended to be one of those chaps that can charm the ladies. Too blunt by half and no charm to speak of. Thing is, I wish I knew what to do. I rather like Miss Ingram, you see."

"I suspect I see far more than you realize. You want to be dashing and find yourself in a bit of a pickle when all you manage to do is squash all hopes."

"You think it that bad?"

"Well . . . I doubt it is good," Sidney replied after some thought. "You have but a few days to mend your fences before Althea takes herself off to Vienna." He reflected some moments, then said, "Now that's a city I should like to visit. I understand the pastries there are out of this world. Chocolate as well. Fine food to be had. Sure you don't want to go to Vienna?" he added with a gleam in his eyes while he rubbed his hands together.

"How you can remain such a bean pole when you eat more than a horse is beyond me," John grumbled. He wandered toward the door, first offering a good night to the comte and Mrs. de Lisle. "I'll see you later, or perhaps in the morning. I have some work to do."

Sidney stood by the door, watching his friend march resolutely up the stairs like a soldier going off to battle and grinned.

Alone in her room, having sent Susan to bed, Althea stripped off her gloves while staring out at the lake and distant mountains. There would be more mountains, more cities even greater and more interesting than Geneva. None would claim her heart, however. She turned, picked up the little music box from the desk, and wound it up. The tinkling tune sounded loudly in the quiet of the room. Placing the little gilt box carefully on the desk once more, she returned to her contemplation of the dimly lit scene from her window. Shadows and soft moonlight, flickering lights from various windows. It enchanted her.

A noise in the hall caught her ear, and she turned her head to listen. Cecily, perhaps?

She watched in horrified fascination as the knob on her door slowly turned, then the door swung open.

"Woman, will you never learn?" a familiar and exasperated voice rang out. "The lock—where is your lock?"

"Hush!" she exclaimed. "Whatever are you doing in my room? 'Tis most improper—but then you seem to think you can do anything you please and no one will complain."

He shut the door with a faint snap and crossed the room in long strides to confront her by the window. Checking the desk at their sides, he found and lit a candle, then faced her again.

"You ought not be here," she reminded him, although she could not stir up the anger she supposed she ought to know at his high-handed ways.

"Why not?" he said, a lazy grin stealing over his face and lighting a gleam in his eyes that even the candlelight caught.

"Well," she sputtered at him, refusing to back away from him even if he intimidated her half to death, "it is highly inappropriate for a gentleman to enter the bedroom of an unmarried lady. And you know it." She jabbed a finger at his chest to emphasize her point.

"And you are a lady? What with riding astride, hiking your skirts to reveal your legs—nice ones, too, I might add—haring off across country to picnic alone with a man not your husband or betrothed—just to list a few of your sins. I think not, my dear."

"And I am *not* your dear," she snapped, feeling as though she stood on slippery ground that was fast disappearing from beneath her feet.

"Ah, but you have such a lovely lap. I should like to have that lap for my permanent use." He took a step closer to her, and she retreated a half step, almost tripping on the hem of her gown.

"Well, you cannot," Althea said, although not quite as angrily as before. "You had best leave." She wanted to stamp her foot, but slippered feet made such a small noise.

"But your door was unlocked," he reasoned. "It is a good thing I checked on it, or who knows what might have happened to you during your sleep. Do you have a good bed?"

"Lovely," Althea said with a wary look. Had he gone mad, taken leave of his senses? "Are you all right?" she asked in desperation.

"Never better," he said, taking the final step that brought him tantalizingly close to her, almost touching.

"Please go," she whispered. "I . . . you . . . we . . ."

"Now that is an interesting progression of thought." He tilted up her chin with a hand that seemed to appear out of the air and studied her face. "Yes," he said with clear satisfaction in his voice.

Before she could ask what that meant, she found he was kissing her again. Oh, how she wished for the strength of character to push him away, shoo him out of the door. Why, if Jemima learned of this, she could dine out for weeks on the tale when once again in London.

Then Althea was forced to admit that when it came to the art of kissing, Lord Montmorcy was most accomplished. She felt like the first snowdrop of spring opening up to radiant sunbeams.

"Let me see," he mused when at last he released her from the deliriously wonderful kiss that had her clutching the front of his coat for support, "we shall go to Venice and marry there—I should like to have my mother attend, she will lend us a certain amount of propriety, you know. Then after seeing them, we can travel on to Rome." He wrapped his arms about her in the most comforting embrace she had ever known, one that spoke of love and cherishing. "I believe you will like Rome, my love. It is wildly passionate like you. The Romans are certain to adore you. Doubtless I will have the Italian dandies cluttering our salon while they pay homage to the newest goddess in town."

"Marry? Did I hear you correctly?" she cried, backing away from that precious embrace. "First of all you never *asked* me to marry you. Secondly, I doubt it necessary to give up your single blessedness just to satisfy propriety. And thirdly, I cannot fathom why you would wish to establish the most remote connection with me. You have called me"—she raised her hand to tick off the list of hated appellations—"an Amazon, hardy, brave, resolute, sturdy," and she made a face at that one, "practical, dutiful, and sensible. And, oh yes, you damned me with the faintest of praise by saying I possessed a *unique* appearance! How dare you ask me to marry you, sirrah!"

She placed her hands on her hips and glared at the dratted man she loved with all her foolish heart.

"I suppose you would not accept that I might love you?" he said with a hopeful note in his voice.

"Not in the least," she declared. "You just want a convenient pillow for your head," she cried, recalling something else that had irked her.

"I see it is worse than I feared. Sidney was right."

"Out," she hissed at him. "Out, and I shall be certain to lock the door behind you—as I was about to do before you barged into my room without so much as a by your leave."

She was almost disappointed—although she insisted to herself that she was pleased—when he turned and quietly walked from her room. With the door securely locked, which she admitted she should have done earlier, she walked to her bed and plunked herself down on the edge of it.

"You are an out and out fool, Althea. You love that man, and he will undoubtedly run as fast as he can, thankful to have escaped your clutches." With that observation she hurled herself against her pillow and sobbed her heart out.

Much later she hiccuped, wiped her no doubt swollen eyes, blew her nose, and sighed. "All I wanted were a few words of love, nice things—like he thought me pretty, or a few kind words about my gown. Instead he calls me practical and resolute; what dreary words." Although—her conscience reminded her—he had told her that she had lovely legs, shocking as that might be. And he had said that she was a delight and graceful. She had cherished every conversation they had held and remembered much.

While she undressed and hung away the pretty gown that had given her such high hopes, she thought on those memories.

But, she decided as she slipped beneath her covers and pulled them up to her chin, he must understand that she liked to be petted and adored just as much as dainty Cecily. And with that sensible, resolute thought she fell asleep.

The following morning she awoke feeling muzzy-headed and cross as crabs, and wondered why. Then she remembered everything. That wretched man had informed her they were to marry in Venice and honeymoon in Rome. It was the outside of enough that he be permitted to behave as though he could command the world and it would obey.

Besides, she admitted as she crossed to unlock the door to admit Susan with the pot of hot chocolate and rolls, Althea wanted more from him than marriage.

Shortly after that while she was still sitting at her little desk and enjoying the last of her chocolate, Susan went to the door to answer a rap. Upon opening it, a maid proffered an enormous bouquet of summer flowers. Their fragrance filled the room, and a hint of honeysuckle could be detected.

"Oh, how nice. It is about time," Susan said with a wise nod.

Before Althea could decide if she might agree, for the card tucked into the bouquet bore Lord Montmorcy's name, a knock was heard again. This time Susan opened it to find another maid with a small box.

Inside Althea found a bowl of strawberries and thick cream. Upon closer investigation she found the topmost strawberry to be a jeweled pin made of rich red rubies with a few emeralds for leaves.

Susan gasped with delight.

No sooner had Althea set the jewel aside and stared at the delicious-looking berries than another knock came. She beat Susan to the door. Opening it, she found Lord Montmorcy standing there, leaning against the wall and grinning at her like a cat that has his mouse cornered. She gazed up at him, wondering what she ought to say now.

"My final offering," he said, nudging her back into the room and giving a nod of his head to the romantic Susan. She whisked out the door with a shy smile at Althea.

"It is even worse this time, for it is broad daylight and here you are!" It was so difficult to say no to him. Her heart cried out for her to say yes, but her head said not on your life, my dear.

"And here I belong," he teased. He dug into his pocket and came up with a small box. Althea held her breath.

"This," and he opened the box to reveal an extremely beautiful emerald ring, "is for you, and I hope it will remind you of a certain kiss in a pine-scented glade as well as a particular kiss in an alpine meadow, occasions that I will treasure all of my life—which I devoutly hope will be a long one. Now—will you marry me, my dearest love?"

Satisfied beyond her wildest dreams, Althea replied, "Oh, yes." And she permitted the ring to be placed on her proper finger and allowed her betrothed to kiss her all he pleased—which lasted a considerable time—and in the back of her mind decided that some day she would see to it that her daughter would also have a Grand Tour of her own, for they were extremely rewarding, to say the very least.